BETWEEN
TWO WORLDS

BETWEEN TWO WORLDS

A NOVEL BY

Simone Schwarz-Bart

translated from the French by Barbara Bray

A Cornelia & Michael Bessie Book

HARPER & ROW, PUBLISHERS, New York
Cambridge, Philadelphia, San Francisco,
London, Mexico City, São Paulo, Sydney

1817

This work was originally published in France under the title Ti Jean L'horizon. © *Editions du Seuil, 1979.*

BETWEEN TWO WORLDS. English translation copyright © 1981 by Harper & Row, Publishers, Inc. All rights reserved. Printed in the United States of America. No part of this book may be used or reproduced in any manner whatsoever without written permission except in the case of brief quotations embodied in critical articles and reviews. For information address Harper & Row, Publishers, Inc., 10 East 53rd Street, New York, N.Y. 10022. Published simultaneously in Canada by Fitzhenry & Whiteside Limited, Toronto.

FIRST EDITION

Designer: Ruth Bornschlegel

Library of Congress Cataloging in Publication Data

Schwarz-Bart, Simone.
  Between two worlds.
  Translation of Ti Jean l'Horizon.
  I. Title.
PQ2679.C43T513   1981   843'.914   81–47249
ISBN 0–06–039002–6   AACR2

81 82 83 84 85 10 9 8 7 6 5 4 3 2 1

"The words of the black man harm not his tongue; it is his heart they erode, from his heart they draw blood. He speaks and is left empty, his tongue whole in his mouth and his words swept away on the wind. By dint of talk, the torrents, the streams, the air itself have turned, and suddenly they are poisoned. But we cannot live without the tongue's ceaseless labor, without the crop of stories that are our Shade and our mystery. And as the leopard dies at the same time as his spots, so we fall together with our Shade, which is woven by our tales and is forever resurrecting us in another guise."

Thus said the Ancients years ago, before that batch of creatures who know "neither high nor low, center nor source": so they called us, the younger generation. And they would always add, half sad, half mocking, "But what you chase after, on this forsaken island, is but the shade of the clouds, while your own you consign to oblivion."

But I do not say, no, I do not say they were right.

BOOK ONE

Which tells the history of the world up to the birth
of Ti Jean L'horizon, and of our hero's early life.

1.

The island on which our story takes place is not well known. It floats, forsaken, in the Gulf of Mexico, and only a few especially meticulous atlases show it. If you were to study a globe you could wear your eyes out peering, but you'd be hard put to it to find the island without a magnifying glass. It arose out of the sea quite recently, a mere couple of million years ago. And rumor has it that it may go as it came, suddenly sink without warning, taking with it its mountains and little sulfur volcano, its green hills where ramshackle huts perch as if hung in the void, and its thousand rivers, so sunny and capricious that the original inhabitants called it the Isle of Lovely Streams.

Meanwhile it still floats on a sea that brings forth cyclones, on waters always changing from calmest blue to green or mauve. And it supports all kinds of strange creatures, men and beasts, devils, zombies and the rest, all seeking something which has not yet come but which they dimly hope for without knowing its shape or name. It also serves as a stopover for birds that come down to lay their eggs in the sun.

To tell the truth, it is a completely unimportant scrap of earth, and the experts have once and for all dismissed its history as insignificant. And yet it has had its bad times, its past great upsurges, fine copious bloodlettings quite worthy of educated people's attention. But all that was forgotten long ago. The very trees have no memory of it, and as for the people, they believe nothing happens on the island, never has and never will until the day it goes to join its elder sisters at the bottom of the sea.

They have adopted the habit of hiding the sky with the palms of their hands. They say that real life is somewhere else, and even that this speck of an island can reduce anything to nothing; so much so that if God were to descend there in person, he would end up like all the rest, up to his neck in rum and women.

In this back of beyond there is a place yet further remote, and that is the hamlet of Fond-Zombi. If Guadeloupe itself is hardly more than a dot on the map, it may seem even more hopeless and futile to try to summon up an atom like Fond-Zombi. And yet the place does exist. Moreover, it has a long history, full of wonders, bloodshed and frustrations, and of desires no less vast than those that filled the skies of Nineveh, Babylon or Jerusalem.

The first inhabitants of Fond-Zombi were men with red skins who lived on the banks of the Leafy River, beyond where Ma Vitaline's hut now stands, just after the Bridge of Beyond: you can still see great rocks there carved with suns and moons. They had their own special way of looking at the landscape; hence the sparkling name they gave to their own little world—Karukera, or, as I have said, the Isle of Lovely Streams. The name Guadeloupe came later, with the arrival of pale, long-eared men, harassed and uneasy, who seem not to have noticed the beauty of the rivers, though they made a great fuss about the heat of the tropical sun. Having driven out the men with red skins, these philosophers turned to the coasts of Africa for men with black skins to sweat for them. And so, just because of the sun, slavery came to the ancient island of Karukera, and there were cries and supplications, and the sound of the whip drowned the sound of the mountain streams.

But all that was a thing of the past when my story begins, and the blacks of Fond-Zombi thought there was not a single event about the island worth remembering. Sometimes, deep down, some of them wondered whether after all there might not be some glory in their past, some radiance which might reflect on them a little; but fearing ridicule, they were careful to keep their thoughts to themselves. Others went so far as to doubt that their ancestors had come from Africa, despite the little voice whispering in their ear that they had not always lived here, that they were not native to the country in the same way as the trees and stones and beasts that had sprung from its pleasant

4

red soil. And so, when they thought of themselves and their fate, arisen out of nowhere in order to be nothing, hardly more than shades roaming Fond-Zombi on a tuft of wild grass, these forgetful ones would be seized by a kind of bitter, feverish longing, which would make them miserable for a moment or two. But then they would drearily shake their poor battered heads, and reassured by a familiar face or shrub or a broken-down hut still standing among the rocks, would send a great shout of laughter skyward. All was well: they knew where they were again.

For, you see, they were men of sand and wind, born of words and dying with them. They knew life as an ox knows ticks, and they did their best day after day to make it anew, even amid the sharp sugar cane and the itch of the red ants among the bananas. Their feet were not quite firmly on the ground. And when two village women parted after one of those little chats when time is forgotten, instead of bidding each other "au revoir" they would shorten it to "au rêve"—meaning "till the dream."

In those old long-gone times, the days before light and tarred roads, before the electricity posts that give no shade, Fond-Zombi was quite different from what it is today. The only ones who still remember it as it was are the few old white-haired mongooses who every year convey the latest news underground.

Listen, youngsters: The Fond-Zombi of those days was not the forest, but beyond the forest, not the back of beyond but the back of the back of beyond. The traveler would leave the township of La Ramée with its town hall, its school, its graveyard with the flame trees, its dilapidated wharf humming with mosquitoes. Then he would go along a little wandering path that led off the main road and seemed to take off like a bird toward the mountains, as if it could not wait to disappear into the clouds. There were bananas on the left, cane fields on the right—all the property of the white man, one single estate from the sea to the first foothills of the volcano. On either side of the track there sprang up little wooden shacks supported on four stones. They looked as if they were joined together in big clumps, but these groups grew sparser as you left the coastal plain behind and went farther into the interior. Then the clumps became only thin tufts, two or three thatched huts shimmering in little mud yards, smooth and shiny as marble.

After an hour's journey the forest sprang up on all sides, fighting a rearguard action against the sugar plantations that inched farther up every year, over one hill after another. And there were shadows lying easy and dense across the track—mahogany and galpas, genipaps and locust trees, the now extinct bois rada, and balatas entwined in lianas, screening you in, shutting you away in a separate world. Then came the little Bridge of Beyond, hanging over a dried-up gully, a dead river haunted by a troop of evil spirits writhing and beckoning in the hope that some human being would miss his footing, slip, and come and join them below. And then you reached Fond-Zombi itself, in a fantastic clearing of light, built on a string of hillocks, its little cabins dotted about crazily and seeming to hang from invisible ropes: a mere handful of human habitations, the dwellings of zombies abandoned in the great forest and clinging to Mount Balata, itself apparently about to collapse into the void.

The actual village was no more than a row of shanties beside a dusty track which petered out there below the solitudes of the volcano. Strung out like that, they looked like the coaches of a little train setting out to climb the mountain. But this train didn't go anywhere. It had come to a halt long ago, half buried under the vegetation, and had never started off again. The huts faced the sea and looked out at the world; but the world didn't see them. From wherever you stood you could see a distant strip of water below, about five miles away, a longish cycle ride for those who made their living by fishing. Most people worked on the white men's estates, flatlands spiky with sugar cane or rich slopes planted with bananas. But there were also a few fishermen, craftsmen, shopkeepers who sold oil and rum and salt cod; two or three women who hawked fish; and, holding themselves somewhat aristocratically aloof, some sawyers who cut planks in the forest, on scaffolding up near the mist-shrouded peaks.

All these people seemed to have ground to a halt, like the track. Everyday life was hardly any different from what the oldest among them had known in the days of slavery. The shape and arrangement of the houses went back to the same period, as did their poor and wretched appearance: mere boxes perched on four stones, as if to signify how precariously the black man was rooted in the soil of Guadeloupe.

And yet it was a land of verdant hills and clear waters, beneath a sun every day more radiant. When there was no wind, clouds would form and slightly veil its splendor; but usually it shone as bright as could be, the breezes and trade winds keeping heaven clear and solacing man.

These people of wind and sand were not the entire population of Fond-Zombi. Beyond the village, across the Bridge of Beyond, a narrow path rose up hills piled one on the other like a giant ladder climbing the hazy steeps of the volcano. There, on an almost inaccessible plateau, lived a small group of real solitaries, people who had cut themselves off from the world once and for all, and who were called the folk Up Above.

The hermits of the plateau were the poorest of all the inhabitants of Fond-Zombi, of Guadeloupe and the neighboring islands, and perhaps among the poorest people in the whole world. But they regarded themselves as superior to all, for they were the direct descendants of slaves who in the past had risen in revolt, and had lived and often died bearing arms on the very spot where their dilapidated huts now stood. Unlike the villagers, these people did not fret or wonder about the color of their guts; they knew, they knew that a noble blood ran in their veins, the blood of the braves who had built these same round whitewashed huts. Nor did they ask themselves whether Guadeloupe was of any importance in the world; they knew, they knew that rare happenings and unparalleled glories had been seen in the wretched forest they now haunted, and that these deeds had been the exploits of their ancestors.

Every evening the wild folk would sit by the edge of the

plateau facing the twinkling lights in the valley, and tell their children stories of African animals, stories about hares and tortoises and spiders that thought and behaved like human beings, and sometimes better. And then, in the middle of one of these stories, some old veteran would point at the grass which the evening breeze pressed down under their naked feet, and say earnestly: "Look, children, that's the hair of the heroes that fell here." The people would speak then of the dead blacks, and of their fate in this world, on this very spot, the desperate battles in the dark, the hunt and the final fall. And suddenly, at an always unpredictable moment, a strange silence would descend from the sky, during which the heroes rose up out of the earth and were visible to all.

These people were very tall, much taller than the people of the valley, with impassive countenances, broad yellow cheekbones and slanting, elusive eyes. They did not go in much for cultivation. They did not work in the cane fields, and they neither bought nor sold. Their only currency was crayfish and game, which they exchanged in the villages for rum, salt, paraffin, and matches for the days when it was too damp to use flints. After the abolition of slavery they had tried to talk to those in the valley, the folk Down Below as they called them, to tell them of the heroes' flight in the dark and the final defeat and fall. But the others had laughed, a strange shrill little laugh, and said that these things were never of such great importance—they couldn't be, for where were the books they were written down in? Some of the villagers even cast doubt on the truth of the stories. They said that as far as they knew, never, since the devil was just a little boy, had any fool of a black ever done anything so incredibly illustrious. Though free, they uttered these words with a kind of triumphant bitterness, as if they prided themselves on admitting their own insignificance, and found secret pleasure and special virtue in being beyond all doubt the lowest of the low. But the wild folk thought otherwise, and as a result there was considerable animosity between them and the people in the valley. They did not marry or intermingle their blood with one another. They did not drink together. If they happened by chance to encounter one another in the forest they would ostentatiously avert their eyes. In short, their paths no longer crossed.

The folk Up Above called the people of the valley chameleons, snakes continually casting their skins, experts at apery—not to put too fine a point on it, consummate imitators of the white man, delighting in doing just what they were not born to do. For their part, the respectable villagers sneered at the barbarians up on the plateau, steeped in ignorance, madmen of the dark who still wiped their arses with stones. But they were careful to stop there and lower their voices, for the "people of the dark" had the power of changing themselves into dogs and crabs, birds and ants, which could come and spy on and plague you even in bed. They could also strike from a distance and make you fall into nonexistent pits. And no sorcerer in the lowlands could counter their spells or undo what they had tied up or fastened up there in the dark. For their lore came straight from Africa, and against the blows they struck there was no defense.

Their chief had been present at the struggles of the heroes of old; his powder had added to the smoke of the battles fought ages ago in the wild woods. His comrades' bones had whitened, turned to dust and been washed deep into the earth, while he still told the children of their exploits, every evening, facing the setting sun. The man's name was Wademba, the same name he had brought with him from Africa in the hold of a slave ship. But after it became known that he was immortal, the people of the plateau just called him the Green One, or the Green Eel, because he had coiled himself up on the heights like his namesake in a hole in the rock, and nothing would ever get him out again.

Things dawdled along like this for a hundred and fifty years, with now the sun and now some flashes of lightning, until the day when the tarred road and its electricity posts shot Fond-Zombi right into the twentieth century.

2.

That fateful day found the man still perched up on his plateau with his old comrades from the deluge, who were still holding out, though they didn't quite remember against what. When the tarred road went through Fond-Zombi and got as far as the Bridge of Beyond, the former rebels realized the battle was lost; and two or three of the gloomier ones, shattered by the spirit of defeat, crept down the path, followed by others and yet more in a positive cascade, leaving behind only the wildest ones, in other words all the green eels. Most of the women had drifted down, drawn by the magic of the plain, the tarred road and the electricity posts. So the majority of those who remained were men, and the traditional balance was upset. But after a period of indecision a new system was established among them, a strange and unexpected harmony whereby several men's houses were grouped around one woman who serviced them all alike.

For a long time Wademba enjoyed the privilege of having a wife to himself, a woman called Aboomeki, also known as the Silent One. She was a very simple creature, completely lacking in coquetry, whose only definite liking was for the long grass skirts she would make twirl and eddy about her hips when she thought no one was looking. But after a few years she began to hanker after the exciting life of the folk Down Below, and she asked her husband's permission to leave, to go down the path now referred to as the cascade.

The man agreed, but on condition that she left him the little girl they'd had together, to keep him company: the child was called Awa.

Awa, Aboomeki's daughter, was scarcely ten years old when her mother went down the cascade. She was rounder and curlier than a breadfruit, with eyes far apart like hanging droplets—drops of water after the rain, trembling, quite willing to fall.

With her two sous of hips behind and her little Chinese

dates in front, she nevertheless gave off the radiance of a woman, and the old Negresses would smile as she went by. "See how flesh springs from flesh all of a sudden," they would say, enchanted by the sumptuous, promising curve of her hips, which might soon bring new strength to the plateau. Fortunately these crude old ladies never dreamed of the fancies filling the child's brain. Her eyes already looked for what they could not see, and perhaps that was what made them so fine so young. That was why, when she indulged in love play, instead of flailing around softly in the grass as convention required, she would suddenly take off into the air and float mentally, at a height of at least fifteen feet above the ground, toward a youth from another place, whom she had never seen but whose countenance attracted her more than anything else in the world.

Perhaps that was the only pleasure she got out of rolling in the hay—that all-powerful attraction that drew her away elsewhere.

She dreamed also of the plain, of her mother's skirts now seen no more; and she wouldn't have been ashamed to go down the cascade herself in due course. She had never had the feeling that noble blood ran in her veins. From the middle of that round head she secretly looked at the folk Up Above and the folk Down Below with the same affectionate eye, full of both melancholy and desire, as that with which she saw the creatures of the air and the water and the forest, who all belong to the great family of the living, and who all die. But she never said anything of all this, but concentrated on anticipating the wishes of Wademba, who tended to treat her as a servant, or some domestic pet to fondle or kick out of the way as the fancy took you.

The Immortal One might let whole weeks go by without saying a single word to her. Despite the fact that she lived in his shadow and in his smell, lit his fire, did his cooking and his washing and wove his cotton belly bands, he just did not see her. Every now and again he would seem to remember her, and then he'd take her into the forest and teach her about the plants and their secret virtues, their subtle connections with the various parts of the human body. Often, in the middle of the lesson, he would fly into a rage and heap on her all the insults he could lay his tongue to: she had no talent for this sort of thing, her head was full of water, and as for her brains . . . just beads without a thread, all jumbled up together. But if she'd been a good pupil he'd tickle the top of her head and ask her to tell him what she'd like as a reward—anything, so long as it wasn't to do with the degenerate existence of the blacks Down Below. Awa knew what she wanted, but lowered her eyes and kept her own counsel. One day, however, when he actually smiled at her with a sort of affection, she plucked up her courage and confessed her long-felt desire to know what fish from the sea tasted like. Wademba, surprised, gave a mocking laugh. "Is that all?" he said. Then he picked up a basket, drew the outline of a boat on the side of the hut, stepped coolly into it, and vanished as if swallowed up by the soot-blackened wall. Soon afterward, Awa saw him return by the same magic means, his naked body streaming with water leaving little white trails, and the basket full of small fishes of various colors.

Another time, when she'd been to fetch water and was coming back with a calabash balanced on her round frizzy head, the Immortal One's slanting eyes suddenly gleamed with a strange light. Pointing as if to show her to beings present but invisible, he proclaimed that she was like a little black vanilla bean, able to perfume the whole world. Then he broke a twig off the pawpaw tree that grew by the house, dipped it in carapa oil, led the child inside and made her lie down on the bed. Then very gently he slid the pawpaw twig into the most secret hollow of her being. He seemed pleased to find she'd already been opened by young scamps of her own age. He continued this procedure for several weeks, gradually widening and shaping and easing the opening, until the child could receive him as a guest at the narrow table of her body. In his big hands she felt light, absorbed in her role as a properly opened vanilla bean giving off its perfume. But a sadness came over her because of the unknown youth whose face had suddenly ceased to appear to her on the crest of the wave. And more than ever her eyes would turn toward the little lights that shone up from the valley in the evening, as tales were told of heroes of the past.

She grew bolder now, and would sometimes slip away to a little hill near Fond-Zombi from which you could see the villagers without being seen yourself. She would have liked to walk along the tarred road—her feet tingled at the thought of it—and go into one of those funny wooden houses, get to know the people, find out at last what those folk thought about life. From a distance everything about them charmed and excited her, including the exuberance that made them bubble like boiling water, and their way of sending up roars of laughter into the sky, as if to mock the judgments always raining down on them from the wretched thickets up on the plateau.

To her their young men looked smoother and shinier in the sun than those of the plateau. It was whispered that they made love more delicately. And this thought disturbed and bewildered her as she stood there on her little hill, for she didn't really know what it meant.

Growing from Chinese plums to guavas, apples of Venus, her breasts swelled gently in the sun. The year they reached the size of mangoes, two young sawyers set up a scaffolding in the mountains, a stone's throw or so from the plateau. They streamed with sweat, shining all over, even to their short oiled hair. Each wore a leather thong round his wrist and a large-linked silver chain round his neck. The poor girl, lurking behind a clump of trees, compared them bitterly to the shabby youths of Up There, all hairy and unadorned, their fingernails blue and hooked like claws.

She liked best to be there about noon, for the pleasure of watching this brilliant couple eat: they used a metal fork to select morsels from a bowl held between their knees, and then popped the food into their mouths without ever letting a spot of grease fall on their chins. One day they quarreled in the middle of this ceremony, and one of them flung off, cursing his friend, while the other just shrugged his shoulders and went on with his meal regardless. He ate like a great artist, sitting up straight and putting the food away in small mouthfuls, chewing slowly and judiciously, the veins in his temples scarcely moving. Awa, bewitched, emerged from her refuge and went over to the stranger, who stood up in the still air of the clearing, his skin shining like lacquer in the sunshine, the sort of skin that looks cooked to a turn and transparent as a grilled corn cob. At first he stepped back, rather startled at the sight of this wild, barefooted creature. Then she laid her hands on his shoulders and pressed down, smiling, cool, a slim straight red canna, and he, dazzled, forgot all fear and dropped unresisting onto the grass. She had already pulled up her shift, and with her legs bare to the sky was politely opening with her fingers the pearly edges of her shell. But to her great surprise the young man quickly pulled the fold of cotton down again, saying with a worried expression:

"You are pretty, more charming than a coconut flower, but I don't hold with such goings-on. I belong to the L'horizon family, and that's not how we set about it."

"How do you do it, then?" she asked with a sigh of delight, enraptured at the thought of a world where people made love delicately.

"We start off by saying sweet words. . . ."

"Words?" she stammered.

Tears ran down Awa's cheeks as he declared his eternal passion for her. Then they had something to eat, went down and drank from a spring, then returned to the clearing and did the same things to the same music. Awa now knew, and followed, the proper order to be observed in making love. And when at last she took off from the ground, she was not at all surprised to find that the face on the crest of the forty-foot wave was that of the sawyer.

He still gazed at her dazzled, fascinated, unable to credit this manna fallen down from heaven practically naked, wearing just an old shift with a vine instead of a belt. Awa, fulfilled, bright-eyed as a tench, now examined him at leisure, and saw that he was tall on his legs and well set up, perfectly proportioned from head to foot. But somehow she felt there was something frail about him. Then she suddenly realized that he belonged to the nebulous race of the blacks Down Below, creatures of sand and wind who according to Wademba were upset at every tremor of the earth. But wasn't that true also of herself, who had always found it so hard to maintain the shape of her body in space?

When darkness fell she went down with him into the valley, where he had just built a little hut of new, sweet-smelling planks.

The coming of Awa sent a wind of panic through the anxious souls of Fond-Zombi. Her sweetheart's many friends advised him to send her back home right away; otherwise her father's spells would reach him, Jean L'horizon, even in the shelter of his own house and no matter how many charms and countercharms he weighed himself down with. When the evil day came, the loftiest and most subtle protections would avail him nothing, for no one could set himself up against the Immortal One. Run away? Cross the sea? But distance did not exist for that old mesmerizer of darkness. He might be that fly there on the table, apparently preening itself in all innocence. Or that ant on your arm, listening to what you say and its jaws really grinning all the time at the useless ploys you were inventing. The young man listened to all this in a dream, not taking his eyes off Awa's face, determined to follow his misfortune through to the end—his complete and final undoing, people called it, but he called it his fine one. So people gave way before that fateful smile, and one smooth peaceful morning overflowing with serenity the whole population accompanied the new child of God to the church at La Ramée, where the priest made her promise to renounce the devil and all his works. Then, without warning, the white man flicked a few drops of water into the wild girl's eyes; and that was how she became Eloise.

In the twinkling of an eye she had learned to wash and mend, how to make a nice Christian stew and lay the table, and how to eat with a fork as daintily as if she'd never done anything else all her life. Then she squared her shoulders and went into the blaze of the sugar canes; and that was her second victory in the eyes of the people of Fond-Zombi. But her real hour of triumph was yet to come. For one night before Lent, an especially warm and sweet-scented night, the neighbors were woken up by extraordinary cries, full and splendid, enough to carry even the most unwilling away.

Musicians of the dark were not rare among the village women, and sometimes their cries would answer one another from house to house.

"Ah, what a journey!"

"Yes indeed. But let's keep on, my lass, further, further!"

And the cries would go on with renewed vigor, for what was the use of having a man if it wasn't to journey with him, sail, float, fly?

Musicians of the dark were not rare among the village women, but from the latest one, from the throat of Eloise, there came such a wealth and variety of sounds it was like a whole orchestra, with drums and violins, flutes, guitars and rattles, all mounting up toward the sky. Other voices were immediately caught up in it, rising up in the dark and rolling from roof to roof as far as the outskirts of the village, like a living wave forcing all, willy-nilly, into the concert. People talked long afterward of the night when human beings started to fly together like angels hand in hand. Even the shyest and most modest of the women, whose cries usually sank to the soles of their feet, let themselves go. And more than one of them came and thanked poor Eloise, and congratulated her on the heavenly beauty of her song, which had almost plucked Fond-Zombi up off the ground and sent it whirling among the stars.

In their enthusiasm everyone had quite forgotten she was a sorcerer's daughter: that was ancient history, a useless trifle, to be put away on the shelf with the broken china. But Jean L'horizon remembered night and day, and sometimes he feared he would be stricken with some horrible disease, a vile snakelike thing that would for a long while writhe unknown in his heart and then suddenly burst out in the sight of all. What he was most afraid of was the "tying of the knot," this of course being particularly apt as he had led into wrong courses the precious blood of the Immortal One. This fear always came upon him unexpectedly. He would seem quite content with life and glad that his mother had borne him, and then suddenly two fingers would stray between his legs and he would say sadly:

"Here I am, eating and drinking like a fool, but who knows? Perhaps my glory will never rise again."

Then Eloise would stretch out a helping hand, and there would be laughter and eternal vows, soft bread and sweet words, as it was under the scaffolding in the clearing, the first time.

But Eloise could see he was soaking in a brine of sadness, and every day that God wove, as the people in the valley used to say, she was tempted to go up the path and ask her father's consent, as Aboomeki the Silent One had done in her day. But she was afraid he might keep her, having grown used perhaps to her young live body and her scent of ripe vanilla. And she loved her sawyer, who dazed her with the soft words he lavished on her day and night, for, he said, a kiss without words is like a pretty black girl's neck without a golden necklace. And as she could not bear to lose him, every day that God wove she put things off till the next day.

Their bloods went so well together that she became pregnant the same year as she was baptized. But there was no weight in her womb, which felt full of air, like a gold-beater's skin; and in the sixth month all her hopes turned to water and blood. Ten years went by like this. Jean L'horizon became like a man gone mad over the spell, in which everyone recognized the brand and the touch, the unique claw mark of the Immortal One. And when his wife was with child again he looked thoughtful, and people saw he was giving up and getting ready to haul down the flag. One day when Eloise was asleep, worn out with carrying another dead child, he quietly packed a case and went to the main road to wait for the bus. It was driven by one Max, Max Armageddon, well known as having the easiest and luckiest hand at the job in the whole service. Max could drive drunk as an owl, or leaning

17

back with his feet on the steering wheel to amuse the passengers; but all his charges always arrived safely. On this occasion, however, just outside La Ramée and the bend where the ice factory stood, a rock suddenly appeared in the middle of the road, forcing the driver to swerve right into a tree. One of the doors flew open and one of the passengers, as if propelled by an invisible hand, was thrown onto the horns of an ox grazing peacefully a few feet from the road. The man flying without wings was Jean L'horizon himself. The driver looked back along the road. The rock had vanished.

At that very moment Eloise was sitting in her hut, swollen with pain, her hand on the enigma in her womb, thinking of the years that had gone by and been lost with the man who, according to what a neighbor had just told her, was now on his way to Point-à-Pitre. Suddenly something forced her legs open and she felt herself being assailed and penetrated by an invisible body; and as she recognized the fabulous drive and attack of the Immortal One, she was carried away on a wave of foam, and dimly knew that this child would live, would not, not this one, come unstuck from her womb.

Once the departed was buried, Eloise began to contemplate her womb, which already thumped and leaped about like a second heart. Then her sorrow abated, and she even tried to smile from time to time, for it is well known that a mother's sorrow is not good for her child. And when the time came, moved by some obscure piety, she gave birth in the manner traditional among the people of Up There, kneeling at the foot of the bed, her hands joined at the nape of her neck, her elbows finding support and courage in the wooden crossbar. When she was shown the *ti-mâle*, the little boy, she at once recognized the thick, obstinate frontal bone which projected like the peak of a cap from the ancient skull of Wademba. But the attendant matrons paid no attention to this sign, for they were overcome by the enormous length of the infant and the darkness of his gleaming skin. One of them clasped her hands together and said:

"If he'd been a bit longer the scoundrel would never have got out."

"Yes," said another, "and he's already eager for the fray."

And she pointed out how the *ti-mâle* was clenching his fists, thumbs tucked well inside, as if to strengthen the blows he would one day rain on her, that madwoman who runs through the streets seeking whom she may devour, that madwoman called life.

After a tortuous and passionate debate in which some of the old women exhibited the wildest imagination, it was decided that the young warrior should simply bear the name of his father, the late lamented Jean L'horizon. But this seemed useless to Eloise, a farce which left the child without protection in life, like a nestling without beak or feathers. An African name was what she wanted, a real and effective shield which would give her son weight and prevent him from being upset at every tremor of the earth, like the people of the valley. And so on the eighth day, after taking the baby to be baptized, she left him with a neighbor and went secretly along the path that led Up Above.

It was a long time since it had rained and the earth was dry, shiny, coppery. Eloise went through limp vegetation listlessly trying to struggle against the sun for no other reason than that it had gone to the trouble of putting down roots. She stopped on the edge of the plateau, taken aback by the picture of abandonment that confronted her: dilapidated huts open to the sky, on ground broken here and there by mounds of termites. A single hut still stood upright amid the desolation, and the old man sitting in the shade of the sooty walls on a carved wooden stool seemed to her eternal. She immediately felt certain that the ancient mesmerizer of darkness was waiting for her behind those old tortoise-like eyelids.

"You know why I've come," she whispered.

"I know why you've come. I also know you've come for nothing."

"But the child is yours, sprung from the foam of your loins?"

"So you say, Awa," he answered with a sarcastic smile.

"It is your child—the evening breeze itself knows it. It is

your child, and have you no name for him, nothing to put over his little shoulders? Do you want him to be at the mercy of the forces of evil, to go through life unprotected, the prey of anyone who wants to take his soul and throw it to the dogs? Do you want him to be exposed to the weather like an animal—is that it?"

"Awa, Awa," he said, "don't waste your breath spitting at me. There is no name I can give to your child, for as you yourself said, he will go through life like an animal, a wild animal that finds its own path. And if I gave him an African name it would wind itself round his throat like a collar and strangle him. You don't want anything like that for him, do you?" He ended with a sneer.

"I went down among the people Below, but you wanted me to, or else you could have stopped me with a lift of the finger. And now you take your revenge on the child you yourself made, on your own flesh and blood, Wademba. Why did you let me go if you wanted me to stay? And why did you make the child only to abandon him to the Powers of evil?"

"The way these young females carry on!" he said. "Now listen, little water flea. Dry your tears and try to understand what I say. There is no name for this child because his name is waiting for him, his name is somewhere in front of him, and when the time comes it will come and alight on his head. Do you see?"

But Eloise was far away and no longer listening. She had clasped her hands over her head, covering her face, and was rocking mechanically to and fro like a mourner. After a while she heard a strange sound, and coming back to earth saw her father's mouth opening in frail laughter. Sitting up scaly and naked on his stool, with his knees drawn up to his shoulders, shining like an old tree trunk polished by the wind, Wademba was gazing at her with his eternal eyes and laughing.

Then for the first time in her life the young creature was swept by a wave of anger. She had fallen back a step, trembling all over, and suddenly she had an inspiration and said, her voice still tearful:

"I see now. It was you who sent me among the people Down Below, and now you're laughing at me, eh?"

She was like one distracted. She saw the old man's stick leaning against the door of the hut, seized it, and gave him a violent thump on the head.

"You sent me down there, and now you laugh?"

Then she hit him again, and yelled in stupefaction:

"You dried my babies up in my womb, and you laugh?"

She said a lot more that day, going back over her despoiled childhood, her darkened youth, and finally the strange flight to death of the late Jean L'horizon, whose only sin was to have made her happy. And she punctuated each grievance with a great ringing blow which disheveled the white tufts on the unfathomable skull of the Immortal One.

"The way this young female carries on!" he said suddenly, as if absentmindedly.

Then there was a great dark gush, and he toppled slowly off his stool onto the ground, like a tree. Eloise looked vaguely at the huge body lying at her feet. But the old man raised himself on one elbow, wiped the blood away from his eyes, and started to laugh again, louder and louder, with a sort of terrifying gaiety that made Eloise draw back, drop the stick, and draw back further still. Then she turned and took to her heels, across the ruined plateau and down through thickets and sharp-grassed undergrowth, pursued by the laughter, which only stopped right down below, with the evening and the first gleams of light in Fond-Zombi.

3.

He had been baptized with his father's name, but the people of the valley avoided calling him Jean, Jean L'horizon, lest the departed take the opportunity of answering in his stead. Eloise didn't like mixing up the living and the dead like that either, and to avoid the confusion her son for a long while answered only to the names of Hey, Hi, and Psst. Then someone had the idea of calling him Little or Ti Jean, and it was under this modest appellation that our hero made his entry into the world—he who was one day to overturn the sun and the planets.

As a child, scarcely fallen from the breast, he had the somewhat ponderous grace of a young pachyderm, with legs like small bronze columns and round feet which had difficulty getting a purchase on the ground and made him stumble. He was a fierce animal, his fists always clenched tight as in his mother's womb. Eloise, seeing him look so surly and discontented, wondered how it was she had not given birth to the joy of living personified. In fact, as she discovered later, the lad's whole being was concentered then on his muscles and bones, which still had need of him, of his constant attention, in order to reach their full perfection. He had so many things going on deep down in his body that it made his mouth forget to smile or speak, and he didn't utter a single word until he was four years old. But once he did make up his mind to it he spoke whole sentences straight away, in a high, clear, precise voice strangely reminiscent of the tones of the Immortal One.

This gave Eloise an opportunity to see that the valley people were cultivators of forgetfulness. The child moved among them with the face of Wademba, his voice, and the same excess of spirit emanating from his slanting, impregnable eyes; and no one seemed to notice it. The only thing they did remark was how his little tail stood up when he got into fights, as boys of that age will, and returned to its usual position when hostilities ceased. Ti Jean was still going about quite naked when this phenomenon first occurred. The people, amazed, took pleasure in making him angry just to see his organ stick up stiff as a spike. But this glory didn't strike anyone in Fond-Zombi as suspicious, and after the show the men would just say to one another with a touch of wistfulness:

"The world is full of all sorts of rods, some that are sumptuous and others that are less so, and even some that are supposed to be forked, apparently. In short, God always provides more than the mind of man can imagine, that and more." And they concluded that Eloise's child had inherited a veritable rod of gold!

Although the boy grew quickly, he made little more use of his tongue than Ma Eloise did of hers, and their hut was the quietest in Fond-Zombi, if not in the whole of Guadeloupe. Sometimes he would prick up his ears for no apparent reason, as if he had just heard a call, but although Eloise looked all round the hut she would see only an ordinary fly on the table, or an ant running over the slats of the floor, or some bustling insect. Then she would ponder, strangely uneasy, wondering whether Wademba had ever let the child out of his sight since the hour he was born. And whenever a big black dog came wandering nearby, she would panic and throw stones at it.

Yes, the child was about as talkative as an oyster. But as soon as he could stand up on his round feet he was always to be seen out of doors, trotting about and nipping under the verandas, on the alert for anything that was said in the village. Sometimes his mind would draw strange conclusions from what he heard. One day he was there when a neighboring housewife said, "Ah, if the earth could speak it would tell us some things we don't know!" It was just one of those throwaway remarks one makes without thinking. But later the same day Eloise found her son lying in the garden, his ear to the ground, listening for mysterious voices rising from the depths. Another time someone said that only the trees know what man is, and unfortunately they are dumb. Eloise turned at once to her son, and saw him making off, with his slightly clumsy, hesitant step, and a little while afterward couldn't help laughing when she found him clinging lovingly to the guava tree in the yard, his face all lit up with expectancy as he listened for the voices lurking in the knots of the wood. She laughed again during the days that followed, every time she saw him clasping the trunk of the guava tree. Then suddenly the laughter died on her lips: the boy had taken to rushing round the village, with eyes that looked as if they had become sightless and didn't recognize anything, and open-mouthed as if asking, "Is it really true—what I see, what I hear?"

The rushing about stopped the day he first went to school in La Ramée down on the coast. He came back wearing an air of deep serenity. And then came the second surprise for the people of the village: despite his dislike of speech, Eloise's boy had a brain as vast as the belly of a whale, a brain just like a white man's, with columns for arranging everything in his mind. In the evening, by the light of the oil lamp, she watched with amazement as he sat immersed in his books, touching them with the same look of radiant expectation as that with which he used to caress tree trunks in order to hear the voice of the world. Things went on in this way for one or two seasons, and then the joy in books vanished and Eloise found herself once more with a child who came home from school silent, who would work a bit in the garden, fetch a drum of water for his mother, and then sit in a shady corner with his little hands clenched on his knees, suddenly still and stiff as death.

It was plain that the books had fallen silent and that the boy had given up the voices of the world; he no longer went out, even to bathe in the river. Sitting there in the dark, his eyes quiet and dull, he seemed to be constantly pondering and cultivating some insult or outrage committed against him. And seeing him like this, Eloise wondered how it had happened that she had not brought forth the joy of living personified, when during her pregnancy she had tried so hard, so hard, to smile.

So it went on until Ma Justina's fall, which for a long while provided a topic of conversation in Fond-Zombi and round about. Ma Justina was not a real witch but a sort of reservist, one of those people weary of human form who sign a contract with a devil so as to be able to change themselves at night into a donkey or a crab or a bird as the fancy takes them. One fine day she was found drowned in her own blood on the way into the village. Returning from a nocturnal flight, she had been surprised by the first rays of dawn and immediately flattened on the ground, struck down by the holiness of the light. As she lay in the middle of the road her bird's body slowly resumed its human form: hands sprouted at the tips of her wings and long dazzling white tresses mingled with the lusterless feathers on the head of an owl. The people stood a little way off taking note of all the details one by one, for it was a sight extremely rare, to be recounted carefully to those who happened to be away, to distant relations, even to strangers who might be met with later along the road of life. It was a Thursday, and the children slipped between the grownups' legs, but they didn't seem unduly surprised at the spectacle. They'd seen much more in dreams, they seemed to be saying, since they drank in such stories with their mother's milk. Only the oldest among them made any comment, the "doctors" studying for their school leaving certificate, each with his or her pen sticking proudly out of a mop of hair. According to them, people turned into dogs or crabs as naturally as water turned to ice, or as electricity was changed into light in lamps or into words and music on the radio. In their view Ma Justina was just a little slice of a life which wasn't mentioned in books because the white men had decided to draw a veil over it.

The police from La Ramée, alerted by the secretary at the town hall, arrived after the battle, on the stroke of noon. Ma Justina had just finished with the birds, and all the policemen found was an old Negress lying shattered in the middle of the road. Despite all the witnesses present, the police refused outright to listen to the explanations offered by the people of Fond-Zombi, determined not to understand and getting angry and rough with them as if they were concealing something unmentionable, perhaps some crime in which the whole population was involved. And it was only after spending weeks combing the entire district, joking and mocking and straining the charity of not a few, that they resigned themselves to the mystery of the tall naked Negress lying in the middle of the road as if fallen from the sky. This persecution was painful to all the blacks, but those who felt it most bitterly were the schoolchildren, especially the "doctors," who could not understand why the testimony of the people of

Fond-Zombi had been rejected. Did not they themselves, at their desks, accept the white men's stories about the earth, the sun and the stars, which weren't all that easy to swallow?

Yes, the whole population was present at the metamorphosis, but it was our hero whose eyes opened the widest. Ti Jean seemed to be contemplating at last the secret sought in vain under the earth and in the trunks of trees and in books brought back for one or two seasons from school. By the following day the little fellow was reconciled with the world, and returned to the river and the games appropriate to his age. From his whole person there flowed a sort of happy magic, and when they saw him people said: "Well, well, Ma Eloise's boy is coming out of his cocoon. Is he making up his mind to take his place in the sun?"

BOOK TWO

Which tells of the encounter with Egea, the fight with
Anancy, the oath on Ma Vitaline's veranda,
and other marvels.

1.

A few years earlier a strayed hunter had inspected from a distance the last ruined huts on the plateau, and the people had concluded that the accursed Wademba was now long dead and buried, his soul writhing in some remote corner of hell. They breathed freely again. And once fear had fled, the whole thing became just an affair of the tongue, just a flight of words floating up into the sky like bubbles. Gradually the younger generation forgot the once dreaded name, no longer to be heard except occasionally on some aged and moldy tongue. It was all ancient history, and people gave themselves over more than ever to the fury of the new times and the thousand tricks that appeared with the tarred road and the electricity posts.

But the old folk still remembered the obliterated, extinct story, and they liked to tell it to Ma Eloise's son because of his good manners and the flair he had for listening to them in silence, waiting for the words to drop from their worn lips and fall right where they wanted them to inside his delighted little skull. Actually, none of them could boast of having seen the man in the flesh, and those who spoke of him were only echoing older words. As the tale was passed on from one to another, the river became a majestic stream overcoming all obstacles, and some even said that from up there on the red gash of the plateau Wademba had controlled the weather, unveiling the sun or unleashing a downpour over Guadeloupe as the fancy took him. For a long, long while people had thought he was immortal, the old folks would say, smiling, with a relaxed and satisfied expression, and you could see they were just talking for the sake of talking, embroidering their former fears to add a spice to life.

Returning home after these conversations, Ti Jean longed to question the only person who had really experienced life Up Above. But all questions died on his lips at the sight of Ma Eloise, the bony little black woman with her sad, dim, almost funereal face, and the eternal white kerchief around her head as a sign of permanent mourning. Whenever Wademba's name was uttered in her presence her cheeks would grow ashen, and she would open her mouth and appear to be gasping for breath. She seemed always on the alert, as if in perpetual danger. Her ideal was to have the house locked up and the shutters closed against every living thing, including marauding insects: she would stare at a fly or a butterfly as if it was the devil. Whenever she left her own four walls Ma Eloise ran as if fleeing from something, and she returned in the same hurry, still on the qui vive. And yet she liked the singing and murmur of people. When she had no visitors to calm and reassure her, she would spend hours with one eye glued to a crack in the wall overlooking the street. She liked watching people go to and fro, and could learn as much from their faces and frowns as she could from hearing their confidences. But she always pretended to know nothing about anyone: it was not her business to watch over what happened to people; the only person she knew was herself, and she often wondered about that.

For as long as Ti Jean could remember, Ma Eloise had always toiled up hill and down dale in search of medicinal herbs which she sold to the chemists in the town. She was a nature healer herself in a small way, dispensing herbal baths and potions and soothing such human ills as were within the scope of her dry little sinewy hands, their fingers green from contact with the plants. She liked looking after people, but wasn't too fond of gathering simples in the darkness of the forest. She often came home soaked with sweat, her heart thumping as if she'd met a ghost. Later on Ti Jean, by then a connoisseur of "leaves" himself, took over this, the disturbing part of his mother's job. She had initiated him into the art of gathering leaves and wrapping them in separate scraps of cloth according to their kind, so as not to mix their virtues. And then one day—he remembered all his life that it was the Thursday after Ma Justina's fabulous fall—she solemnly handed him a little basket, leaned down, and breathed on Ti Jean's feet that they might always lead him to a propitious spot. She had never made use of this ritual before, which meant, as she pointed out, that her breath had kept all its force and power intact.

So now every Thursday Ti Jean spent long hours wandering through the dark cool undergrowth pretending to be interested in gathering herbs, with his nose glued to some shrub or other, then whirling round to see a spirit that had been tailing him vanish in a phosphorescent flash. Ever since he was small Ti Jean, made sensitive by Ma Eloise's behavior, had felt the existence of an invisible presence around him. But he had never been able to put a face to it. And now here was the spirit revealing itself if only he turned round quickly enough to catch it. The boy would give a little cry of delight at this, and his heart would beat fast at the sight of the enormous crow with red eyes which froze for a moment as he looked at it, then faded away like a vision in a dream.

During the week, when he got back from school, Ti Jean, after having played the man of the house—knocked in a nail, lifted some heavy weight, dug two or three sweet potatoes out of the garden, and complimented Ma Eloise on her beauty and eternal youth—would go down to the river to join the children of his own age. The place was downstream from the Bridge of Beyond, behind a little hillock that hid it from sight. There a stray branch of the river tumbled in a waterfall into a pool which seemed to embrace the whole immensity of the sky in its center, while the trees on its banks colored the air with their shade and gave it its name, the Blue Pool. Grownups did not go there, nor children capable of doing wrong, of giving or receiving seed. The place was strictly reserved for innocents: little girls not yet women, and little boys with dry pricks, not yet men.

Most of the children larked about in the pool, but sometimes they would form pairs and go off to learn love play, either in the water, under a rock, or on dry earth, behind a big coco plum, or again in some neighboring tree, like the birds, which was then the fashion. Because of his rod of gold Ti Jean was the center of attention for the little girls who went bathing. They would splash him and tease him with their slender nakedness, laughing, smooth as the palm of your hand; or they would brush against him caressingly under the blue water. But he went off with none of them, for every time he felt he would like to an inner voice told him that another awaited him who was not in the middle of the pool, or who was there but not yet properly seen by him. Some of the girls, vexed by his attitude, told him with a matronly air that a man ought to see women and pay attention to them, otherwise he would lose his eyes. And then they would dive under the waterfall in search of a crayfish, with which they would take it in turns to pinch their nipples and anticipate the future.

Ti Jean laughed to see and hear them, with the grave, fresh laughter that still stood stead with him for words, for a universal answer to all that could be said under heaven, and especially around the Blue Pool. And then he would go and stretch out on a flat rock lying across the current and burning in the sun, or stroll naked along the banks with his nose in the air, pretending to inspect the landscape and turning round unexpectedly to see the spirit at his heels disappear. One day when he was walking along like this, deep in mystery, he saw a couple of children fondling each other behind a rock, the boy lying on the grass and the girl straddling him, head thrown back a little, eyes closed, silent in her blind course to the sun. As he went by, the girl opened her eyes and gave him a look that rent his heart: for he had just realized that she was the one he wanted for his friend. Yet he saw her every day God sent—Egea, old Kaya's daughter. And she wasn't very different from all the other little black tots around the pool, with her steady eyes slanting gently toward the temples, and her hair fluffed out around her face in a sort of helmet that elevated and protected her. Often she dived into the water when he approached, as if she was scared. But once, as he now remembered with pain, she had emerged streaming with water and offered him a little red fish which she'd just caught in the foam of the waterfall. The fish seemed redder than it really was, in the middle of her black hand, and she'd smiled, as if to say, Doesn't it look splendid between my fingers?

The next day Egea Kaya was waiting for him by the river, sitting trustingly in the water. The boy went up to her and touched her cheek. Then they both walked away from the pool amid calls and mocking laughter from the other children, who'd waited a long while for Ti Jean's time to come.

A bracelet doesn't tinkle by itself, and the just betrothed pair, lying down behind a friendly clump of siguina, noticed that together they gave forth a goodly sound. Perhaps their music would last for only one season, as sometimes happens on the banks of the river: just until a new batch of innocents came to drive them away from the Blue Pool. But perhaps not, they said, smiling, their eyes full of tears at the thought. Then, impatient with the childish bodies in which they felt restricted, they spoke of the cries that haunted the night in Fond-Zombi, waking even the drowsiest. And the lady said that for him she would utter such glorious and triumphant cries that they would startle all the birds sleeping round about—just as Ma Eloise had done once, that night still remembered in the annals of Fond-Zombi.

They vowed that this should be so, and from then on they could be seen clinking against one another on the dusty road to the school in La Ramée. At the end of the day they would bend their steps toward the river and swim with the others, play under the waterfall, or dance to an impromptu orchestra of hand-claps, clicking tongues, glottal stops, old tin cans and pebbles, all of which combined to produce a splendid effect. Then they would take leave of the rest and go off to their tree, a bushy old mango where they would fondle each other until dusk, taking care not to break their necks in the process. Up there, arms and legs entwined like the branches that surrounded them and seemed to spring out of their own being, they felt linked by invisible threads to Fond-Zombi, glimpsed through the leaves: to the mountains, to the distant sea, to the golden waves of the cane fields, and to all that lived and throbbed in the sky, on the earth, and in

33

the depths of the waters. Egea knew about the spirit who dogged her friend's footsteps, and when Ti Jean's attention was caught by a rustle among the leaves the little girl would turn and look in the same direction, gaze for a while, and say: "It's the wind." Or if the boy's heart started to thump against hers because of a bird alighting on a branch, Egea would peer attentively toward it until she could say with certainty: "It's only a thrush."

To all appearances the spirit was that of a dead person who came back to earth. Probably a very powerful dead person, up to the neck in power, for the ordinary dead visited the living only in dreams, and then only on very dark nights. Then both of them thought of the ruins on the plateau, rumored to be buried in vegetation like the porticoed mansions people sometimes found in the forest, indistinguishable from the trees and vines. And clinging together, they called to mind Wademba and the hidden face of things, the part of the world that didn't appear in the schoolbooks because the white men had decided to draw a veil over it.

Egea liked the dark halo surrounding her friend, giving him a history of his own whose reflected glory fell on her since they had become one. And on Thursday mornings, a wicker basket on her back and her head bound tight in a kerchief so that the whole forest shouldn't get tangled in her hair, she used to go with him on his alarming errands up hill and down dale. When they had collected a week's supply for Eloise, they always went home across the Bartholomew Hill so as to see, on the other side of a dark valley, the little gash of red earth that was the plateau Up Above. One day as they stood hand in hand on the edge of the valley gazing intently and dizzily into the mysterious distance, the sound of a tom-tom met their ears and then ceased. This happened two or three times running, but getting gradually fainter, like a dying echo. The two children, surprised, stood for a moment, waiting. And suddenly a light breeze blew in their faces from the mountain and the plateau, while again they heard that other-worldly music. The drum beat to a rhythm they did not know, monotonous and insistent, as if on metal. And suddenly there was a human voice singing in a language equally unknown, but with such sadness and peaceful majesty that Ti Jean knew he would remember that tune and metallic beat and that wind-borne voice all his life long. Then the sky was silent again, and Ti Jean murmured, not looking at the little girl because of the embarrassing tears rolling down his little boy's cheeks:

"Egea, did you hear?"

"I heard," she whispered.

"Say again that you heard."

"I did," she said.

There were all sorts of stories about the ruined plateau, and people took care not to go near it, so that it was as if protected by a circle of darkness and secret horror. But Egea was ready to accept anything that came her friend's way, and she now accompanied him in her blue spotted apron to the foot of Mount Balata, as if to say, If we have to climb it, climb it we shall. It was getting late. The sun shone high in the sky. The children had long left Bartholomew Hill behind, the golden waves of the cane fields, and the river which acted as a boundary between human worlds and wildernesses. Suddenly Ti Jean looked at the little girl awkwardly, and asked her to wait for him here, or rather hope for him down by the Blue Pool, near a creek they knew. And setting his basket down in the grass by way of a swift and silent farewell, he plunged into the brushwood concealing the entrance to the path leading Up Above.

To his great surprise the undergrowth on Mount Balata was much the same as in other forests, with its ever-damp moss which rarely saw the sun and its masses of restless, twisting vines which fell like snakes unwinding out of the sky. But dread rose in him as he approached the heights. Memories and shreds of thoughts took shape, scraps of stories fell into place, and in his mind's eye he saw again some of the expressions on Ma Eloise's face, and her ashen cheeks when anyone spoke Wademba's name. Then his legs trembled, and his whole living body, trunk and arms too: his very bowels yearned painfully to go back down the mountainside.

After some hours had passed it began to drizzle, and fine rods of silver slanted through the air. The path was suddenly swallowed up in a dense hedge, nearly ten feet high, of aloes, cadasses and other prickly plants, together with climbing vines throwing out shoots, and tufts of orchids, pink, mauve or blood-speckled. All this lay at the foot of a narrow slope skirting a series of precipices, and high above rose the impressive mass of the plateau. It looked like a keep or citadel standing out in the void, keeping vigilant watch over the valley. Try as he might to find a way through the hedge, Ti Jean could see no opening or place where anyone might have passed through. He concluded that if the plateau was still inhabited at all, it could only be by apparitions.

At that moment, looking round him, he saw the winged spirit of his dreams, apparently asleep, its beak tucked down, on the lowest branch of a mahogany tree. It was a very aged crow, with little frayed feathers over its eyes like bits of yellow cotton. It was pretending to be asleep, dreaming, but Ti Jean knew it was wider awake than a bag of fleas. And lest it vanish in smoke as usual, he stretched his arms out gently toward it and said imploringly:

"I'm Ti Jean, Ti Jean, and you needn't be afraid of me."

As soon as it heard the boy's voice the spirit began its metamorphosis, fading and becoming as transparent as glass. Then it seemed to hesitate on the branch, opened its beak in a brief cracked squawk like a laugh, then slowly, as if reluctantly, resumed its original appearance, feather by feather right down to its claws. It gazed at the boy with a melancholy expression, and suddenly, without knowing why, Ti Jean began to weep, rubbing his eyes with his fists.

The winged spirit went back with him down the mountain-side, flitting from branch to branch through the undergrowth while Ti Jean's tears flowed and he remembered the sad and majestic song of Bartholomew Hill. Through the shadowy apertures in the trees, white stars shone in a cloudless sky, then turned yellow as the sky grew dark and dim.

Egea was waiting by the river, sitting on the sand. She was all blue in the darkness, with gleams of liquid silver on one arm and shoulder caught by a moonbeam. She seemed far away, motionless and lost in contemplation. Her dress was damp with dew; everything about her was as fresh and cool as a young lettuce. With a little cry, twisting round to see him better in the dark, she said:

"The whites of your eyes are all red. Have you seen . . . something?"

Ti Jean had just come back from another world, the world he had once sought in vain under the earth and in the murmuring crooks of trees, and he smiled vaguely at the little girl who had pierced his heart.

"I saw," he said, "a man who slept face downward on his back. On a day when it was night, and the thunder pealed in silence."

She put a finger on his lips.

"Don't speak, don't say anything," she said. "I'm only a woman with a little tongue in my head; but remember, and never forget, that my eyes may see Christ."

"I shall never forget," replied our hero gravely.

2.

Egea's mother had died a few years before, drawn down into the grave by a woman dead earlier, a rival of her youth who appeared in a dream and asked her to go with her on her way. Instead of refusing, insulting her and telling her to go back where she'd come from, instead, in short, of making it clear that she wasn't yet ready for the journey, the unfortunate woman had made the mistake of holding out her hand to her enemy, thus signing her own death warrant and extinguishing her own sun. The next day she had told her dream to a neighbor, in despair at having to quit life before her hour had come. Then she had begun to perspire, and despite all the efforts of doctors, witches, seers, frequenters of other worlds, not to mention Ma Eloise's nimble green fingers, she was dead in less than a week, regretfully leaving her two children in the charge of her husband, old Kaya, who was a bit simple and saw no ill in anything.

Anancy, Egea's elder brother, was about twelve and in one of the top classes at school. He had a mild, rather crooked face; the features looked like those of his sister reflected and slightly distorted in running water. But the mildness of the rest of his face was in strange contrast to his eyes, full of secret fury. With them he constantly shot the same rejection at everyone, friend or foe. Ti Jean was charmed with Anancy's way of looking like an offended prince, and sometimes thought that hidden deep down, the brother's soul was like his sister's, only more turbulent, flowing in a torrent instead of in a peaceful stream, as hers did. But Ti Jean took care to keep out of this stripling's way, for his eyes looked more daggers at him than at anyone else since he and Egea had started walking hand in hand.

It was an old custom, at the pool, that if a brother came upon his sister with her sweetheart it was his duty to fly into a terrible rage and even fall upon the guilty party and thrash him. Hence the children's choice of a bushy old mango tree whose branches lent them their protective shade.

One day when they were in their tree, deep in a delicious torpor, a flying pebble drew their attention to the presence of that fool Anancy, who was literally dancing with rage on the grass as tradition required. Without hesitation Ti Jean jumped down from his perch and planted himself before the elder brother, whose surly countenance lit up with an incredulous grin at the sight of the rod of gold pointing gaily skyward. The statutory battle began. Both combatants aimed listless punches that missed, and each time they waved up at Egea on her branch to reassure her about their intentions. But suddenly Ti Jean, carried away with martial ardor, seized his adversary by the throat and brought him to the ground in a murderous grip. Anancy's eyes were beginning to turn up. Then a cry rang out, and Ti Jean, letting go of the other boy's neck, became aware of the slim figure squawking down at him from the foliage like a quail in a snare. He wondered, aghast, what devil had forced his hands round Anancy's neck. And the girl slipped quickly from the tree, grazing her naked body, then bent over her brother and breathed on his eyelids.

Now, as you know, each one of us comes into the world with a gift, and that little snippet Egea had a breath that was very refreshing. Eventually, as a result of this breath, her brother bounded up and dealt Ti Jean a great blow in the belly with his head. Our hero's own head encountered a rock sunk in the grass among the surface roots of the mango. A dark veil rose up toward the sky, like a fishing net thrown out from the gaping wound in his brow, a big swirling net that suddenly ebbed back again, revealing a strange sight: Anancy standing over him, foaming at the mouth with fury and holding a big stone with which he was about to smash his face in.

At that moment a second cry rang out from Egea, and the boy's blazing eyes grew softer and seemed to be surrounded by a halo, as if he remembered the grace just granted him when he was in Ti Jean's amazing grip. At last, letting the heavy stone hang harmless in his hand, then putting it down slowly on the grass, he said with an air of calculated indifference:

"Well, shall we stop the contest, brother-in-law?"

"Stop or carry on—whichever you like, brother-in-law."

"I'm not too keen on carrying on," said Anancy, touching his throat meaningly.

"I'm not very keen either," said Ti Jean with a smile. "In fact, to tell you the truth, I'm not keen at all, brother-in-law."

The two adversaries stood stiff and upright, looking at each other, silent, more taciturn than night, their arms hanging idle in the glory of their budding friendship. Egea, seeing them thus, rolled delighted on the grass, all beautiful and shining.

"Heavens above," she cried. "There's never been such a mad pair as these in Fond-Zombi. Heavens, heavens, heavens—what will become of me with a couple of customers like this?"

From that day on, Anancy accompanied them as a matter of course on their way to school, chatting to his new friend indirectly through Egea, who listened to what each said and passed it on, turning from one to the other like a mirror. Anancy also joined them on the way to the river. But when they got to the fork in the road he branched off to a bathing place used by children old enough to be able to do wrong, while the two innocents went straight on along the path leading to the Blue Pool. On the riverbank Anancy's eyes became suddenly peaceful, and all the gentleness in the world seemed to flow beneath his bulging brow. But once past the Bridge of Beyond on the way back to the village, the same eyes became like vicious dogs again, growling and raging against everything they saw. He had found a rusty old pistol which he secretly polished from morn till night, pretending, impossible though it was, that he was restoring it to working order. As he rubbed away at his bit of old iron he kept saying that Guadeloupe was at war, a secret war that the people of Fond-Zombi could not see. But whenever Ti Jean plucked up his courage and asked who on earth the war was against, that fool Anancy just shrugged his shoulders dejectedly and said he didn't know. It wasn't a war against anyone; no, it was just a canker in his breast, a spirit gnawing at him, that's all.

One evening as they were coming back from the river Anancy assumed his hunted air and made them go with him to Ma Vitaline's veranda, where an endless conversation was carried on about the black man, his insignificance and folly and the unfathomable mystery he was in his own eyes. Dusk crept up from the street, an acetylene lamp sent out greenish rays from the bar, and you could tell that many words had flown through the air and fallen where they might. Some people's faces were thoughtful, others watched one another furtively with a glint of malice in their eye, inwardly congratulating themselves on their cleverness at getting the better of life. It was the old, eternal refrain. Someone said God doesn't love us because we're only his bastards and the white men are his real children. Someone else said life is a wheel, and that if it had turned differently the white men would have been where we are, our slaves perhaps. Fat Edward, speaking through his sweaty mustache, said as usual that the black man is his own curse—moody, incoherent, flamboyant, tainted in his very blood, a savage good for nothing but cutting capers and pulling faces. Then, picking up a glass of rum to loosen a tongue still stiff from a day in the sun, Fat Edward, the devil, laughed quietly and continued:

"So you suffer, do you, you useless lot? Well, go on suffering, my little wingless angels, and just let me tell you your suffering will get nowhere, and no one in the world, no one, has the least idea it exists."

At that point old Filao bent his thin body toward him and said in a low voice, as if afraid to raise his Ancient's voice:

"Hey, Fat Edward, smasher of other people's delight, won't you ever have a pleasant word to say to people? We know we're outcasts, but does that mean we haven't got souls, as you seem to think? Won't you even let us have a soul, my friend?"

"You feel you've got a soul, do you?" cried the other.

"I may well have, I may well have," said old Filao doubtfully. "Don't you feel you've got one?"

"Me? A soul? No, it's only men who have souls, old Filao. And I may look like a man, but I'm not one."

"What do you feel you are, then?" asked the old man.

"Sometimes a donkey and sometimes a horse. Now one and now the other," answered the drunkard with a sarcastic pretense of regret which succeeded in finishing off his audience.

Never in all the generations that this dreary refrain had been heard on Ma Vitaline's veranda had black men been rated so low, and the people gazed at each other in dismay and self-doubt. Then old Filao, deciding that Fat Edward had gone too far, cleared his throat, and in a faint voice which forced people to follow the lapping of his thin lips, a dead voice that sounded as if he were afraid of wounding someone or of wounding himself with his words, he said:

"Fat Edward, my friend, you breathe an air in the forest that doesn't agree with you. We are what we are, and the disaster

41

is complete, naked, without any trappings. But it's because we've been beaten and beaten again—don't you ever think of that? Yes, we were men once, whole men, like everyone on earth. And we built their sugar factories, we worked in their fields and built their houses, and they beat us and belabored us until we didn't know anymore whether we belonged to the world of men or to the world of the winds, the void, and nothingness."

Then there was a long silence, and from the Bridge of Beyond came a mountain breeze which blew onto Ma Vitaline's veranda and did everyone good. They all looked at old Filao, with his hollow cheeks, mumbling away, suddenly angry, and upset at having spoken out for the first time in his life. Many visions had been born, many theories hatched during those slow late afternoons, about the black man, his insignificance and folly and the mystery he was in his own eyes. But the one they'd just heard was the strangest of all, and everyone was spellbound. Then, as they sighed and scratched their heads, not wishing to break the spell of the Ancient's words, a shrill clear childish voice was heard.

"Why did they do that to us, old Filao?"

"Boy," said the old man, turning in surprise toward Ti Jean, who had stuck his head up over the third step of Ma Vitaline's veranda, "no one can say, my little flute, for those who beat us have kept the dagger in their hands and their reasons in their hearts."

The boy turned pale and put his hands to his head, and strange words fell from his lips, words he did not recognize although they were uttered with his own voice, his own tongue.

"Old Filao," he said, "with all respect—there are no birds left in last year's nests, and I, who am not afraid of death or the dagger, I shall wrest it from their hands."

"Ti Jean, my poor child, what raging sea is your brain swamped in all of a sudden? Do you think you are a new generation in yourself?"

There were hoots of laughter from all sides, but Anancy's eyes sparkled above his sharp cheekbones, two bright patches in the darkness beside our hero. And then to Ti Jean's rescue came the furious, slightly cracked voice of his friend, rising above the din.

"Old Filao, it is true that one alone can't be a new generation. But two can, as surely as I am Anancy Kaya and a good colleague of death myself."

And then, while Ti Jean still stood amazed at the words that had fallen from his lips, a shade rose from the roof of the veranda, and the old crow with the shabby yellow head flew over the road, and with a sound like the sighing of a wave, vanished almost immediately in the darkness, making for the mountain.

The two boys, suddenly awkward, ran off into the night, followed by Egea, who hung onto one of their sleeves, laughing without knowing why. Ma Vitaline's bar fell silent. Inside, the men drummed their fingers on the little wooden tables; outside, on the dark roadside, someone under a spell, whose soul flitted about here and there, started to thresh the air with uplifted arms. At last one of the drinkers commented on what had just happened: was it really children who had just spoken, their own children who had been talking that language of death? But the hoarse voice of an old woman soon shut him up.

"Children?" she said. "What children? Have you ever seen children immune from death? When children no longer die, then we'll talk about children."

And the other women, who until now had remained silent behind the railing while generations of men dreamed on Ma Vitaline's veranda, now suddenly looked at each other and smiled, and said with surprise tinged with sadness:

"Do you hear, all of you, how a woman speaks when she gets around to it?"

3.

During the days that followed, the winged spirit secretly shared the children's lives, fluttering here and there at a distance while they feverishly thought how to get the knife out of the hands of the white men. It was a harsh and difficult task, rising up before them like a slippery wall reaching to the sky. And oftentimes Ti Jean, getting depressed, would suggest having recourse to spells of darkness, to the magic which seemed to him the black man's only chance against the invulnerable strength of the white universe. But Anancy laughed at this, saying that while sorcerers could breathe fire from their nostrils, there had never been one of them who could make a simple safety match: in his opinion, the only witchcraft the black man needed was guns and bullets. So Ti Jean said no more, overcome by the force of the argument. He spared a melancholy thought for the bird flitting above him wherever he went, even on the way to school, invisible to all other eyes but his. And in the evening, before he barred the door, he would slip quietly over to the guava tree in the yard where since the incident on Ma Vitaline's veranda the winged spirit was in the habit of perching. And there, looking reproachfully at the little blue-black ball which trembled at his approach and shifted from foot to foot at the top of the tree, he would ask it why it had inspired him with such great words about the black man on Ma Vitaline's veranda. Why had it done it, eh?

Now one dark cloudswept evening an old man, a stranger, presented himself at Ma Eloise's hut and asked to speak to her. He was curious-looking, long and lean as a day without bread, with a big bacua hat flopping over his shoulders. His body was draped in vegetable-fiber shorts and shirt, the latter in shreds like a badly cured goatskin. Ti Jean hadn't seen the crow for three days, either on the way to school, or when he was out for a walk, or on its chosen branch in the guava tree. He was beginning to wonder anxiously whether the ghost hadn't gone back to the other world, tired of hearing his reproaches. Now, his heart in his mouth, he thought he recognized his winged companion in the stranger waiting on the doorstep, with his emaciated features as of an eternal wanderer between heaven and earth forever in doubt as to where to set his transparent, ghostly feet.

Meanwhile Ma Eloise trembled at the sight of the man, and leading him into the hut with a hesitant hand, as if touching some relic, sat him down at the table with signs of the utmost respect. Then she set before him a plate, a dram of rum and a jug of cold water, and he started to eat peacefully with his hands, apparently not noticing the fork shining there in front of him. Ma Eloise stooped over him, and whenever he went to fill his glass or break off a piece of bread she anticipated him in a flash, a dragonfly divining his slightest wish. And when he had finished, belched and rinsed his hands in a bowl of water, she turned her face away and breathed:

"So here you are under my roof, Old Eusebius?"

"I see you recognize me," he said, sucking at his lips with satisfaction. "You know who sent me, my girl. The Master. He said, Go down among the people Down There and find Awa. Tell her I smell of the grave, that I shall die at dawn, and I must see the boy before I go. The Master also said, As the poor woman won't want to trust her pup to you, tell her she can come with him."

"Is that all he said about me—'poor woman'?"

"No," he said with an embarrassed smile. "The Master also said, I'll be glad to see her anyway, one last time."

"Glad? He said he'd be glad?" Eloise repeated in a shrill voice, her arms dangling, a look of catastrophe on her face. And then her eyes started to shine with such delight that she laid her hand on her heart as if to help it bear the shock, and her delicate pursed lips opened in astonishment.

The three of them left the house and slowly climbed up among the deep lanes that vanished into the dusk and only existed for their feet. When they entered the outskirts of the forest the moon had risen a notch in the sky, and its rays flecked the leaves and spread in luminous patches over the moss. In the unreal light the boy turned his eyes toward his mother, who was climbing eagerly, making every effort, her mouth wide open and her hand on her heart, still gripped in the same emotion as had seized her in the house. And remembering her ashen face whenever anyone uttered certain words or names where she could hear them, he thought that she must always have known the truth about the Immortal One. Several hours passed in this fashion. Then at a certain moment the man leading the way signed to them to stop, and whispered: "Don't be afraid—Powers are passing by." A few seconds later a hollow rumble rolled down the mountainside, followed by a streak of light that circled a rocky peak, fell toward the sea, and faded away. Silence restored, the man heaved a sigh and set off once more. And as he was lit up by a moonbeam, Ti Jean could see beads of sweat suddenly covering his face as he murmured bitterly:

"This is the blackest night that has ever fallen over Guadeloupe. Heaven and earth are shaken, but the sons of slaves have heard nothing, and just go on sleeping while the last black man from Africa departs. A hundred and a hundred years ago did you leave your village, Wademba, old warrior, and now you are going home and leaving us to the dark. You say there is no longer a path, you say the road has stopped, and that it is time, and more than time, for you to return to the Old Country. But were not you the path, the only path left to us? And now we are left in the dark, left in the dark."

Farther on, at the foot of the plateau, he pushed aside a clump of aloes and revealed a narrow opening, a kind of corridor through the mass of briars which Ti Jean had thought impenetrable the day he went in search of a voice borne by the wind from the other side of the valley. Then came a dizzy slope between two cliffs, a stretch of ruins overrun with vegetation, and they came to a round hut lime-washed in moonlight, an African Negro's hut as in the pictures, with a roof like Old Eusebius's hat. A halo encircled a number of still shapes by the door: men and women revealing aged nakedness, with the haunted faces of ghosts. And there were all kinds of wild animals too, all sitting in their own particular manner in an attitude of expectation. Some seemed to hesitate between the two worlds, with human noses and human mouths, but great black ears sticking oddly out among feathers or fur, just like when Ma Justina crashed down on the road. Old Eusebius took one great stride with his strange, youthful, springy step, and his gangling shape took its place among the rest, suddenly frozen in the same absence. Then a deep bass voice rang out inside the hut in sad, majestic harmony, and it was the voice that had sung in the wind on Bartholomew Hill. It said: "Come in, come in quickly, child, for those outside are not fit company for you."

Ma Eloise passed by the troop of spirits, bowing her head politely to them, and thrust her son inside the hut. The child had to blink for a while. It was like a cave with dimly shining walls, ancient soot gleaming in the faint light of the little oil lamps burning smokily on the mud floor. They showed a few pots, a hearth of unworked stones, and a bed of palm leaves and dried grass at the back of the room; also, in the conical shadow of the roof, all kinds of phials and bunches of herbs dangling on strings from the rafters.

A huge black man was sitting in the middle of the hut on a little stool of carved wood, his knees hunched up to his shoulders and completely naked except for a leather belt and a ring round one arm. He was the tallest man Ti Jean had ever seen. But his torso was all hooped together with bones, like an old cask crumbling to dust, and his skin, with its blotches of lichen, made one think of the tree trunks that are washed up on the beaches at the mercy of time, seared through and through by sun and sea. The massive brow rested on his knees, and all that was to be seen was his exuberant, luxuriant hair, like a bush of yellow cotton, like the tuft of feathers above the beak and red eyes of the crow. The man looked lifeless, and Ti Jean thought he must have died just as he himself entered the hut. But then the great brow was slowly raised, and the man said:

"You see, boy, as long as you can still twist and turn you

47

haven't yet reached the other world. Come here, my little vine, and let me look at you for a while with human eyes for once."

The worn eyes began to shine with a painful, dazzling light, and Ti Jean saw again the look that had seemed to him so sad in the face of a crow. He took a step forward, and the old man stretched out the wattles of his neck to see him better, the pupils of his eyes already darkened by death. He must still have been unable to see all he wanted, for he reached out for an oil lamp which he moved around Ti Jean with a sort of lingering greed, giving clicks of satisfaction with his tongue at every stage of his examination. Then he took up an ancient gun which lay at his feet, and lifted it in a gentle gesture, his eyes pink with emotion.

"Look," he said, "look well at this musket. It belonged to a black man who lived on this plateau in days gone by. His name was Obé, and I am honored to say he was my friend. Just that: Obé. You've learned your letters at school, but you won't find that name in any book, for it was the name of a fine, a valiant black man. How could you have heard of Obé? Only the people Down Below could have told you of him, if they hadn't done all they could, for nearly two centuries, to forget him.

"And yet," went on Wademba dreamily, "what is the spirit, the shade of man but his stories, those which constantly follow him and without which no race survives? But all that these wretches chase after, stuck on this forsaken island, is but the shade of the clouds, while your own you consign to oblivion."

The boy, fascinated by all this, looked with religious awe at the musket's emblazoned butt, its silver pan, and the strange hole through which some old Fond-Zombi hunters still introduced their black powder. Meanwhile the enthralling voice of the old man went on:

"This weapon is endowed with great power, for into it I have put all I know. Tomorrow morning it will go with me into the grave. But one day you will have need of it and will come and dig it up—such is the will of the gods. And since you will use it, for that is your fate, do not be afraid, my son, but take this old gun in your hands and tell me: do you want to hear the story of Obé, my friend Obé, the man who used it before you?"

Ti Jean seized the gun with both hands and was filled with a strange light. It was as if he were being shown the hidden face of things, the majestic though invisible universe he had always suspected of existing under the mask. And though he had never seen the name of Obé in a book, nor even heard anyone speak it, he knew he had always been waiting to hear his story, and that he had come into the world to hear it tonight from his grandfather's lips. Tears blinded him, and the old man said that was as it should be—he had reacted perfectly. Gently he took back the musket and laid it on the floor, setting it down beside him with affection and respect, as if it were alive. Then, raising one arm from his side, he reached out carefully and cupped his huge hand around Ti Jean's face, without actually touching it, in a sort of immaterial caress.

"Listen, my little buffalo," he said. "My time is near. Already I smell of the grave. So I shall not tell you about Obé's childhood in the plantations and the mud—mud of the body and mud of the soul, for my friend Obé was the son and grandson of slaves. Nor shall I tell you of the deeds he did among us, before our very eyes, after the black man had taken to the woods. I shall begin his story at the end, when he came down this plateau with a bullet in his chest and one arm broken by a shell. We were surrounded, and short of ammunition. Obé held a spear in his good hand, and two others between his teeth. Suddenly he dashed into the ranks of the French and stuck his spears into the chests of three soldiers. As he did so, he just had time to say: 'For my grandfather, for my father, and for me!' "

His head thrown back slightly, gazing absently into the distance, the old man swayed to and fro as if to some inner music, throbbing, nostalgic, playing behind his heavy lids with their tufts of white lashes.

"Yes, that was how he descended the rocks of the plateau

for the last time, in the years that followed the great light of the Matouba. I myself came to this country when I was your age, right in the middle of the Revolution—I mean the white man's, not ours. My eyes were not yet ready to appreciate the light of the Matouba, and it was only later that it appeared to me in all its splendor. But the whites had seen that light and remembered it forever, and didn't want to see it return. And that was why they beat the soles off Obé's feet before they led him to the guillotine, a rusty old contraption they'd set up by the harbor at La Pointe, as in the good old days. They hoped, you see, that he wouldn't be able to walk to his execution. But the slaves they'd massed along the streets noticed nothing that day, except for those at the front, who could see the footprints he left. And when they laid him on the guillotine, the knife got stuck twice, and Obé said coolly, sardonic as a prince to the last: 'If you go on like this, gentlemen, you'll end up really hurting me.' "

Wademba's lids, with their tufts of white lashes, fell suddenly, heavily shut, as if he had fallen asleep where he sat.

"So," he said, a touch of harshness in his voice now, "that was how my friend Obé went, a long, long time ago—more than one lifetime, more than two, more than three, for ten generations have gone by since I was brought as a child to this forsaken island. I've seen many suns rise, and there are many other black men I'd have liked to tell you of: Ako, Mindumu, N'Deconde, Djuka the Great, who came on the same boat as I did, and many, many besides. But no matter. If you ever come back here, bend down and breathe in the scent of the grass, for the grass is the hair of the heroes sleeping under the earth."

Wademba remained there sitting upright in a dream, his two huge fists planted on his knees with the thumbs tucked in—like Ti Jean himself when he was thinking. This resemblance made him look at the giant's sleeping face with its slanting eyes, the square shaft of the nose, the high cheekbones, the round skull like a helmet and jutting brows like a visor. Then his head started to swim, for it was as if he were looking at his own face, reflected in the gulf and unfathomable well of time.

A musky odor came from the great slumbering body, a smell as of a fierce and solitary beast, and Ti Jean sensed behind him the discreet presence of Ma Eloise, who on stepping into the hut had taken refuge by the wall, in a dark corner. A sudden rage seized him at the thought of her shining eyes as she had hurried through the night to see this great man who did not remember her until the hour of his death. He saw again in his mind's eye how she used to close the doors and windows on her little frightened soul. She had lived in a boundless terror, on a bottomless sea, and she had accepted it as her natural environment, like the air she breathed, like the fine braids that seemed to sparkle on her neck, and like her beautiful eyes always full of trembling water ready to ripple at the least breeze. And the boy said in his heart: Ma Eloise, don't forget that for me you are as tall as the sky, and your least little tremor is dear to me. And his fists were clenching and stretching out mechanically toward the old man as if he were about to fall on him and destroy him, when the sleeping lips opened to say:

"Ah, Powers, are these the questions my own flesh and blood asks me when I am about to go and lie down in the heart of darkness?"

The eyelids rose to reveal a great peaceful gaze, the same distant pink as the setting sun, and he whom men had thought immortal smiled for the first time.

"There's no need to hate me, child," he said. "I sent your mother among the people Down Below, and didn't want you to get to know the smell of these woods too soon because otherwise you would never have gone down again. And as you can see, there was nothing for you here but solitude and death. But you have just taught me something, and if I could give you a name I would call you vine, vine of the yam, for it is the vine that links one yam to another. Tell me, little flute, what do you think of the people Down Below?"

He scrutinized the silent child for some time, then said in astonishment: "You find them . . . beautiful?"

The child nodded.

"What else?"

The child bit his lip, perplexed.

"You find them . . . more than beautiful. Is that it?"

The child bobbed his head up and down, delighted at having been understood so well.

"Ah," said Wademba gravely, "I see you are like the elephant, which has several homes and several wives. To tell you the truth, I have often pitied the people Down Below, for of all the birds in the world they are the only ones who have forgotten their nest. But if I looked at them through your eyes I would, with your permission, my child, accuse them only of having short memories. It is true," he added, slipping into reverie again, "it is true I belong to a race whose blood is heavy and slow, and who never forget anything."

Then, smiling once more:

"Go on. What is it you like so much about the people Down Below?"

"Their pretense," the child answered this time.

"Ah, I see you have guessed everything, and if I only could give you an African name I'd call you Abunasanga—He Who Moves in the Depths. Who knows, perhaps one day you yourself will warm the sun."

"The sun?" said the boy, laughing.

The gnarled, tortoise-like fingers stretched out again to cup Ti Jean's face awkwardly, without touching it.

"Meanwhile," said the old man, "get all the warmth you can from it, so that the marrow of your bones will remember it when the time comes."

Then Wademba bent and picked up a jug and poured on the mud floor a few drops of a whitish liquid with little round yellow specks in it. Each time the floor absorbed a drop, he said a few words in a strange language. Then he signed to Ma Eloise, poured out a little pot of the liquid for each of his guests, then clasped his hands around the jug and observed, smiling:

"In the village where I was born there was a song that said the fish of the sea were dumb because they drank water, and that they would sing if they drank pombe. So let us drink some of this fine millet beer together, for the first and last time."

After performing the libation, all three sank into silence and peace. The old man was starting to dream again, one hand held out blindly toward the boy, when the anxious voice of Ti Jean interrupted his reverie.

"Are you sure, Grandfather? Are you really sure?"

He was looking at the musket lying on the floor, and his dilated pupils seemed to see through the relic to the hero's rush through the dark and his final striking down.

"Are you sure, Grandfather? Are you really sure?"

"I was there. I can bear witness to it," said Wademba quietly.

"And what about your own deeds?" the boy went on in the same eager yet faint little voice.

"Don't worry. My deeds were honorable. You have no need to blush for your own flesh and blood."

"But . . . ?"

"Don't worry, my little buffalo. When you have horns, you will know that it is not for a man to speak for himself."

"What about Ma Eloise?"

"She heard stories about me when she was a child, but those who told them were all born several generations after me. None has seen me; none really knows who I am. And it is better so, for people are always telling the story of the dead, dead stories in short, and my story is not dead, for it continues with you."

"Grandfather, no story like the one you have told can happen in the valley. Anancy and I have looked and looked."

"Nevertheless a fine story awaits you, one that will present itself to you without your looking for it."

"A real story of my own?"

"As real as the next, my little flea."

"And can you tell me it?"

"Oh, no, that's not a sensible thing to ask. If I tell you it won't happen. Fate is as thin as a sheet of paper, you see, and a story can be lived only once, one little time in all eternity.

And he who knows his story in advance is doomed to live it only in dream. But while I am not allowed to open your eyes, there is one thing I can do for you, my little buffalo, and that's give you a viaticum for the journey."

The ancient of days paused.

"For your story will not be an easy one, my man; it won't have jam on it. Some days, even, you will think it's the harshest and bitterest ever told under the sun."

The boy smiled at this somber prophecy. And as he wondered, and searched his heart from high to low and from left to right under every span of his dazzled flesh, Wademba sadly undid his leather thong and slipped it onto the tiny arm of our hero. When he had wound it round twice and fastened it by means of one of the little shells that ran along it like a row of buttons, he said:

"I shall no longer be here when those things happen, and you won't have anyone's voice to guide you. But this is a bracelet of knowledge, and it will speak for me. It won't always speak clearly, and sometimes you will have to guide yourself. But whenever it does speak to you clearly you must follow what it says exactly, at all costs, even if it tells you to jump off a precipice. Keep it on your arm and never take it off day or night, in the air or in the water, except if you abandon human form. There, it is on your arm now, and you no longer need me to guide you."

His eyes suddenly wavered, and moving like a sleepwalker he slowly undid the rough leather band from his waist and held it out to the boy.

"This is a belt of strength. Put it round you and never take it off day or night, in the air or in the water, except if you abandon human form.

"So. You no longer need my voice to guide you nor my strength to protect you. But be careful not to do as those dark ones listening to us outside, whose only pleasure is to be like gods. I didn't send your mother down there for you to go in for foolish exploits while the white men abuse our race. Your path among men, remember, is among those Down Below, and its name is sadness, darkness, misfortune and blood."

Then Wademba rose painfully, creaking like a dismembered corpse, and straightened himself up toward the ceiling of the hut. He looked strangely naked and old and helpless without the insignia of power of which he had just divested himself. He absently took a few steps toward the stone hearth, crouched down by a drum, took up some water from it in the palm of his hand and trickled it down his huge genitals, which hung like a dead bird. Finally he reached the back of the hut, lay down peacefully on the bed of dried grass, shut his eyes on the world once more, and said:

"Rest in peace, both of you—you, Ti Jean, and you too, my dear Awa, who drubbed me with a stick because of your love for your son, which was much bigger than your little frightened heart. When the sun rises, unlatch the door and go down, both of you, to the village, without looking back. My friends will bury me at the foot of the mango tree in front of the hut, and lay Obé's gun on my body. And when his time is come, the boy will be able to find my grave."

Ti Jean and his mother stayed up all night, standing there just as Wademba's last words had left them, lost, without doing anything to see if the old man was still alive and breathing. The boy kept telling himself, amid peaceful happy tears that seemed as if they would never cease, that when the oldest man in the world died his eyes were the pink of sunset. And just before dawn a voice rose out of the trembling morning mist, a clear disembodied voice that seemed to have cast off all links with this world.

"It was long, long ago when I left my village, Obanishe, on the bend of the Niger, and all those who knew me sleep in the dust. But if one day you ever go there, you or your son or your grandson, down to the thousandth generation, just say you had an ancestor called Wademba and you will be welcomed like brothers. For I belong to a blood that is very heavy and slow, a race that has a very long memory and forgets nothing, not even the flight of a bird through the sky. Don't forget—Obanishe, on the bend of the Niger."

The boy and his mother did as the old man had told them. At the first glimmers of dawn Ti Jean unbarred the door: there were the troop of spirits who had been waiting all night, still as statues. Mother and son went out of the round hut and down from the plateau without once looking back.

When they got to the foot of the mountain they heard the first beats of a tom-tom. It went on for three days, spreading dismay among the frightened hearts of Fond-Zombi. Then the mountain returned to silence.

4.

Back in the valley the boy found himself in a world without depth or echo, a disenchanted plain, a flat dry basin. Wademba's belt hung useless round his waist, and though he glued his ear to the leather bracelet, the earnest of divination and knowledge, no voice ever came to take the place of the old crow that was gone.

Thus, always on the lookout, bending over his silent arm, Ti Jean passed two years, and one day he saw there was now a man in his trousers. He opened his eyes and saw beside him a girl of thick dark purple velvet, full to the brim of strange, delectable sap. When they walked along the road to school she moved as smoothly as a pair of scales. And when they got to the river she became a flying fish leaping over the waves, her flesh full and juicy, sparkling in the sun and as if radiant with the millions of eggs jostling in her womb. And so Egea was a woman in her robe, and the day of the calm and special pools of childhood was well and truly over.

When all this became clear, a little party was given in their honor by the Blue Pool. And the two children saluted for the last time the waterfall, the white rocks in the middle of the stream and the bushy old mango tree in which they had spelled out love. They could have gone on as before in secret, as many others did. But many bellies swelled too soon, and Ti Jean decided to wait until he was old enough to give the girl a house before he inhabited her living body again. But he was in agony in her presence, and was sometimes afraid of toppling her over in a field without even thinking of it. So instead of going to school he would take down the old cartridge-loading gun that used to belong to his father, the late Jean L'horizon, and scour the woods in search of a turtledove, a raccoon or an agouti. And that was how he became a hunter by trade.

At that time the forest was already in decline, and the old people said that the world was growing tired, that everywhere there was one and the same decay of water, air and earth, and nothing would be spared. The time was long since past when there were miraculous hunts, with peccaries running openly across the plain and wood pigeons cooing away in the surrounding woods. The larger animals had taken refuge on the heights and left their lairs only at night. Up there near the clouds they were under the protection of the spirits of the mountain, and rare were the hunters who dared to go thither; rarer still those who dared and didn't go mad.

At first the boy had hunted over the country nearby, returning just before twilight, the witching hour, with a vast jacket falling to bits over his shoulders and his waist hung about with little birds. And then some strange force had made him push farther, into the middle of the forest. He was attracted by the great trees. Sometimes he would undress near some smooth young trunk and embrace it, losing himself in a dream of Egea. One day as he was watching for a raccoon near the Bradefort waterfall, a woman emerged wringing out her hair, which was longer than she was tall. She was a Maman d'l'Eau, a Mother of the Water, all black with greenish gleams and patterns, and liquid curves that made you think of her as swimming and disporting herself in the water even when she was walking along the riverbank or sitting motionless on the cushion of her rolled-up hair. Ti Jean knew the shapes of all the apparitions—they had been described to him by the old hunters, the ones who used to talk about the days of the peccaries among the canes, and wood pigeons and ortolans sitting within arm's reach on the roofs of houses. The old people's stories did not always agree, for apparitions like to lead you astray and confuse you, so that their image does not remain on mortal retinas. But this one was certainly a Maman d'l'Eau, and there was no need to be afraid of her, he told himself as he approached her. She smiled incredulously.

"Do you know who I am, little boy?" she said.

Ti Jean touched the belt round his waist and the token of divination on his arm, and he seemed to be wrapped in a marvelous shell of power and invulnerability. He took a step forward, then another, and the creature before him went on in an anxious, trembling voice:

"Do you know that to see me is death to mortals?"

As she spoke she backed away and entered the pool, followed by the boy. He couldn't tear his eyes away from the great dazzling corridors that opened up between her lashes. Suddenly she held nailless hands out to him and took him in a weird embrace, burning as hot oil, and started to drag her victim down toward the depths of the Bradefort, under the foaming column of the falls. Ti Jean, almost fainting away, could already see his dead body floating on the estuary. This thought filled him with rage, and he tried to inhabit the body of the Maman d'l'Eau, to show her that there had been a man in the trousers of this wretched little mortal. But as he was setting about this in the proper manner, she let out a cry of despair, and slipped from between his fingers in millions of bubbles, all black with greenish gleams and patterns, which were swept away by the current.

This incident emboldened our young fellow, and from then on he ventured farther toward the heights in his quest for big game, sometimes even spending whole nights in the mountains, alone with only a wood fire for shelter. A bitch he had taken with him at first had gone mad, because of the Powers which fell on her soul and which she couldn't resist. The boy himself had difficulty standing up to the nocturnal apparitions—zombies, devils' horses, balls of fire that whizzed right up to his feet. Animals with human faces would lurk round his camp, and one day as he was making his way through a thicket he felt a thump on his back from a stick, and turning round, nearly fainted away at the sight of the phosphorescent face of Filbert, a black man long dead and buried. But the worst of his trials was an apparition that came from inside himself when he was asleep. Try as he might to stay awake, sitting by the fire and putting more wood on it from time to time, he never succeeded in seeing the day break. Terror itself couldn't make him keep his eyes open. At a certain moment, angelically gentle fingers would be laid on his eyelids and his whole body would enter into darkness like a house with the shutters closed, a little piece of night within the great night of the world. But there was still a little candle burning deep inside him, and he knew he was asleep, and waited in dread for what was going to follow: the swirling in his chest, the bubble that would form on his sleeping lips and turn into a big yellow-beaked crow which took a few steps in the grass to stretch its legs, then spread its strong wings with relief and departed, flying straight up above the world.

The breath of Ti Jean himself would be behind the bird's eyes, and he was enchanted to see rocky peaks and ridges rushing past below him as if flattened and smoothed by the height, the slopes falling away to the plain and its vast cane fields and its tiny clusters of huts, with every so often coconut palms waving their tresses over the roofs. The earth was the earth no longer, and the moon hung in the sky like the fruit of a tree which stretched up to the vault and whose trunk and branches he could dimly discern. And so they both sailed beneath the stars, the crow and the child's soul perched behind the bird's little round eyes. Then, always before dawn, the bird would bring him back to the paling embers of the fire and to the shape that seemed not to have moved, that even seemed to have stopped breathing, the nostrils pinched and the mouth half open on the darkness. The bird would flap its wings again, but this time with a suggestion of regret. And then it slipped between Ti Jean's lips and down into his sleeping breast.

When he woke he would find an insect's wing case on the corner of his mouth, and fragments of something unidentifiable on his tongue. And when he ran his fingers over his body, icy with fright, he suddenly felt nothing but wandering and insubstantiality, insubstantiality and wandering. But his head was still there, still well screwed onto his shoulders as it should be. And at the height of his terror he felt a strange satisfaction at being there off his own bat, and able to tell himself that if, with one thing and another, his brain became unhinged, at least the defeat would be his own.

When he came down from the mountains, his eyes blurred and uncertain, people murmured that Ma Eloise's son had a lump of dry earth instead of a head, a lump of hard dry earth that didn't absorb the rain. But they were reassured when they heard his laughter, as smooth and fresh as ever, perfectly innocent. So that taking it all in all, they thought he couldn't possibly be a Power of Evil, no, not with a laugh like that.

He was about fifteen when the time predicted by Wademba came, and he was already one of the tallest men in Fond-Zombi and the neighboring districts—Valbadiane, La Roncière and L'Abandonnée—if not in the whole of Guadeloupe. But when, one day out hunting, he met his own story, our hero didn't recognize it.

BOOK THREE

Which tells how the Beast swallowed the sun,
shedding darkness over the world;
and how, to end up with, it swallowed Ti Jean.

1.

It all began with a flight of wild ducks at the start of the rainy season. The travelers' arrival always caused a stir in Fond-Zombi. When they appeared in the sky, flying in a first circle around the volcano, the village was seized with secret envy of these wordless creatures who came from so far away and never made a mistake about where to stop. They seemed to know their way better than men did on earth. People were jealous too of their constancy, of the regularity of their flight, and even of their formation in flight together—an arrow bearing within itself both its starting point and its destination. Such a journey, and what had they seen, discussed, flown over with their green silk wings? What more did they know about life than the black man did?

Ti Jean also had a passion for the ducks. When the time came, he could spend whole days watching for them in the mud of a swamp, fascinated by creatures that had the regularity of the stars and seemed to contemplate from on high the course of all the universe. And he fired his gun with reluctance, as if he were shooting at his own dreams.

That year he was up on the heights of the Bois Saint-Jean, on the edge of a marsh where the visitors from space usually rested. It was dawn, but the sun was still smoldering behind the mountain and there was no cloud to be seen, or patch of yellow or blue; only a great dazzling void. Then a shining arrow appeared above the volcano, as in previous years. The flight of birds, making a huge circle in space, arrived vertically over the lake and stayed there, wings outstretched, while the lead duck thrust a long melancholy neck downward to inspect their next halt. Ti Jean gently raised the hammer of his gun, his heart touched by a vague regret for man or bird of passage. And suddenly the marvelous arrow broke up, and flew out to sea in a fine disarray of feathers and cries.

The hero wondered what could have alarmed them so, these seagoing ships, these creatures who had covered so much distance with their green wings. Pushing forward a little way among the reeds, he straightened up and saw a strange shape on the other side of the marsh, just within range. It was in fact an unknown apparition, one the old hunters had never told him of. It resembled a cow, but it was as tall as several ordinary cows, with a human-looking muzzle and two rows of lyre-shaped horns on its head forming a sort of crown. It was lying on its side, its bright white coat sparkling with long, silky, transparent fair hairs like the hair some old women have. Its head lay in the grass, the mouth open at ground level, and all sorts of creatures were entering it in silence. Field mice, mongooses and toads all hopped up to where the cow lay, then onto its chops, before disappearing inside. They seemed to obey the command in the apparition's eyes, which were of an extraordinary blue and pierced right through the hesitant light of dawn. The apparition rolled its orbs slowly in their sockets, and when they lit on Ti Jean he felt a strange desire to cross the marsh and throw himself like the rest into the Beast's gaping jaws. He dived face down in the mud, and the ray passed above him, producing a sort of electricity, the crackle a black woman makes when she tongs her hair. Ti Jean was weeping and sighing and trembling in every limb, thinking he hadn't been born to encounter a Power like this, one the oldest people in the village had never told him about. Then the ray grew weaker, the terrible gaze turned in another direction, and Ti Jean, struggling free of the mud, saw that the swallower had stood up and was looking at the distant sea with her great damp weary eyes which seemed to be imploring, making complaint into the face of day.

That was really too much hypocrisy for one person, even one as tall as several ordinary cows. Ti Jean, in a rage, shoved a charge of buckshot down the barrel of his gun and aimed at the hollow below the shoulder, the place where he thought the heart would be. At that moment a winged shape emerged from the Beast's monstrous ear and flew off into the vegetation around the marsh. Then came the explosion. A round dark patch appeared in the hollow below the left shoulder and the steel pellets bounced off and flew in all directions. The animal hadn't even flinched, and went on looking at the sea. Ti Jean knew then that he was in the presence of a spirit so lofty that it didn't even notice the agitations of human beings. It was as if he'd just fired his deadly charge into the sky in an attempt to hit the sun.

As he made to withdraw, the winged shape flew down again toward the Beast and alighted in its ear. The bird seemed very agitated. It cackled something, then poked out a great yellow pelican's beak as if to bring the mortal to the attention of its master. At once the incredible mass went into action, stretched to its full height and with its tail flung fiercely in the air. Ti Jean forgot all shame, turned, and rushed down the slopes without more ado.

When he got within sight of the village he plunged into the Rivière-aux-Feuilles, the Leafy River, and washed off the mud with which he was still bedaubed. His ears pricked up from time to time, surprised not to hear the trampling of hooves. When he had recovered himself he wondered if he ought not to tell the people of the valley about the apparition. But the longer he thought about it, the more it seemed to him that the folk Down Below were not in the right frame of mind to accept such a strange phenomenon. For some time now, young people back from France would explain the world to you as if it were a little bit of clockwork they knew inside out, putting it together and taking it apart in the palms of their hands. At first the black people of Fond-Zombi were taken aback by these new whites, their own children, flesh of their flesh and the jewel of their loins, but who now looked at them with affectionate mockery just as their former masters did. And then the young people had uttered the word "revolution," and after asking its exact meaning the old people of the village laughed and said: "Children, have you ever seen ghosts bring about a revolution?" But the word had found favor and everyone started using it as if it contained an as yet unknown magic, as if there were really going to be a new earth, a new world and new men at last, at last, just through the bandying about of those divine syllables. Ti Jean himself had been attracted by them, enchanted even, and had had some difficulty in continuing his solitary expeditions over the mountain. And now he was coming down from the mountain with a story that belonged to the old days and was not even guaranteed by tradition.

He shrugged his shoulders and crossed the Bridge of Beyond into the village. As he advanced between the two rows of huts the giant shadow lurking in his mind grew indistinct and lost its shape. He could hear outlandish brayings and deep and frantic appeals: human life in all its strength and detail was there beside him, the life of men and women who suffered and yet laughed in the sun. On Ma Vitaline's veranda a group of modern young men were chatting. They were talking about a recent strike to the death, and saying that everything about the black man needed changing, his head and heart and bowels, and perhaps also his speech should be organized, for, they sighed bitterly, the black man talks and sees the moon at noon. Anancy was there with them, tall, red and rather gawky, with his left cheek scarred by the butt of a policeman's gun outside the sugar factory. At a discreet sign from Ti Jean he came down the three veranda steps, approached his childhood friend and studied him with troubled but piercing eyes. Ti Jean would have liked to throw his arms around his shoulders as in the old days, but instead he just told him quietly what he had seen on the heights of the Bois Saint-Jean. Should he tell the people of the village about the Beast, or warn the authorities? He didn't know what to do and had thought the best thing was to consult his friend, he concluded painfully, his mouth dry and his heart beating fast. Anancy assumed an ironical expression.

"I don't know if I'm your friend," he said coldly. "But you are still mine, and that's why I advise you to keep this story to yourself."

"Why do you say 'this story' like that? Do you think I dreamed it?"

"Listen, great hunter—I know very well you are an extraordinary person, one who can see only extraordinary things. You come and go through life, you don't eat like other people, you don't drink like other people, you don't work like the rest of us, you go up into the forest and talk to spirits if you feel like it, for you are not afraid of anything or anyone, either friend or foe. What is it to you that a girl weeps secretly at night? A shadow, a wisp of smoke that rises before your eyes for a moment and then disappears. You say you've seen something strange? Bravo. I'm only an ordinary person, and all I can say to you is: Keep what you've seen to yourself, my friend."

Ti Jean, his eyes shining with tears, went slowly back to Ma Eloise's house. The hut was empty, all the doors and windows open onto the street. Probably the poor woman was out performing her duties as a leaf doctor, rubbing with herbs, squeezing, pinching and driving out pain with her long green lizard-like fingers. The lad, moved by the thought of Ma Eloise's consoling hands, laid aside his hunting equipment and went and sat on the doorstep. A fine rain rose and fell in the breeze; the leaves on the trees still shone in the rays of the sun, sparkling in the water and the light until they resembled anything rather than leaves. Strange weather, thought Ti Jean. The sort that spirits take advantage of to prowl the earth. Under the porch of a neighboring hut a little girl with a fat bottom was feeding a kid tied to her wrist. She was giving it dittany porridge in the palm of her hand; the animal sucked it up at once, its tail thumping its sides. A little boy stopped to watch what was going on. He was stark naked too, laughing, with a protruding navel, and without looking up the girl said to him curtly:

"Never out of the way, are you, Anatole?"

"So what? Am I annoying you?"

"Yes, your mouth annoys me," said the little girl, as if this were the most ordinary conversation in the world.

"Why?"

"Because no good food ever goes into mouths like yours, and I bet you have no idea what fish tastes like."

"Let me tell you I *have* had fish, and what's more, we have fresh meat once a month."

"Well, *I* say you're lying, Anatole. They say you killed the pig at your place last week and sold the whole of it, so that again you haven't got any meat to eat. But when people kill one of their own animals, it's usually for the family to eat it, isn't it?"

"So they say, but they say a lot of things. For example, it has occurred to me that you might have been carried off by a devil to the top of the mountain, into the mouth of the volcano. And even that he played with you, and you let him."

The little girl stuck her fists in her cheeks and whispered happily:

"Let him?"

"You're not really a little girl," the boy insisted. "You're a woman, Elvina, and you already go with men, for sure. Just look at her with her bare behind—how many men has she had, eh? Not that it's surprising, with a mother like yours—every child with a different father. Shall I tell you what? Your mother's a house that lets itself be covered by any corrugated iron, any straw. All the men go to her—she's a slut. That's what I had to tell you. Answer if you can."

For a moment the girl seemed nonplussed. She shut her eyes, her fists still stuck in her cheeks to hold in the joy that arose from the whole of her cool black body, round as an apple. At last she made an effort and said:

"I needn't say anything for your words are only empty cartridges, blank charges in a rusty gun. But do you know why men go to my mother?"

"It's not difficult—" the boy began.

"My dear fellow," she interrupted, not at all disconcerted, "allow me to tell you that if men go to my mother it's simply because they find her good. Whereas your mother—what unfortunate would want anything to do with her? She's a fruit that's lost its taste and is turning to water. She could be there forever and no one would go to see her. My mother has never climbed up on a roof to call a man, but take care, Anatole, take care that doesn't happen to yours."

Whereupon the little girl gave a strangely beautiful crystal laugh and the boy spluttered and flung up his hands to show he was throwing in the sponge. Then the loser bowed politely and went off merrily, his navel sticking out in front of him. And the human child, turning back to the goat child which was clamoring for its dittany, began to sing, softly, a light gay tune as frothy as lace, which lent an aura of cheerfulness to the great melancholy of the ancient words:

> "My mother has gone away
> With the jar of sugar
> And now every morning
> I drink bitter coffee
> But if you see my mother
> Don't tell no don't tell her
> What a fine blind crab without a hole
> She has brought into the world."

Ti Jean, sitting on the doorstep, was beside himself with delight at this little example of everyday life in Fond-Zombi, which he had neglected these last few years in order to contemplate the tall trees. He had thought he was going along a path of courage, fighting up there in his way just as Anancy fought down here in his. But perhaps he had been wasting his time up on the heights, a little boy who'd seen the world as a flat tabletop while many hitherto unsuspected strata lay below. And suddenly, as he sat on the doorstep, he felt for a moment that the huts of Fond-Zombi had no real foothold on the world. They could start to wobble at any moment—fall apart, be torn from their four stones, and disappear into the sky without leaving any more trace than a flight of wild ducks.

And so an hour or two passed away in a dream, interspersed with a few everyday acts such as splitting wood, digging a trench for yams, threading a batch of leaves for Ma Eloise and hanging them in streamers from the ceiling. It was almost noon when the first shouts rang out from the entrance to the village. The rain had passed over. The earth steamed gently in the sun. Hurrying outside, Ti Jean saw the spirit from the marsh galloping calmly down the middle of the street, each step sending up nebulous whorls of dust.

The Beast's back rose above the rusty roofs of the village, but its open muzzle was at ground level and emitted a soft and funereal wail that froze your insides. Shapes could be seen rushing for the huts or diving, howling, into the ditch. Others at first stood still as statues, then, as the swallower passed by, threw themselves into the enormous dark mouth, which lapped them up carelessly yet delicately. Shots were fired, and one man attacked with a cutlass from the sugar plantations; but it shattered as if he'd struck at the sides of a locomotive. Ti Jean felt very weak, and going back into the hut, he dreamily propped his gun on the windowsill. The whole street was empty, doors and shutters closed against the Beast, which advanced, lowing, neck and nostrils flung up, light eyes gazing at the top of the mountain in inexpressible desolation. When it came level with where Ti Jean was hidden, he tried to greet it with a second charge of buckshot, but to his great surprise his finger froze on the trigger. At the same moment the figure of a child issued from the hut next door, caught up in the still air like a straw in the wind. And then the little girl with the kid was whirled around and set down on the huge heaving tongue and disappeared, swallowed alive and whole.

When it reached the middle of the village the Beast swung suddenly round in the direction of the little cane-covered hill that overhung the road at this point, with one eye on Fond-Zombi and the other on the sea. And there, bracing itself on all four hocks as if to leap a ditch, the apparition rose swiftly up into the blue air of that immortal forenoon, its tail stuck straight out behind and its four legs flung out toward the four quarters. The sun was high on the horizon, and several people who were out of doors saw the Beast approaching the planet, mouth open and white hair becoming a halo of gold as it drew nearer. Then it swallowed the sun, glug, as it had swallowed the children it met with along the road.

But night did not fall at once. First there was a sort of hesitant ebb, like a tide which halts for a moment and sprays out some of its foam before receding toward the depths. And through the stagnant light thus shed over everything, Ti Jean saw a great radiant yellow flame inside the Beast, high up there at the end of a dusky corridor in an already darkened part of the sky.

Then it set off on a downward path, alighted on the other side of the mountain, and suddenly was extinguished like some fabulous firefly as the earth plunged into complete darkness.

It was obvious right away that this was no ordinary night, was not the great black hawk that swooped down on the world when the sun passed over to the other side of the mountains and left Guadeloupe in a warm and living darkness, made up of thousands of sacred words. To begin with there was the silence of all the animals of day, while the animals of night still lay waiting in their lairs, knowing it was not yet time to come out. After that, the colors died away one after the other, and it was then that the real night began: a night more gray than black, a sort of thick vapor which enveloped everything like a fog, slowly separating animals and men, trees and stones, and reducing each one to its own solitude.

The people who were indoors sat trembling, not daring to stir or turn their heads or do anything that might plunge them deeper in the dark; they were like drowning men, not moving lest that drag them down more quickly. Those who were out in the street or in the immediate neighborhood also stayed where they were, reassured and comforted by the nearness of a familiar tree or house. But there were some whom misfortune overtook a long way from home, in the woods or the cane fields or doing their washing by the river. Not knowing what had just taken place in the village, not having seen the Beast flying toward the sun, not even having heard the sound of its hooves on the road, they all seemed suddenly plunged in a terrible dream from which they must escape as soon as possible, no matter how. They went up to one another and touched, pinched, bit till they drew blood, to make the dream stop. Some threw stones at each other, some lashed out randomly with their cutlasses, at the ground or the back of an ox or at a neighbor. And some turned their weapons against themselves, taking pleasure in gashing their own bodies fiercely, as if they'd been waiting a long while for a chance to destroy themselves in dream, sure of coming alive again when they woke up. Later on it emerged that there had been horrific scenes in Pointe-à-Pitre, with rows of cars crashing into one another, breaking down the walls of houses or knocking electricity poles over; there was panic in the department stores when the lights went out. Meanwhile a ship entering the port went straight into the main jetty, setting two or three cargo boats alight; suddenly the whole roadstead was covered with a layer of flaming petrol.

The wave of panic died out when real night came, the night that had come every day since the beginning, the lovely night, queen of the world, with her scarf of stars. Then everyone calmed down, and those who had animals fed them, and afterward got together with other human beings, to talk to them and to give and receive warmth. And because the moon, the stars and the Milky Way had been restored, some people came to think that the sun, master of ceremonies all, would rise next morning as usual.

But many of the inhabitants of Guadeloupe kept vigil that night because they were no longer sure the sun could be trusted. This was particularly so in the country, especially among those who had always believed themselves accursed and so always expected disaster. Not having the wireless, and so not knowing what was going on in the rest of the world, they thought they had been specially afflicted because of the blackness of their souls and of their blood.

2.

That night, a night of nights, Ma Eloise's hut was never empty.
There was always a crowd, a delirious bacchanal. People clustered
round Ti Jean asking over and over again for the story of his
adventure in the marsh, as if they were awaiting a revelation.
He had had time to see the Beast, to examine it with an expert
eye, one used to the nocturnal spirits of the mountains. Perhaps
he would finally make up his mind to deliver a word, an oracle
that would make all clear? But he wouldn't. He would only stu-
pidly stick to the facts, so that in the end they had doubts about
his straightforward description of the monster. Soon everyone
had his own beast, different from all the others. One person would
suddenly remember a gold chain round its neck; another a pair
of arms stretching back openhanded from its spine in a sort of
eternal plea; and another, thin scales of glass which covered its
body and tinkled together like a crystal chandelier when it moved.
According to some, what they had seen was not a cow with
long white hair but in fact a demon, something evil, unclean
and murky, a devil, an Ashtoreth and a cloven hoof, a Satan
like the one Saint Michael was slaying in the picture over the
stoup in La Ramée church: a great black thick-lipped devil, bristling with seven heads that were really seven souls in torment,
each endeavoring on its own account to maintain the state of
evil in the world.

People couldn't keep still. They would come in, listen, give
their opinion and then rush out again, a lighted lantern in their
hands. In they came and out they went, and it was just one
great tongue-wagging—a canter, a cavalry charge of news passed
on at random, just for the pleasure of giving form to a dream,
a sudden terror. During the first few hours discussion centered
on the Beast, its secret reality and its multiple appearances, and
the casual way it flew off to attack the sun. But when the radio

came on again on the stroke of midnight, a large proportion of the crowd hurried to such of the huts as possessed these musical boxes, and when they heard what was going on in the world the happenings in Fond-Zombi at once ceased to seem important. Disaster had struck everywhere. Whole cities were on fire—Paris, Lyons, Marseilles, Bordeaux. Such things defeated the imagination, and it took the good people of Fond-Zombi a long while to accept the fact that the sun had gone out for the whole world without exception, including the famous cities of France itself. They too had witnessed its sudden disappearance, its abrupt extinction like a candle when someone pinches off the wick. At least, they thought as they heard all this on the wireless, at least this time we shan't be the only ones to suffer. But some were rather sorry, sorry and yet not sorry at the same time, if you like, but still sorry not to be the only ones in the world who were afflicted. For what up to then had seemed an unquestionably unique event, a catastrophe of the first magnitude which gratified their hearts, hungry for ostentation, all that was now vanishing miserably in the universal darkness.

On the stroke of two in the morning, people came in with their mouths full of words heard on the radio, strange and learned words like humming tops, which they uttered slowly and solemnly as if they were brilliant explanations of the disaster. There was no need to panic, they said, wringing their hands with dread, no need to go off your head because of an ordinary eclipse caused by a comet passing over the face of the sun. And those who claimed to be the best educated, the "doctors," talked knowingly about the hundreds of rockets that were being sent up into the sky to bring back the lost planet. The radio never mentioned the events which the villagers had witnessed, never made even the slightest veiled reference to them. And gradually a shadow of doubt came to hang over the memory of the Beast, its furious rush and its ascent into heaven. Some talked of it now as if it were something rather ridiculous, a quirk of the imagination, a vision typical of drunkards and marsh dwellers, a lot of bunk that inflamed the minds of a few idle blacks. Even those who had seen it hardly liked to believe in it anymore; and those who still did believe in it, having seen a friend or relation disappear before their very eyes, hardly liked to talk about it in the general cataclysm. After all, perhaps it really was a sort of vision they'd had, a dream, an idle dream of old black men, a story they'd told themselves to lend themselves a bit of importance in the world. And as they thought about this, their great pupils burning with sadness, embarrassment and bewilderment, they slipped furtively out of the hut, leaving Ti Jean to his mulish, cranky stubbornness.

Egea was the only one who didn't come to inquire. And while the neighbors were badgering and pestering him, Ti Jean saw again in his mind's eye a little girl emerging all wet from the water holding a red fish in the palm of her hand. He had hearkened to a hint of his story, the fine story Wademba had promised him, and because of that he had shunned this treasure, this proffered flower, this garden of wild herbs that had waited for him night after night while he kept vigil absurdly on the mountains. He had always known that the black man was part of the mysteries of the world, being a mystery in his own eyes. It was a vague feeling that struck him from time to time, observing certain behavior on the part of the people of Fond-Zombi, their maundering, their love of the extravagant and the useless: now he realized that the maddest of them all had sprung from the womb of Ma Eloise.

When he was alone in the deserted kitchen Ti Jean put both fists on the table, the thumbs tucked inside, and fell into a gentle reverie. Ma Eloise was sleeping in the next room, her pipe in her mouth and one finger on the stem as if to draw from it a puff, a breath, of hope. The boy's mind was completely empty, waiting for a voice to emerge from the magic ring. It was some time before he noticed a series of light little knocks on the door.

"It's us, boy—old Kaya and his daughter. Not wandering spirits, but two of human flesh who want to talk to you about them."

Old Kaya stood outlined in the doorway, a tall gangling body with a floppy iguana's head, absent lips, and pleasant round eyes that looked at you with an expression that was not bewildered but permanently astonished and ecstatic. Ti Jean smiled to himself. Despite what he had just said, the old man did look like a wandering spirit, straying between heaven and earth. He had got himself up in state with a white shirt, a ragged old pair of trousers carefully pressed and sandals made out of bicycle tires. Suddenly he stretched out his lips and confidentially, as if hordes of enemies were hanging on his words, said:

"Things take their course. They only take their course. And if life comes to an end tonight perhaps it will begin again tomorrow. For anything can happen on this earth, and man is but a great wind. He passes, he blows, and disappears. But where to? No one will ever know."

After this strange and rambling speech old Kaya squashed a tear against his nostril as smartly as if it had been a mosquito. And shrugging his shoulders in despair, heartbroken at not having found the words to exorcise evil, he gave a little wave of the hand and was engulfed in the darkness.

Egea had remained on the doorstep, gazing at him with the calm, cautious expression of a suppliant before a sorcerer, before him who is going to lift the veil concealing the spell and hurl back the arrow whence it came. She seemed to be waiting for him to bring back the lost planet and put it in the lap of her dress, there in the middle of the hut. He gave a gesture of helplessness, and she turned her face away and sat down on the top step. Ti Jean blew out the oil lamp and came and sat beside her. She was looking up at the stars, as if to find some reflection or distant trace of the brightness of the sun.

They stayed like that all night long, side by side on the doorstep. The girl's breathing was calm, but Ti Jean knew that terror haunted her convex brow. He recognized the old scent of spices and damp sand and the ilang-ilang perfume she had put under her arms since she was a child, against perspiration. She had scarcely changed at all since then, despite her secondary-school dress, her rings, and the beehive hairdo that now and again for a few brief moments made her look like a woman. But perhaps the chin had got thinner, the brow fuller, lending her a kind of gravity which had been lacking in the child he used to know. And now the voice of the lost years rose up in him, and he said to himself bitterly: You went hunting, boy, and you lost both the dog and the agouti.

In the distance, toward the harbor, spurts of smoke shot up, exploding into a huge yellow flower blotting out a whole expanse of sky. Here and there shadows flitted along the road, transistors pressed to their ears; some were followed by other shadows who questioned them and asked for the latest news. One of them stood still, and Ti Jean recognized the tall red Negro with the mark on his forehead, the scar from the famous blow from a rifle butt he'd got from a policeman outside the sugar factory gate. Anancy's eyes moved wildly and indefatigably in their deep sockets, like two thrushes who refuse to see the bars of their cage. Then he made a great sweeping gesture in the darkness as if to encompass both Ti Jean's folly and his own, each equally futile. And suddenly, overcome by embarrassment, he pulled a face and scurried off under the stars.

Egea seemed to have been waiting for this moment to speak.

"Perhaps the sun will come back tomorrow," she said.

"Perhaps it will."

"But I don't think so," she said without looking at him.

Her cheeks were taut with delight and her hand discreetly hid her mouth, her teeth, her strange giggle. And as no sound came from her throat, her eyes shone in all their brilliance.

"My dear Egea," Ti Jean said jestingly. "You don't seem very worried by all this. You must have the stomach of a crayfish."

"Don't talk like that. You know I have the stomach of a woman. And a woman can never be altogether surprised at what happens."

She still avoided looking at him. Then her voice resumed, with a sort of damp quiver in it as if on the brink of tears:

"I've always known that life is the sea, not the river, and

that it goes nowhere. Have you found what you were looking for, at least?"

"What I was looking for?"

"You remember—you were always looking somewhere else, keeping watch on the clouds like Anancy."

"Yes, I kept watch on the clouds, but the rain I expected didn't fall. But why do you talk to me of Anancy?"

She thought of the lost years, and smiled in the dark to hide her emotion.

"He wanted to save the black man too."

"And you, my little green lettuce—what did you want to save?"

She gave her silent laugh again.

"I just wanted to be saved."

The stars went out one by one, doors opened and faces were turned up eagerly to the sky, which turned into a sort of chiaroscuro shot with intermittent gleams, like splinters of mica in black sand. Then the same cloud as the day before came down again over men, alighting gently on the tops of the trees. And all nature fell silent, till the mist covered everything like a muslin veil, an invisible mosquito net that filtered, isolated and divided. The girl had hoped till the last, despite everything. But when the veil of shade reached them, her and her man of the woods, when it covered them both and separated them, she gave a little sob and ran away to her father's hut.

3.

A little while later, in despair at Egea's silent flight, our hero, pondering in the dark, thought he heard something click inside him, a warning sign. At once he wondered whether he hadn't just encountered his own story, the one predicted by Wademba. Until now he had only imagined a story of black men, rebellion and blood, a story that seemed to have come from his grandfather's lips, with a chase through the darkness and a fall, a destruction. And now, he said to himself, somewhat taken aback, here's my story merging into the fate of the world and the course of the sun in the sky!

When the stars came back he set out on the path to the plateau to take possession of his heritage, the precious gun that was waiting for him on Wademba's grave. He could see himself already, shooting a hole in the Beast with his magic musket, and the sun would return to its place over Fond-Zombi, over Guadeloupe and the rest of the world, while he himself went down into the eternal darkness at once victor and vanquished, as is the fate of heroes. He could see himself, he could see himself already, looking on at the show from the front row, when suddenly abject fear overwhelmed him and drove him down the mountainside, his mouth open in a silent cry.

In Fond-Zombi night had just started to blink its eyes, but that day Ti Jean plunged with one leap into pitch darkness. Fireflies shine at night, says the proverb, not so much to light up the soul of the world as to light up their own. Whereas Ti Jean, through trying to bring the sun back to earth, had only succeeded in sinking deeper into the dark.

While our hero was moping and looking for his heart in his breast and not finding it, a new life had begun in the village. The people stayed at home all day with the doors and shutters closed, waiting for the moon to rise and let them go and find out the news, dig a few vegetables up out of the garden, or cadge some oil at the shop. And then the gray blanket would fall away from the heights, and the people would all rush out without speaking, spellbound by how everything looked in the mist— lonely, frozen forever outside all life and motion. The trees themselves seemed made of some inert foreign matter, great frightening objects taken out of their packing cases and set down here and there, their branches still swathed in cotton wool. The days were long, very long, and each minute was a long space of time in which flesh dissolved and bones turned to dust. The radio had completely stopped broadcasting, and the birds themselves, suddenly struck dumb, were silent. They fluttered around the torches in the gray darkness, the silk of their wings filling your heart with apprehension. People caught them with their hands and shot at game from their doorsteps: the animals, attracted by the light, came up to the guns of their own accord. Then the clockwork which connected this world with the stars also broke down; and gradually the birds grew rarer and finally disappeared, taking with them in their silent retreat all the animals that had come down from the mountains and learned to turn time upside down like the humans, for whom the moon was now the star of day.

Once a week trucks from Pointe-à-Pitre brought flour, sugar, paraffin and casks of dried cod to the town hall in La Ramée. Rations were given out on Sunday when the moon rose. They were distributed individually, and hundreds of torches would come down from the surrounding hills toward the seashore, guiding ox carts jolting a cargo of old people, invalids and expectant mothers. There, in front of the little local church, first mass was now attended by huge congregations kneeling in the square, where loudspeakers fixed to the trees proclaimed the word of God. When it was time for the sermon a wave of panic would sweep over the hundreds of frizzy heads, for they were afraid the priest might say they were responsible for what was happening. But to their great relief he didn't, and though he inveighed more than ever against the devil he seemed to take a less gloomy view of him and included the whole human species in the same damnation. A sigh swept through the crowd, overcome with gratitude. They all stood up, brushed the sand off their knees and went to line up outside the railings of the town hall, where the provisions were given out. Lights hung from the railings and the trucks were parked at the back of the courtyard, guarded by soldiers from the garrison in Basse-Terre. You had to go up between two rows of submachine guns to a table where the mayor checked your face and put down a cross on the list. Then you went to the back of a truck and the police gave you your rations for the week. The whites in their uniforms and the blacks in their rags seemed equally exhausted. Each time he stood there at the tail of a truck Ti Jean would think that whereas hitherto the only thing blacks and whites had shared was death, they were now united also by the bond of fear. Then he would take his dole of flour and paraffin and wander through the town among the hundreds of torches weaving back and forth between the church and the town hall. He did not seek out familiar faces but let himself be borne along with the crowd, with that mist in his heart that isolated him from the whole world except Ma Eloise, whom he still looked on kindly. Behind the church, under the flame trees in the graveyard, an odd handful of folk would be exchanging the latest news about the comet. Each week there was plenty of lively comment: everyone found the whole thing as clear as crystal, except that the eclipse was dragging on rather. One Sunday, looking at the transports of old Kaya, who also had views on the comet, our hero, unable to restrain his astonishment, whispered to him:

"How can you say that, old Kaya? Were you at the bottom of the sea playing with the fishes when that accursed cow went through Fond-Zombi?"

Old Kaya turned toward him, his eyes like those of a wood pigeon in a tree, eternally vigilant, and said in a faraway voice:

"Have pity, boy. Don't add to the load my boat has to carry in the rough sea where we are foundering. All I know is that the whites know the sky better than I know the seat of my pants. They fly up there in their rockets, they count the stars one by one and call each by its name. Is it for me, Augustus Kaya, to tell them what has happened to the sun? And finally, to tell you all I have on my mind—do you think the people of Fond-Zombi have better eyes than everyone else, and that they were the only ones to see that . . . that thing rise up into the sky, if it really did?"

Ti Jean shrugged his shoulders wearily.

"What was it we did see, then, pa?"

"My son," old Kaya answered gravely, "I'll tell you. What we saw were the dreams of idiots."

One of those Sundays the people of Fond-Zombi, coming down from the mountains, found the church deserted and the courtyard of the town hall empty. Not so much as a trace of a policeman. All the white authorities had disappeared, vanished into the darkness.

They went home without benedictions and without any rations but desertion and distress. They had to fall back on the last sugar canes, the last root vegetables lying forgotten in the ground. But even the plants looked strange, all streaked with gray and dark, and people wondered what would become of the poor things if the comet went on sticking to the face of the sun. Amid the mounting confusion Ma Vitaline's shop and Cyprienne's little bar were ransacked. The next day the white people got out their guns and handed them round to their servants; a word to the wise. From then on people kept their distance from the houses with big gates and colonnades, said to be fantastically crammed with the finest grub, enough to feed the whole of Guadeloupe and its dependencies. The planters' way of life seemed safe, and no one took exception to that, for they knew deep down that while the days of the black are light, unsure, and at the mercy of the smallest breeze, no star wandering through the sky could ever stop the white man from going on his way with the direct approval of God. No, there was nothing to object to: people might tend to have forgotten because of the darkness, but they'd always known there is no equality save in death, and only men's bones have the same color and the same fate.

All this was confirmed by those who waited at the planters' tables. After the depression of the early days the Lord's favorites suddenly perked up again and seemed to find a new assurance in the midst of the disaster. Between coffee and liqueurs they would raise a finger and talk of past splendors, of the incredible deeds of their ancestors in the days of the whip and the spiked barrel. And then they would dip their elegant hands into a trunk and take out papers, weapons of chased silver, clothes belonging to another age and fearsome blazoned bells which they would strike gloatingly with their fingers, muttering cock-and-bull phrases about becoming strong and powerful in the darkness— all this in strange voices, according to the watching servants. For the time was approaching when the strong would be strengthened, and the weak . . . The sentence always ended there.

At the same period, metal fences sprang up around the large estates, now guarded by police and soldiers from the garrison in Basse-Terre.

After the last yard of fence was put up no one knew anymore what was whispered around the masters' tables, for the gates were closed on the black servants and they were no longer allowed out. The people of Fond-Zombi watched one another, frightened by their own dreams. No one knew who was the first to take up the words let drop from the masters' tables and make them his new law. But immediately all was confusion and division, neighbor against neighbor, each trying to steal a drop of oil or paraffin or a bit of dried cod. Instead of bringing everyone together under one shelter, darkness seemed to have stolen in between the living bodies, making them look just like dim shapes to one another, bereft of their weight of flesh and blood and old alliance.

One by one the bonds of soul came undone, snapped, or were roughly severed. One black hated the other and strangers entered remote huts and helped themselves to necessities and even luxuries, often cutting the throats of any witnesses. Even the bonds between man and wife were broken. Before, what passed between man and wife was a very important matter, high politics and diplomacy, virtuoso cooking, fine, always served on the best china. People got married for a day or a year or a lifetime, in the town hall or out of it, and sometimes there were shrieks and hamstringings, and distracted women rushing along the street in distress. But nothing was ever done without words, at least at the beginning, without all those subtle and delicate ways learned on the riverbanks; whereas now a woman's beauty or a young girl's freshness might be exchanged for a glass of rum in a ditch without any trimmings, without even the polite forms observed in the coupling of animals.

No need to say more: evil had forced its way through men's ribs, and people realized that as well as the outer night there was an inner one that hardened the blood and stopped up and caulked the auricles of the heart. It was as if, by tacit agreement, the two darknesses had met.

This was the state of affairs, people were rheumy-eyed and their mouths overflowed with gray night, when a rumor arose that the whites were offering jobs again, but on condition that their employees live inside the fences as in the old days. They had found out how to grow crops—not so well as before, but the plants did grow and the sugar was rising. People quoted the case of Bartholomew village, to which most of the families, together with their animals, had been transferred, inside the enclosure surrounding the house of the D'Arnouvilles. The operation was carried out with lift trucks and cranes, which could whisk a hut up off its four rocks as if it were a box of matches. Some soothsayers whispered that the old abomination was returning, they could smell the horrible scent in the air. But no one listened to them; most people just shrugged derisively and said, "What abomination? Oh, slavery. You must be gaga."

4.

When the first trucks entered the village the very people who'd shrugged their shoulders shuddered, and you could see they were throwing the doors open to fear, to the fascination of evil. The whole population fled into the surrounding woods. But after waiting awhile the whites withdrew, leaving three bags of flour by the side of the road, with a barrel of dried cod and a large container of Lesieur oil. Black men of goodwill were won over by this lordly gesture. The next day several heads of families watched for the headlights so as to have a chat with the planters. They were given such answers that one, two, three huts flew up like birds, showing the underside of their wings for a moment before alighting on the platforms of the trucks. The same thing happened to others in the days that followed. Some modern young people talked of getting together and forming a united front so as not to end up lock, stock and barrel inside the tall metal fences. The drain had to be stopped before Fond-Zombi disappeared, became a dead river, they said in weakness and anguish. But it was only a fleck of foam, a last play upon words before silence, a final halt before the precipice toward which they were being slowly but inexorably drawn.

Anancy alone hadn't given up. He rushed wild-eyed through the village, arms outflung as if to try to stop the river leaving its bed. Pale-faced and disheveled, he looked like a refugee from the world of madness, buttonholing people, laughing fiercely, suggesting breaking into the white men's houses and killing everyone inside so as at least to be our own masters in the darkness. Other people made fun of him, saying that wouldn't bring back the sun, and that anyway they'd be dead before they had time to break down a single door. Anancy in his frenzy didn't see that as an objection. They'd be killed? So what? But at that the young men turned away awkwardly, and the old smiled and said in voices grayer than the gray darkness:

"Boy, we don't know what we expect, but we do know we don't want to die. We want to see where it will all lead. Man is descending, man is ending. Let us see his fall."

Many felt a lump in their throat when Anancy suddenly announced his intention of climbing up on the lift trucks. His madness flared out one last time the day before his departure. Taking up his stand right in the middle of the village, he burst out into insult and abuse of the black man, scattering him to the wind for hours on end until the mist swallowed up the orator entirely. People thought he had said his say. But after a silence the still childish voice could be heard again, reduced to a thread by the mist, wavering, an absurd appeal that seemed to come from another time, another world.

When the moon appeared, Ti Jean rose quietly in a hut that was entirely shut up, double-barred, not as in the past against the spirits of darkness but to keep out the cruelty and wickedness of the living. After having a drink of water he put on what remained of his shirt and trousers, carefully ironed by Ma Eloise the previous evening to give some sort of an air to the ceremony of farewell. All his movements were extremely slow—more like those of a robot than of a human being. Since the fateful day there had been a void in his head, and he had tried to maintain it, to be nothing but void and silence. Before he left he put his cane cutlass in his belt in case friend Anancy should have another attack when the lift trucks arrived. Finally he glanced into the next room. He smiled at Ma Eloise, who'd fallen asleep fully dressed, fully armed against evil, her eternal pipe in her mouth and her finger curled round the stem as if she were puffing away in her dreams. Then, lifting the latch of the door, he stepped out onto the tar of the road, his face toward the light flowing gently from the sky in a creamy white rain as the stars gradually pierced the gray night.

A large crowd was gathered outside old Kaya's hut. The men wore funeral clothes, short jackets and bowler hats. The women wore hats with veils, lace and goffered skirts as if for a wedding. Old Kaya, seated in the middle of a great heap of parcels, was explaining calmly that the whites had managed to produce crops, not as plentifully as before, but some anyway, by using a new kind of manure that gave the plants a jolt like an interval of sunlight. As he held forth, the old scatterbrain wagged his scraggy beak of a nose to and fro and looked delightedly at his audience out of his little eyes. You could see those eyes had not yet been touched by evil. Brother and sister were busily putting the last touches to the family luggage. Ti Jean thought of making his way through the crowd for a last greeting, at least a handshake or a smile. But he was held back, drawn away from the crowd, by a feeling of shyness at the thought of what had become of the three of them, Egea, Anancy and himself, since the glorious days by the river. Wind, hot air—all their hopes had been no more than that: waste and frittering away of time; and the weapons they'd forged in their hearts would never be used in any battle. As he stood on tiptoe looking on from a distance it seemed to him that Anancy regarded the whole scene as if he were a stranger, not an actor in the drama that was unfolding. As for Egea, he hardly recognized her in the girl with downcast eyes going slowly to and fro between the hut and the road, apparently seeing nothing but her hands and her naked feet chilled with the morning dew. He recognized and yet did not recognize her: in recent months she had gradually changed into a stranger, a shadowy profile, a reflection in stagnant water of something he couldn't put a name to.

Meanwhile the crowd gazed eagerly at Anancy, that great felled tree, that stricken palm now swathed in silence. Then a youth of their own age spoke to him, one of those who had had so much to say about revolution. From where he stood Ti Jean could hear him expressing his surprise at seeing old Kaya's son in this situation after all his fine speeches about the black man. Anancy gave a curt laugh.

"What is it that surprises you, brother?" he asked.

"You," answered the modern young man. "You, who used to talk to us about becoming our own masters in the darkness. And now here you are waiting at the side of the road."

"Don't you worry about that."

Anancy's lips broadened in a mysterious smile, an enigma of a smile, a devilry, and people thought for a moment he was going to speak, to tell of some terrible plan to do with the houses with big gates and colonnades. But the sound of an engine interrupted him and headlights approached, piercing the road with sulfur-colored light that plunged the banks into darkness. The lift truck stopped and a little sedan just behind it switched off its lights. The crowd at once made itself scarce. The only ones left were those determined to drain the cup of bitterness to the dregs. The engine of the truck was still turning over. White soldiers, armed, surrounded the little space filled with those who were leaving, carrying their last items of luggage, fowls and rabbits all hustled together, family photographs still in their frames. The crane turned and let down its hooks on the four corners of the hut, which rose with a creaking of old wood and was set down on the platform. Ti Jean stepped forward, rapt by the memory of a little flat-bodied girl, her face covered by a film of blue-black lacquer reflecting all the colors of the light. But the glare of the headlights showed him only a stranger with a convex brow, cheekbones patched with yellow and brimstone orange, and eyelids lowered in a dream.

Suddenly she noticed his presence and drew back, giving him a glance that was without life, scarcely tinged with a distant sign of remembrance, of abstract recognition. The luggage had disappeared, and old Kaya's voice could be heard imploring his daughter to get in. But Egea shook her head and stepped back, arms dangling, into the beam of the headlight, which suddenly lent her eyes an enormous radiance, the flash of water red in the setting sun. A soldier came over to the girl as she clung to the mudguard. A planter got out of the little car parked behind the truck and complained about this waste of time. Then, seeing Egea and her beauty, he softened and said to her reassuringly in Creole:

"No one will hurt you. You won't have to work in the fields. You'll come to the big house and be happy there, happier than a thrush in a guava tree."

As he said this he took her by the wrist and pulled her toward the platform as one might haul a refractory heifer. Egea, her head thrown back, looked as if she were being swept away in a great turbulent current, and you could see that at any moment she would just let herself go with the stream. The neighbors stared and stared, and some fell back a pace as if to keep their distance from harm. And it was then that they saw Ti Jean for the last time with their living eyes until the hero came back to the village after having given them back the sun. It all happened very fast, at the full gallop of madness. A machete flashed and a white hand flew through the air still clutching the butt of a pistol. Then came the gleam of a gun barrel and it was the turn of a human head to fly up as in a horror puppet show, to fly up, I say, in a fountain of red death.

Egea and Ti Jean plunged into the darkness of a cane field. Behind them shots exploded one after another, leaving traces like falling stars against the sky.

5.

When they reached the forest Egea suddenly changed her mind and wanted to go back to the lift truck. She was sorry she'd come, and pulled sobbing at the hand that held her prisoner, with the gentle, ineffectual obstinacy of a harmless creature. Then she gave in and hitched her skirt up so as to make her way more easily through the undergrowth already lapped in mist. Now their silence merged into the growing darkness, the somber tide of shadows rising round their feet. Meanwhile Ti Jean kept folding and unfolding the girl's fingers, wondering where it came from, this feeling so light that it was a mere breath, so obscure that he could not give it a name, and so heartrending that it was indistinguishable from the dark night stretching over the earth.

At nightfall Egea lay down under a tree and went to sleep. Ti Jean stayed awake to watch over her, lest she slip through his fingers and go back to the lift trucks. Sitting by her, staring into the darkness, he stroked her hair, wondering what remained of the Egea of the past in the Egea he had found again today. This seemed to him the grayest night since the Beast swallowed the sun. But had it really swallowed the sun? It seemed to him that one day the mist had risen up out of the human heart, where its roots had long run deep without anyone suspecting it.

Next day at the boy's suggestion Egea gently removed her big earrings, which kept getting caught in the bushes, and tore a strip from her dress to make a band for her unruly hair. She was upset by what had happened and kept imagining things, seeing Ti Jean as one returned specially from the dead to tear her from her family and drag her down with him into the eternal dark. It was as if the story of her mother were playing tricks on her. And no matter how often Ti Jean said he was alive and swore that his body belonged to the world of men, she just shook her head without answering and walked on through the thickets and hollows in the everlasting smell of decomposing vegetation. By the third day, lack of sleep made Ti Jean so light-headed that he kept tripping over roots, falling full length as if into an abyss and dragging the girl down with him. She, tired out, was scarcely conscious of anything but him; now and again she even lost track of where she was and resigned herself to what she thought was the other world. Then, not knowing how to express death and her new state as one of the departed, she sang a song the old folk often used to sing, remembering the days of the whip and the spiked barrel:

> "Not life yet, friends
> Not life yet
> Turn this way and it's water
> Turn that way and it's the same flood
> And the sea that can never be filled
>
> Not life yet, friends
> Not life yet."

They were by a river when Ti Jean fell for the last time. He dragged himself along, scraping the ground with his nails, smiling, rambling, thinking it was centuries since he'd heard the sound of water trickling over the stones. Suddenly he came to a steep slope and rolled right down the bank, at the same time falling fast asleep. He dreamed he was watching over Egea while she slept. When he woke up an ashy mist still floated at ground level, but the vault of the night was pierced with bright moving gleams that made him blink. Egea lay near him, watching him in silence. When she saw that he was awake she smiled as in the old days and stroked his cheek, saying:

"It's me—Egea. Don't you know me?"

One glance had driven away the darkness. As they set off again she gave him her hand, a little hand that didn't have to be imprisoned but rested freely in his, and there were no more stones under their feet, nor sharp grass or thorns. It was as if the earth were covered with a great velvet carpet.

After a week up in the mountains they came back in secret to the village, to the other side of the Rivière-aux-Feuilles, where they found shelter under a banyan tree with big gnarled branches that enclosed them in a sort of ark. Here a strange life began for the fugitives. Ti Jean combed the woods as though they were his own house, looking for wild manioc and Jerusalem artichokes and adora berries, hunting game which he tracked by licking the grasses and then aimed at by ear as he had learned to do in the mountains. Afterward, using devious animal paths and wading through the river to throw the dogs off the scent, he would go to find out what was happening in Fond-Zombi. But he went only at night—what was now called night but which used to be day—and the only person he saw was Ma Eloise. For now there were people, neighbors—likenesses, semblances of people and neighbors—whose chief delight was to denounce you and get you into the worst possible trouble.

Ma Eloise didn't like the smell of the forest anymore, and preferred to await the end here in the hut of adegonda wood which the departed L'horizon had built for her, and which still held the scent of her youth, of her good time on earth. Usually Ti Jean would find her sitting on her small old woman's bench, her face covered with a layer of white clay which she did not remove even to go to bed. Had it not been for this sign of mourning, you might have thought she was unaffected by all that had happened. And she would often say, in a calm happy voice scarcely belied by the plaster mask that lent her immobile features such a strange effect of youth:

"Let desolation rage—it is balm to people's hearts. But as for you, don't be unduly troubled, and if you're asked where you get your strength, just say, 'My bowels are of lead and my heart is of iron.'"

But whatever Ma Eloise said, Ti Jean knew that madness shrouded and enfolded her like a cloak, and when he drew near her hut his heart was wrung at the sound of the song she'd made up, the dim litany she hummed ceaselessly in her solitude with a tinge of mystery in her voice, now and then descending into a confidential murmur as if to deliver a message as yet unknown to humanity:

> "Madness
> Mere madness to go away like this
> While death was giving birth
> The dread shadow fell on the earth
>
> Oh, it was not the night
> Not the darkness
> It was the shadow of life itself
>
> Step over it, step over it
> Travelers of the plains
> You who go far away
> Right into remotest lands."

She would stop on catching sight of him. Her eyes would begin to gleam in the dry plaster like two great drops of water. Sometimes a herb bath would be ready for him and Ma Eloise would undress him, make him get in the tub and scrub him thoroughly from head to foot as freely as in the days when she used to play with his infant rod. Then she would sniff him intently like an animal, and going back to her bench, puff her pipe and mumble her everlasting song of darkness, which seemed to wrap her in a matching veil of thin and scented smoke that was wafted away at once in the wind.

Her whole attitude showed that affliction, broken bones, even hope, were far behind her now. Every now and again, going off into dream, she would take her pipe out of her mouth and pour forth a flood of dim words about Wademba, talking of him now as a man, now as one of the dead whom she had lived with, now as a special spirit who had possessed some of the attributes that belonged to the gods. Seeing Ti Jean's surprise, she would explain merrily that there used to be such spirits in times gone by in the hills of Africa, when the divine thresher walked the land, going to and fro among the living. Sometimes his spirit would pass into a man and amazing things would happen, for people didn't know if God was the man or the man was God. She told of miracles, like that of the fishes springing out of the wall of the hut. She tried to remember the sparks of light that had dropped from Wademba's lips. But her memory was fluid and her little watery head had retained one sentence only, which for no particular reason floated yet on the surface of oblivion and abandon, still glistening with mysterious and even impenetrable meaning. It said that men must fight the light of the thunderbolt with the light of their eyes.

Then she would stick the stem of her pipe back in her mouth, and her great eyes would start to float there again in the middle of her countenance like two balloons adrift in the sky. And as she returned to her song of darkness, which together with the plaster mask was the only visible sign that the night had passed over her little lost soul, Ti Jean would smile and think that Ma Eloise had always had one heart that suffered and another heart in which to rest from her suffering.

The words of her litany followed him for a long while as he groped his way back through the mist, through fields sleeping like a flock of strange beasts and trees that seemed alive with eyes.

He would cross the river and break out in a cold sweat as he got near the refuge, a little shelter tucked away in the mist, right in the midst of the banyan. He used to whistle in a manner prearranged with Egea, but the door did not open until he whispered through the wall:

"Little Guadeloupe, it's me, Ti Jean, not a wandering spirit but human flesh that wants to tell you what it's been doing."

Then she would laugh, the door would swing open on its vine hinges and the two of them would clutch at each other and embrace as if they hadn't seen each other for a hundred years. Egea looked very slim in her school uniform. But when she took her clothes off her figure assumed an amazing fullness, and Ti Jean would remember the little girl who had given herself to him in the trees. Then regret would steal over him for having abandoned her all these years, for not having followed the rising of her breasts and hips, which he would never again see as they used to be, in the clear light of day. This thought haunted him, and he would lift the torch up over Egea's face to drive something away from her cheeks, as one tries to skim the foam off stagnant water. Usually the foam would not go away, and darkness still hung like a veil over the girl's face. But there were some days when Egea, even in the deepest shadow, was suddenly decked in all the colors of the rainbow, and Ti Jean rediscovered with her the innocence of their play in the trees. He lived now in a sort of strange happiness, a good time full of mild and desolate melancholy amid the shadows. It seemed to him he was born to sail like this through endless night, flanked by the two women who loved him, each in her own way. This was the world he had always expected, and it was good—one couldn't wish for anything different. All the rest—the Beast and the villagers and what was happening in the plantations—all this vanished as if by magic and became improbable, unreal.

Ti Jean had always been told that the first growth of redwood was the strongest and the most difficult to uproot. But during these weeks on the riverbanks he was obliged to admit that it was the second growth that took the tree up into the sky. Egea struggled, aroused abysses and landslides deep inside herself, and then one day announced triumphantly that the earth of her womb had closed around the seed of a child. They were under the banyan, under the great gnarled branches that enclosed them in a sort of ark. Egea was naked and dry and her hair had the pungent smell of wood smoke. In her enthusiasm she seized the youth by the hand, advanced with ceremonial deliberation to the river and tossed a handful of water over her shoulder so that her sins should be carried away by the stream. They laughed, and Ti Jean suddenly saw a strange shape in the depths of the river beside the well-known image of Egea herself. It was a tall figure with an incredible mop of hair and a face still new, with eyes that were astonished and childlike despite the fair amount of whisker on its chin.

6.

Meanwhile half the huts of Fond-Zombi were gone, carried off to the high fences and bells of another age. And one day the soldiers surrounded the village and drew up a census of the remaining population, marking each person down separately in a large ledger. They also counted up the last remaining pigs, the sad rabbits and fretful chickens that some people still kept in secret enclosures, well in among the palms so as to stifle the noise they made. Most people answered truthfully the questions put to them. Some even claimed possessions they didn't have, so as to seem important. But when the soldiers had gone it suddenly occurred to them that the idea was to come and take them by force, clear them out of Fond-Zombi altogether along with the last remaining pigs and their imaginary rabbits and chickens. But all this was only supposition, said those black men of goodwill who are always the same. But still, trouble was in the air, its side effects were familiar now, and next day a dozen or so young fellows took to the shelter of the neighboring woods. They stayed less than a week, after which they returned in terror, frightened half out of their wits by the spirits that swarmed there among the trees much more numerous than before, as if they now ruled over the earth.

Some of the youths didn't come back. And their companions said they'd been swallowed by a fabulous creature that looked like a cow, the one there'd been all the talk about before the darkness began, before it attacked the sun. They said they'd seen it from a distance, all lit up from inside like a lighthouse so that you could see its joints and muscles.

This incident filled our two young friends with particular terror. They stayed in their ark all the time now, except to go and set fish traps or look for roots and wild fruit in the immediate neighborhood. When they fancied some meat, Ti Jean had only to climb up into the branches of their tree and wait till he saw the shadow of a raccoon or agouti coming to drink in the ravine. The silver bullet would hit its target at once, as if somehow guided through the darkness, and the two children would cross the river together, hand in hand, and then bring back their bag, still holding hands. But one day they heard the grunt of a brown pig on the other bank, then the hollow sound of an animal thrusting its way through the undergrowth. It was a tempting prey, too sumptuous a windfall not to grab before it went back up the mountainside. Ti Jean, his mouth dry with excitement, pushed the girl inside the banyan, arranged the branches adroitly around her and said:

"Now don't move—don't even smile."

"Why?" she asked.

"Because it'll see my sweetheart's teeth," he jested, though he felt horribly tense. Then he rushed off into the darkness.

He located his prey by ear, and realized that his wild pig was rootling beneath a huge adora tree for acorns scattered about amid the undergrowth. Although he approached very skillfully, the animal sensed his presence at the last moment, threw up its heels and vanished. The same thing happened again a hundred yards farther on, and again after another hundred yards: the beast would give a grunt and disappear, drawing deeper and deeper into the forest the pursuer who could not resist this mysterious attraction. After an indeterminate length of time had gone by, Ti Jean, emerging from a thicket, fired at point-blank range and saw the animal vanish before his eyes, a streak of silver quivering in the grass at his feet and then disappearing into thin air. Ti Jean, the burden of the spell suddenly lifted from his shoulders, turned and ran back toward Egea in her hiding place under the banyan.

Not long afterward, as he reached the top of a hill overlooking the river, he saw a sparkling shape, well within range, on the other bank. Thrusting aside all before it, it was lumbering toward the tree where he'd left Egea. Without stopping to think, Ti Jean raised his gun and fired a silver bullet at the Beast, which continued cheerfully on its way as if nothing had happened. Then a woman's voice burst out through the night, and he hurtled down the hill with long airy strides, as if there were great black wings beating frantically from his shoulders. But he did not suspect, as he flew across the river and up the other bank, he did not know that he would hear Egea's vain cry echoing throughout his whole life, through all the years that would fall like white snow upon him, the traveler bound for afar, for "remotest lands," as poor Eloise had predicted.

When he reached the banyan, all that was left of the girl was a scrap of her shift hanging from one of the lower branches. He gazed at the shred of calico, wondering what the reason could be for the spell that had drawn him away from the girl's living body. Then he was aroused from his lethargy by a groan, and he saw Ma Eloise lying a few feet away, her Lenten face all shrunken in the shadow. She said the soldiers had taken away what remained of Fond-Zombi on the lift trucks, and that was why she had set out toward the river and Ti Jean's shanty. But there she had come upon the accursed Beast, which had given her a great kick in the chest and then gone on its accursed way.

She tried to say something more, but her eyes were already turning the same palest pink as Wademba's had at the hour of his death. Then she drew in a great gulp of air, tried to breathe it out again, but could not.

7.

Ti Jean took up his mother's body, forded the river and entered deserted Fond-Zombi. Most of the huts were smashed in, and bodies stretched out beside hunting rifles, clubs or machetes told the story of what had happened. When he got to her hut he laid the dead woman on the kitchen table and dug a grave beside the guava tree in the backyard, the one on which the winged spirit of the Immortal One had once perched. Then he laid Ma Eloise out and put her to bed in her last resting place, all spick and span in her yellow-check cotton dress, with her three-pointed head scarf falling down behind over the wasp waist she had still. Lastly he put the stem of her pipe between the hands folded on her breast; it was as if she were having a last puff.

Some birds of day strayed around him, pecking at the fresh earth in the light of a torch stuck in the ground near the hole. As he filled in the grave he pondered on Ma Eloise's fate, wondering what could have been going through her mind a little while before when she threw herself under the hooves of the Beast. Never, never would he know who she really was, this person now lying under the earth holding the stem of a pipe. Suddenly he went back into the hut and brought out all his mother's personal possessions: her nightdress; her mug; the long-toothed comb she untangled her hair with; and the enamel saucepan she was so fond of, the one that had been given her by that enigmatic being and fine talker, Jean L'horizon. After further reflection he made a second trip and placed in the grave the big tin box which always stood on the beam inside the door, proclaiming to all visitors that Ma Eloise was a respectable person, a person of standing, who always had a tin of salted butter in the house. Then he drifted off into a long reverie, trying to think what else that little mason wasp would like to take with her. And as he remembered that she was the whole of Guadeloupe in herself, the Guadeloupe of the past, with her scrap of blue sky, her little yellow sun and the bright green herbs she had gathered so zealously with her own fingers, he was overcome by such an access of sorrow that he bent over the grave, tempted to climb in and lie down in it himself to keep the departed company.

At that moment the flame of the torch swayed, and a familiar scent of cinnamon swirled around him, while the voice of Ma Eloise said to him in spirit:

"What you have to do with the dead, Ti Jean, is bury them."

"It shall be as you wish, little mother," he answered with a sigh.

Fighting off dizziness, he hastily filled in the grave. Then he caught up Ma Eloise's old bag and tossed in a flint, a screwdriver, a pocket knife, a machete and a length of wire for setting traps. With one last look back at the guava tree, he threw the sinister spade over his shoulder, went through the village, and set off on the forgotten path to Up Above.

When Ti Jean had taken up the corpse by the river he had thought this grief too heavy for his heart to bear. But now, on the path, he derived some consolation from the scent of cinnamon that still fluttered along before him, not so strong as it had been just now by the grave, but yet enough to keep him company. Dragging along, his limbs heavy with sorrow, he glanced out of the corner of his eye at a red moon spreading its wings among the topmost branches like a bird in flight. It was a fine night, like one in the past, with a fine dusting of stars falling out of the sky all the time over by the volcano, La Soufrière. And our hero remembered what Ma Eloise had said about the Milky Way, which she called the path of the gods: the gods gathered up the stars by the armful and put them into bags, but some escaped, and as they fell broke and formed the dust men saw from below.

> "By the armful they gather them
> By the armful they put them into bags
>
> By the armful
> Like a woman gathering grasshoppers
> Who piles them up in her basket
> And the basket overflows."

So, carried along by the song, he pushed aside the aloe which closed the entrance to the secret passage and climbed the slope to the plateau, and wherever he looked he saw ruins upon ruins, here as in the valley. There was a swelling in the gray grass under Wademba's mango tree. Three feet below the surface the spade struck against a sitting skeleton holding in its arms the musket, tightly wrapped in cowhide. On the skeleton's knees lay a goat's horn full of black powder and a case full of bullets that looked like silver. A sensation of faintness overcame Ti Jean when he found the weapon intact inside the cowhide. His hair was already standing on end at the thought of the Beast, he was bewildered and thinking of rushing screaming down the mountain as before, when a distant breath of cinnamon tickled his nostrils. The smell was so faint it was almost nonexistent— the last breath of the little creature before she went down under the earth—but it restored his spirit.

"Thank you," he said, with a smile at the newly minted soul. "A thousand thanks, little mother."

Suddenly, noticing a slight sound behind him, he turned and saw two strange beings leaning forward and examining him from the side of the hole he had dug. One was Old Eusebius, the man with the face of a ghost who had come to fetch him the night Wademba died: he was still the same in his long pants, his tunic and the big straw hat flopping over his shoulders. The other was one of the creatures who that same night had seemed to hover between two worlds, still as statues, outside the round, moon-blanched hut—an old black man with an enormous crinkled paunch, a human torso surmounted by a boar's head with long bristles that gave forth a frightening sound.

The red eyes glowed in the boar's head, and from its jaws issued a hollow, inarticulate voice:

"What do you think of this lad, Eusebius?"

"A good boy, come just at the right time."

"Do you think he's able?"

"I quite like the look of him. He's the split image of Wademba—if I couldn't see that great skeleton down in the hole I'd have thought the old boy had decided to make a new start. And it's not only his face that's like Wademba's. Look at how his eyes shine with rage: they look straight at you like a devouring fire."

"But perhaps after all there's something lacking: he looks pretty stupid."

"I don't think he's really stupid," said Eusebius with a little laugh.

"A matter of taste, as the man said as he sucked the horn of a snail."

"How do you mean—stupid?"

"Well—like someone who tries to make a rope out of smoke."

"Or kisses the hand he ought to cut off . . ."

"Or a madman who hates his own folly . . ."

"Or like someone who tries to count a chicken's teeth and shave its eggs . . ."

"And hey, friend, what about this? As stupid, idiotic and hopeless as someone who goes to La Désirade to fish for green mares . . ."

They both broke into mirthless laughter, and Ti Jean emerged from the grave, awkwardly leveling the oily musket.

"I'm not going to ask you what you're laughing at," he said. "You seem very pleased with yourselves, and that's all that matters at your age. But what are you doing at my grandfather's grave, and why do you speak his name?"

"We were waiting for you," said Old Eusebius calmly.

"Yeah," echoed the boar. "You may be a bit stupid, but we thought we'd better wait for you."

"So you knew I was coming?"

Old Eusebius gave another grating laugh. "We knew the day, we knew the hour, and we knew what you would look like and what would be the sound of your voice."

Then, giving a little tap on the front of Ti Jean's trousers, he went on: "We even knew the exact weight of your magic wand. But that's enough nonsense, boy—we must go now. We're not the only ones who've been waiting for you, you know, and there are some old baboons it's better not to get on the wrong side of."

Old Eusebius's eyes were bitterly sad, with a sort of abiding deep anger despite the smile stretching his old black lips. Struck by this strange look, the boy put the powder horn and the case in Ma Eloise's bag, and abandoning the tall skeleton to the stars, meekly followed the other two across the ruins of the plateau.

Right on the other side, behind a line of trees facing Bartholomew Hill, ten or so Men of Knowledge were assembled around a fire of branches—the same as those who had kept vigil outside Wademba's hut the night he returned to the land of his ancestors. Among this band of incarnate spirits, extraordinary figures he'd scarcely glimpsed on the previous occasion, Ti Jean now took particular pleasure in discerning a human raccoon and a human agouti; a big dog with flaming eyes and a high wrinkled forehead full of unknown thoughts; also a bat which sat like a cat, all stiff and formal, with two beautiful eyes like a Christian's rolling around a bald and bony head. But really all these nightmare faces were quite familiar to him. And Ti Jean's spirit stepped forward and saw again in those wild eyes the strange fixity which had struck him as a child in the eyes of his grandfather during their long conversation in the night. Then, stepping forward again but this time within himself, he recognized on those goblin faces the expression he had seen on his own face in the past, when he looked at his reflection in the streams after his imaginary crow flights. Then he knew why the people of Fond-Zombi used to say he had a lump of dry mud for a head, and Old Eusebius smiled, saying:

"You've guessed right, Ti Jean—you are one of us."

A hum of agreement ran through the gathering, and the bat, in his emotion, lit a tiny pipe that made him cough and cough again. Then in silky tones that seemed to flow from between his shaggy jaws, he said:

"You heard the voice, you came, and you opened up the grave. That's why you're one of us."

"Not quite," murmured someone on the other side of the fire.

"No, of course not," agreed the bat, drawing himself up to his full height. "The mark is on his brow, all right, but he's only taken the first step this evening, and it's a long path."

The bat had said this with great self-satisfaction, and Ti Jean couldn't help smiling despite his distress.

"I didn't come for your sakes, fathers," he said mildly.

The bat staggered, as if struck by an invisible arrow.

"We know that, child of the valley," said the bat contritely, his old eyes sparkling with pain and regret. "Unfortunately we like to keep company with the Powers, and as you've just realized, we take pride in being like the gods. We can't even blame you for wanting to stay a man, because that's probably what Wademba planned for you. Have we turned into gods anyway?"

Then there arose a chorus of sepulchral lamentations, punctuated with shouts and furious howls, and the bat went on with a stricken smile:

"Yes, all our lives we dreamed of surpassing one another, of performing countless absurd exploits just to terrify the poor folk in the valley. Such was our ambition, while the whites abused our own flesh and blood down on the plain. The fact is that though we were trying to be gods we were acting like toothless old women. And now that accursed cow reigns over the world, and we are more helpless than ever."

"Do you know the Beast, then?" cried Ti Jean naively.

At this, the whole assembly seemed as if it was trying to stifle some unbearable inner pain. And Old Eusebius, borne up by the mournful delight contracting his nostrils, rose into the air and twirled slowly round like a top until he reached the uppermost branches of the trees.

When peace was restored among the gathering, Old Eusebius folded his limbs and swooped down as if perched on a cloud, landing where he had taken off, with his legs crossed and the brim of his huge straw hat floating about him like wings.

"Alas," he said in a smooth voice, as if resuming a conversation momentarily interrupted by a mere shout, a dream or a sneeze. "Alas, alas, it is a long time since we were forewarned of the Beast. But we wouldn't listen to Wademba's warnings. We buried them deep in our hearts, each of us thinking he'd be a corpse by the time it came, and gallantly leaving the others to take the necessary steps. But we're all still alive, and the Beast is here, its heel on our necks."

"And do you know where it comes from?"

"No; all we know is that it comes from far away, from a great House in the heavens where it has been shut up since the world began. People say it broke its tether and burst through the fences that held it in."

"But what does it want?"

"My boy, there's another mystery. When it came we joined together to find out its name and what it wanted, what it was thinking in its heart. But we are only earthly, and it is hard for us to understand a Power which does not belong to the earth. All that the prophecies said was that one day a world-devouring Beast would come and swallow up all in its path—men, rivers, suns and moons. Everything would go into it and stay there: its obsession was to contain all the worlds. You were there. You must have noticed that people went into its mouth unscathed— it didn't harm a hair of their heads. They are all alive inside the Beast. But we know nothing of the life they lead there."

"This apparition doesn't stand much higher than one of the huts in the village of Fond-Zombi. So how, fathers, can it hold whole worlds?"

"Your question is as wrinkled as an ass's behind," growled the boar's head, shaking the menacing hair on his chest with a metallic clank.

Ti Jean gave a faint smile at this irrelevant comment, but allowing for the weirdness of the body regarding him with such an air of affected superiority, he concealed his feelings and went on tolerantly:

"I am only a child, fathers, and to me the world is nothing more than a mystery machine. But, without disrespect, allow me to say that all this seems very queer to me. I can understand a great spirit like that playing with worlds, moons and suns, but what pleasure can it get from swallowing poor folk like Nestor Galba, or Ma Vitaline with her varicose veins, or little Aureola Nicéor, who wasn't five years old when she was gulped down before the light of my own living eyes? And tell me, what's a powerful Beast like that doing in Guadeloupe, a clump of earth, a speck that isn't even marked on the map of the world in the school at La Ramée? Above all, what was it doing in Fond-Zombi, our little Fond-Zombi, a mere couple of feet that not even everyone in Guadeloupe has heard of? Really, does it all make sense?"

"Boy," said Eusebius with a wry smile, "you ask a lot of questions all at once, but that's youth's privilege. But we, whom you laugh at in your heart—that too is a right at your age—we have always known that there are no answers, that since time began there has never been the beginning of a beginning of an answer. The Beast was foretold, and its path lay through Guadeloupe. That path was foretold to us and probably to it too, since such was the path it took. As you see, that's not an answer, it's just the other end of the stick. And now, whatever it looked like and whatever worlds it engulfs, here's the other side of your question: a man's skull is not much bigger than a coconut, but doesn't it too contain whole worlds?"

"I see that you are my fathers," said Ti Jean, bowing respectfully, "and I am only a child newly dropped from its mother's womb. But if all that is so, why have I been summoned to the fire here, and what do you want of me?"

"There's no answer to that either." The man with the face of a spirit smiled. "And it's as well you should know, my lad, that some of us are very skeptical about you. You were foretold to us by Wademba, but we don't know why. In a nutshell, we know no more about you than we do about the Beast."

"Except for one thing," said the boar.

"Yes. We only know that you are of our blood, and that you walk in our ways. And that is why we have agreed to help you, as our Master asked us to do before he departed. Even though, as some of us think, it's all useless and a waste of time."

"Perhaps you're a waste of time for me too," said Ti Jean meaningly. "Who was talking just now about toothless old women? Eh? That's another thing I ask myself, my masters."

He had drawn himself up in fury, the veins in his neck swelling with bitterness and sorrow at the thought of Egea being lost and swallowed up by the world-devourer, while he stood gossiping with these dusty old cynics. But instead of resenting the affront the crowd stood still and gazed at him fascinated, and the bat, tremulous with joy and hope, squeaked out:

"Friends, do you see that fire, that flame?"

"No doubt about it," yelled the boar ecstatically. "This lad isn't the least bit afraid of us."

"He hasn't the slightest respect for our gray hairs," added Eusebius happily.

Then, turning to Ti Jean, the man with the face of a spirit made a sort of protective gesture, a melancholy wave of his hand in the air, as Wademba had done on the night of his departure.

"So forget our words, boy," he said. "They are only damp cartridges in an unloaded gun. Your blood is alive and fine and singing, and we're very sorry you don't want to be one of us. But after all we were told your path is among men, and your strength, little buffalo, in the sadness that fills your heart. This sadness is what bears you along, as we have good reason to know, and if we played with you a little it was to obey the wishes of the Master, who said, before he returned to the old country:

'When the child comes to my grave, tease him a bit and hit him like a drum to find out exactly what he sounds like. And if his sound pleases you, if he is as I think he is, open a vein in his wrist and mix his blood with that of a male crow, for that is the animal that belongs to my clan. Then let him go on his way.'"

"Yes, that's exactly what he said," affirmed the boar humbly.

What followed was swift. The goblins gathered round close to follow the operation down to the last detail with their hard, dry, searching eyes, sharper than claws. Someone picked up off the grass a big bluish crow which looked as if it were dead: its eye was dull, the wattles under its beak all bedraggled. Then with a quick straight cut of the knife, Old Eusebius opened a vein in the lad's wrist; he made no resistance, for he was far away and secretly indifferent to the ceremony. Eusebius drew blood from the bird's leg and put the cut to the wound in the boy's wrist, setting the young human being vein to vein with the animal. Then he held the bird at arm's length high in the air, as if to launch a fighting cock into the arena of the sky. And then the Man of Knowledge, in a voice at once authoritative, monotonous and strangely melodious, sang:

> "Above the leaves
> Above the eyelids of men
> Above the jaws of the lion
> Spread your black wings."

An inner trembling ran through the little bunch of blue feathers. The man's fingers parted, and the crow flew up like an arrow without either croaking or moving its wings, then dropped like a stone toward the trees, which closed about it without a stir. Ti Jean didn't know how he got the impression that he himself had taken off, but at the same moment, though there was no special sign and no pain to mark his passage from one form to another, a wind swept him up from the earth and he was one with the strong pinions beating the black air, the claws stretched forward and open, and above all the beak, firm and sharp as a shaft of steel. He suddenly had a strange feeling of having experienced this absolute strangeness before. Perhaps he was only with the bird in spirit, as before, and perhaps his human body was waiting for him somewhere in another time, lying by a hunter's tent, and all he had to do to be finished with this trick was to slip into the young man's sleeping breast. . . . But look down at the earth as he might, under his speeding wings there was no tent nor anything remotely resembling a hunter, and in the middle of the ring of spirits with transparent eyes a shirt and trousers lying on the grass dimly suggested a human form. Then, with a lugubrious croak, Ti Jean resigned himself to flight, and soared straight up into the sky like a flame up a chimney.

Borne by the wind, he rose higher and higher, and was thrilled to see the shapes of the world become so tiny, though he knew all he had to do was glide down toward them to see them their right size. Fields and woods streamed past beneath him, crushed by a gigantic heel. Sometimes he was overcome with dizziness and descended toward the earth with cries he could not hear because they were immediately swallowed up by the wind. Then he was over a huge void, a sort of sky which looked as deep as the sky up above and was crossed by a few scattered gleams which vaguely recalled the existence of human beings. Ti Jean understood then, or thought he understood, why some blacks used to change themselves into "shuttlecocks." There were gum trees out at sea with lanterns on, and farther out, toward Point-à-Pitre, lighted ships were leaving the port laden with the products of the new slavery. Ti Jean hesitated, swerved slightly toward the Caribbean mountains, then made his way between the valleys that divide the peak of La Madeleine from the crater of La Soufrière, emanations from which covered the mountain passes with a veil of yellow silk.

As he approached the wild heights overlooking Fond-Zombi, he thought he could see the light of a fire in the middle of the plateau Up Above. But he didn't have time to linger over it, for already his attention had been drawn to a small, white, slightly phosphorescent patch like a firefly on the edge of the marsh where he used to watch for duck. At that moment an invisible flash darted forth from that little innocent light, and Ti Jean felt a burning sensation deep down in the most secret recesses of his mind.

Shortly afterward, when he was over Fond-Zombi, he was surprised at the strange picture of it conveyed to him by his crow's eyes, when he knew its narrowest ravine and slightest hillock as thoroughly as the veins and glands in his own vanished human body. Then with a last flap of his wings he landed on the grass of the plateau Up Above, in the middle of the circle of incarnate spirits.

Not far off, beside a little heap of clothes, lay Wademba's musket, together with the belt, the ring, the powder horn and Ma Eloise's bag, its strap still over the shoulder of the shirt lying on the grass. He hastily conjured up a picture in his mind. And just as it seemed to him that human worlds were vanishing and could no longer be contained within his crow's brain, a sudden swirl of air propelled him, upright, into the body of a man, standing on smooth black human legs. Old Eusebius looked at him sadly, his faded eyes gleaming with sorrow despite the smile on his old black lips, and said:

"Now, my boy, you belong to the family, the ancient and noble family of the crows. Go, and may the gods go with you on the road that is sadness, darkness, misfortune and blood."

8.

At these words Ti Jean took his leave of the group, his eyes still full of Old Eusebius's last look. It had been like an appeal, a secret warning, the hand laid on the brow of a child about to die.

As he passed the open grave he bowed to the tall skeleton, and it occurred to him that he might honor its memory with a shot from the gun. Pleased with this idea, he checked the musket's firing mechanism and managed to produce a spark. Then he poured some powder into the barrel, tamped it down carefully with the rod and inserted a silver bullet by means of a small plug of grass, as he had seen old hunters do with their ancient blunderbusses. But just as he was aiming the gun up at the stars, he saw the face of Egea in the sky, and what he had been about to do seemed futile and absurd, just like the hopes vested in his grandson by Wademba, warrior of another age who had prepared for battles that would never take place. In fact there wouldn't be anything but this drop, this dark slope down which the world was falling into an ever deeper abyss. And Ti Jean, putting the musket over his shoulder, left the ruined village, which moaned in the wind like a doomed ship sounding its siren.

The stars were fading when he reached the apparition, by the marsh where he had first seen it. It was lying in the long grass, its hooves tucked under it and its head between its forelegs. The mist rising from the marsh added to the unreality of that great shape apparently resting on a bed of clouds. To Ti Jean it seemed beautiful with some strange, terrifying beauty. Approaching slowly, he saw the pelican in its ear. It too seemed to be sleeping, its eyelids closed as in dream, the yellow pouch of its beak filling and emptying rhythmically. The electricity radiating from the Beast was less strong now, and seen from close, through the long old woman's locks that covered it, the skin looked at once oily and soft to the touch, and like the mother-of-pearl lining of a shell.

Ti Jean walked round the world-devourer, then went up to its head, suddenly hesitant and in a sweat. Its jaws were open just wide enough to admit a man's body. Its lips shone wetly with a frothy yellow saliva; its cow's teeth seemed to be smiling in their sleep with an irony that lent them an aura of supernatural life. Old Eusebius had said that all living forms were there inside the Beast intact. He had said intact, unscathed. Our hero, clasping the musket to his chest, carefully placed one foot inside, on the other side of the row of teeth.

BOOK FOUR

In which Ti Jean arrives in the land of his ancestors, via
the gulf that opened up in the Beast's inside.
This is followed by the tale of the hero's first day—
an ordeal, I can tell you.

1.

So our hero entered barefoot into contact with the other world, on the far side of a row of molars which had never been used and were of the smooth bluish enamel of milk teeth. And he was still wondering how to proceed, his musket clutched to his chest, when the fabulous tongue drew back slightly at the touch of his toes, like the rim of an oyster at a little drop of lemon. At the same moment the huge eyelids were raised and he felt himself slipping right between the jaws, gently as one slips down in the water, without any hurt. And in a flash of distant surprise he wondered what had happened: had he himself leaped into the Beast outright, or had it snapped him up?

At the bottom of the throat, which was as wide as a church porch, he saw two tall pillars supporting a vault which didn't correspond in the least with the Beast's outward appearance. Then he plunged sadly into the darkness of the innards, head over heels, his one idea being not to let go of the musket or of Ma Eloise's bag.

He was surprised by the softness of his descent. The space around him was empty and boundless. There were no shapes to be seen and his body fell as slowly as a bird about to land on the ground. He was stretched out flat, his face toward the abyss and his arms flung wide like wings. This easy fall made him feel peaceful. He breathed slowly there in the void, arms still outspread, legs kicking, cheeks brushed by a cool dark breeze. He was surrounded by a sprinkling of stars, some of which expanded and contracted like jellyfish according to whether he was approaching or receding from them in his tranquil dive, like that of a deep-water fish. Here and there he thought he could see different-colored suns and moons, each operating on its own account in a different-sized quarter and in a different region of space. And as he swam through this ocean he could still see the Beast asleep up above in the marsh, beyond all those torrents of imprisoned stars streaming through its innards.

His body gradually got used to falling, discovering in it a new way of living and breathing, and in the end, slowly, he fell deep asleep, his spirit spreading out into the darkness. When he opened his eyes, refreshed, he was gliding through a huge starry sky. Below him now was a hilly landscape with checkerboard fields and winding silvery rivers. Then he recognized the chief trees of Guadeloupe—palms, coconuts and bombaxes. Landing on a moon-blanched plain, he leaped up immediately to embrace the earth, laughing, laughing and crying at the same time, his cheeks rubbing themselves insatiably on the cool night grass. But all of a sudden the scent of this world struck him as strange and he sat down and gazed calmly at all that lay spread before him.

Everything looked both odd and familiar. The palms and coconuts and bombax trees that he'd recognized in his fall now presented a different aspect. Seen from the earth they looked bigger than those in Guadeloupe, with something rough and harsh about them which they didn't have there. As for the hot acrid air, the space which surrounded him, and the position of the stars in the sky, all these too were foreign to Guadeloupe, though deep down inside Ti Jean felt they weren't altogether alien to him. Hadn't he already, at some time in the past, breathed this air and felt the anguish of this landscape? Had he not looked before at this mysterious arrangement of the stars in a sky which was not transparent like the sky in Fond-Zombi but bespattered with deep black ink like the random ejections of an octopus?

Then as he looked at a tree that was squat, with short, bushy foliage reminiscent of the cap of a mushroom, the sight of it gave rise to sounds within him and he uttered the word "baobab."

2.

He remained on the plain all night, breathing in the smells, old
and new, of Africa. Sometimes he would stroke a stone or a
blade of grass in the darkness, and he experienced right down
to his fingertips the disturbing feeling of being part of the landscape, of having the same right to be there as the blade of grass
and the stone. He had never felt this in Guadeloupe, where everything was enveloped in a fine, distant mist and there were some
days when one had the heartrending sensation of being in exile
in one's own country. And Ti Jean liked the feeling of being so
close to the grass and the stone, at one with the dim voices rising
from the earth. But suddenly he was overcome by visions which
cut his heart in two, and the present moment merged into Egea's
cry there under the banyan tree, beyond the fabulous jaws of
the Beast.

Dawn revealed a prospect of long gentle hills stretching out
as far as the eye could see, like waves on the ocean. Ti Jean
hauled himself to his feet with the aid of his gun, and turned
around on one leg, uncertain what to do. In Fond-Zombi the
sun always used to appear first over the harbor and then sink
behind the mountain, between the volcano and the two Mamelles
or breasts. This thought naturally led the lad in the direction
of the rising sun with the calm certainty of finding a town resembling Point-à-Pitre. Gradually mountains appeared on the horizon. The woods thinned out, with giant trees towering above
the undergrowth, and picture-book animals—does, antelope and
giraffes—looked at him mildly then took off without uttering a
sound. All this was so typical that he wondered whether this
Africa was not the product of his dreams as he walked calmly
through the tall dewy grass. Unless he was unwittingly moving
through the mind of the Beast, who had created specially for
him a dream Africa with the old day and night and the sun of

Fond-Zombi—though the sun here spread wider over the sky, trembled more in the red of dawn, and was more like a bloodstain.

Suddenly, as he was going round a thicket with leaves shining like green flames in the dawn, he saw once more one of the most attractive scenes from his African picture book. A sandy yellow lion was reaching up the trunk of a young tree and trying to get hold of a little black boy perched in the branches. It was a huge beast, with a head that seemed to belong to an animal even larger. Ti Jean was bemused by this latest trick of his senses. The child was laughing hysterically with fright, jabbing with a spear at the animal's foam-flecked muzzle. The lion fell back, clawing down with it great patches of bark. Ten years old he might have been, that insubstantial boy, and his hair was arranged round his head in regular tufts held in golden rings. Ti Jean shrugged his shoulders philosophically. And without haste he loaded his musket with powder and a silver bullet, knelt down on one knee and aimed steadily at the sandy yellow shoulder as if just practicing at a target. Everything froze in the blank silence which every detonation makes in space. The animal fell on its side and rolled over and over, glaring at the invisible enemy who had got the better of it. Then it gave a great wild leap and fell motionless on the grass, its eyes staring. The shot echoed still, fainter and fainter in the distance, as if in homage to the doughty fighter with the flowing mane.

The little black boy rearranged the cloth he wore wrapped around him, came down from the tree and walked over to Ti Jean in a cryptic manner, the tip of his spear directed halfway between earth and sky. After a furtive glance at the musket, he made an apprehensive survey of the hunter's body, lingering over the belt and the powder horn and Ma Eloise's bag, but smiling when he came to the face of the stranger who had just saved his life.

"If I were a puppy," he said, "I'd wag my tail. But as I'm the son of a man, I can only say thank you."

The child's face was smoothly rounded except for the brow,

which jutted out like a vizor of bone, casting a slight shadow over the large liquid eyes. Under the naive and fearless gaze of those two orbs Ti Jean had a sudden intuition.

"Friend," he said, "you seem to recognize my face, whereas we've never seen each other under the sun."

"Do you mean you are a stranger?"

"That's what I mean." Ti Jean smiled.

"Do you mean you've never been here before, even in dreams?"

"Never," said Ti Jean.

Putting a hand politely in front of his mouth, the child stifled a laugh.

"Well, how do you come to understand our language, stranger?"

Two or three vultures had landed near the lion's body and were slyly watching the two youths out of their cold, dissolute eyes. The boy looked at them with indifference, and went on shrewdly:

"I know I'm only a chick who hasn't yet thrown off its shell, but I must say, stranger, I admire the way you speak our language. It's true we live in very, very strange times, according to what the Ancients say."

"Why are these times so strange?"

The child threw back his head and laughed between his fanned-out fingers, courteously and discreetly. Then he said, in a light, bantering, pseudo-confidential whisper:

"They're strange because they're times when the dead come back up out of the earth."

Almost at once, as if he wanted to spare Ti Jean the trouble of denying the obvious, the boy went over to the tree which had given him refuge, picked a fruit up out of the grass and offered it ceremoniously to the hunter. He was quite at ease, not at all put out by the presence of a dead man who spoke, laughed even, and slew the king of the forest as easily as you would squash a flea. His name was Maïari, Child of the Little

Eye. He explained that this name had been given him because of the way he blinked one eye when the light was too bright. But Ti Jean scarcely listened to what he was saying. Instead he bent toward him and asked for the second time, in the unknown language which flowed from his lips quite naturally:

"Friend, you seem to look at me as if I were someone you knew. Have we met somewhere before?"

The boy twinkled his great black becalmed eyes and turned them up mildly toward the unknown hunter.

"As a matter of fact," he said, "you remind me of a traveler who came to my village long, long ago when I was no higher than my navel is now. I'm still only a blade of grass, but I know the leaf never falls very far away from its roots. And that man's blood shaped every one of your features, for I recognized you at first glance."

"And did you speak to him—to the dead man who was like me?" cried Ti Jean excitedly.

"I spoke to him as I'm speaking to you, during the short halt he made in our village before continuing on his way. Of course, we realized at once that he was a dead man from the distant, the very distant past, for he lost no time in putting himself under the protection of the palaver tree, as travelers used to do before the white man spoiled the world for us. The king came to find out what country he came from, and as the refreshments were brought in he tried in vain to get some answers out of this dead man who knew the ancient customs. But the traveler remained silent, and only condescended to give an answer when my father the king offered him a loincloth to cover his old man's nakedness."

"The king your father?"

"Yes, King Emaniema," said the child in astonishment, as if everyone ought to know that.

"And what did the ghost say then? My friend, my friend, do you recall his words?"

"He gave thanks in the ancient manner and said that there

were as many loincloths as he could want awaiting him in his village. Then he kissed my father's shoulder and went, never to return."

"But at least he left his name behind with you?"

"He left nothing at all behind with us. All we saw that day was the light of his eyes. But why do you want me to tell you his name? Don't you know it better than I do?"

"You are right. But I want you to take me to him."

"That's what I was afraid of, traveler."

"Why?"

"Because he no longer exists," said the boy, laying his hand consolingly on Ti Jean's arm.

"But at least you'll take me to his village?"

The boy shook his head in silence, his eyes suddenly drowsy under the heavy lids with their short tufts of blue lashes.

"It would be better for you to come home with me," he said at last, after a distracted glance at a group of hills that seemed to be spying on them from the other side of the plain. "My friend, you must have had a long journey through the nether realms. Why don't you stop and get your breath, and come and taste our curds?"

A wind without ozone, salt or smell arose, a dry, scorching, Lenten wind which told Ti Jean for the first time that he was a long way from any ocean. And as the wind struck him full in the chest, he imagined it was entering his thorax through a gaping hole that had been driven through at the height of his heart.

"Comrade," he said, "I saw where you were looking, and the truth you are hiding from me I shall find beyond the hills."

"You will learn the truth at the tip of a lance. But don't ask me to strike the blow."

"But what could strike the blow more gently than the hand of a friend?"

The boy's eyes looked suddenly asleep, drifting in a dream, veiled by the eyelids with their short flights of blue lashes. Then a little tear ran down to his lips, where it was caught up by an absent flick of the tongue. And Ti Jean realized that it was a bitter truth that awaited him under the sky of his ancestors.

"The people of his village shot him," said the lad mournfully. "They shot Wademba with their arrows."

3.

Turning to the horizon, Ti Jean could see in the distance a group of huts built at different levels on the misty crest of a hill. They were strangely like his grandfather's, all round and white, with a little conical thatched roof from which you almost expected to see the bees emerge. It gave our hero a real jolt to see those huts so like Wademba's. It upset and surprised him more than anything else, more than the does or the antelope or the giraffes; rather as if he were the famous river in the proverb, that ran back up the hill to gaze at its source.

"Is this your village?" he asked in a low voice.

"No, it's only my father's house. The real village is beyond."

Then, beseechingly: "But won't the stranger really rest a moment and taste our curds?"

"I want to go into the hills," said Ti Jean.

"In that case," said the child after a pause for thought, "I'd better come with you to the boundaries of my tribe, for we no longer live in the old days when the paths were kings. You saved me from the claws of the lion, and if you have to die, I prefer it not to be at the hands of my people."

After winding over the plain they went down into the bed of a dead river, deep and shady, their intrusion flushing up crowds of noisy birds. Tufts of reeds and dry grass were caught up in the shrubs along the riverbanks, a souvenir of former floods. The long dangling tresses filled our hero with sadness. It seemed to him—how can one put it to you, you younger generation with smooth backs that have never been laid open?—it seemed to him that his own heart was the riverbed, full of sand and dry grass and bushes.

After a while Maïari observed the position of the sun and then began to clamber up the bank, pulling himself up by the roots of a tree which overhung the absent river. The dawn wind had dropped and the leaves hung motionless, waiting for a breeze that would not come. But a human rustling sprang up around them, all murmurs and whispers and sham twitterings that deceived no one. And the exile smiled in his heart, thinking, old hunter of the forest that he was, that the tall grass might swallow up the guinea fowl but not the sound it makes. Suddenly a man appeared between two tufts of grass, a quiver over his shoulder and his body draped in a cloth of frothy white material that reached to the ground like a wedding dress. The boy stepped in front of his friend Ti Jean and said to him lightly, in a shrill voice that carried far: "Should not the little star accompany the moon?"

But a suppressed gravity belied his smile, and Ti Jean realized that the king's son was shielding him with his body. Then the warrior turned his eyes on the unknown stranger and with a look of incredulity bowed ceremoniously and vanished, as if swallowed up by the earth again. Moments later the sound of a tom-tom rose up in his wake, gay, lilting, booming, though impossible to dance to. And Maïari said simply:

"Our arrival is being announced in my village."

"What does the drum say?"

"The drum says a friend is on the way."

Then, like a fire among the dry canes, the stream of sound gave one great leap and reached the middle of the plain. It stopped, then started again farther off, died away and started again, over and over, to the most distant horizon, where the drumming became more and more animated, like the thin, vibrating fury of an insect desperately trying to plant its sting.

"And now our coming is being announced on the other side of the river, in the land of the Sonanke."

"And what does the drum say now?"

"The drum says a stranger with the face of Wademba is on the way."

Ti Jean, in a trance, no longer paid any attention to the landscape. He looked only at the small shape making its way before him among the grass, its head sparkling with its dozens of gold rings which each seemed to trap a sunbeam. A resolute spirit, a staunch heart, and tear glands that were dry, burned to a cinder, that's what you need in life, he thought, laughing at himself and at his present situation, ensnared in strangeness, midway between two equally impossible worlds. Suddenly the boy stood still and Ti Jean, coming up with him, saw at their feet a river flowing through a valley. In midcourse the waters divided to form a little boat-shaped island. Beyond, the jungle rose in a green impenetrable wall.

"That islet doesn't belong to men," said the boy. "We call it the boat of the gods. But beyond it is the beginning of enemy territory, and if you set foot on the far bank you are walking on the ancestors of another race, and I am no longer accountable for your blood."

"Why should they kill me?" asked Ti Jean.

The boy did not answer, but went down to the riverbank, undressed, and waded into the water, his arms held straight up over his head, the rolled-up cloth held in his hands. The water came up to his shoulders, then his mouth, then the gold rings, and then all Ti Jean could see above the surface were the two forearms. That lasted for several seemingly endless seconds, and then the rings miraculously reappeared. Ti Jean now undressed and joined the little shivering frog, who had begun to dry himself as the children at the Blue Pool did, wiping the water off with the edge of his hand and producing showers of spray.

In the middle of the island, surrounded by rocks, was a sandy beach like finest flour. Maïari tied his cloth round him and sat down bolt upright in this angel meal, his palms open on his knees, suddenly as motionless as a statue. His still wet lips were pursed in a grimace.

"Ow, ow—my lungs won't let me speak, your behavior

grieves me so. All the spears you encounter on the other side will be turned against you. Why won't you accept my hospitality? Look, there's still a hand's breadth of sun left—we could be in my village before nightfall."

The river lapped softly at the prow of the island. Our hero was thinking of what Ma Eloise had told him about Africa, the wonderful country the gods had chosen to live in. Reassured by the indifference of the two humans, the animals nearby came back to life, and on the other side of the river the wall of green opened to reveal a little she-monkey with two babies clinging round her belly. This charming character had carefully parted the leaves, and crouched there for a few moments snuffing the air, her thin, almost human lips thrust forward, as if to judge how great the danger was. Then, alarmed by a sound or some other sign perceptible only to her, she drew back her friendly little head and the curtain of leaves closed again over her mystery.

"And now," said Ti Jean, "I want to know why death awaits me over there on the other side of the river."

"Are you really as keen to know as that?"

"As keen as that, and more," said Ti Jean, smiling.

"Well, then, learn that your death clings as closely to that of Wademba as that monkey's babies clung to her belly."

Maïari seemed to be counting the grains of sand, the leaves on the trees, the last sparks of daylight shimmering on the water. After a long silence he swiveled his head around, atremble with gold, his meekly lowered eyelids damp with sweat, showing that he surrendered completely before the stranger's madness.

"Yes, your death hangs on that of Wademba, for one event is always the son of another, as the king teaches us. 'In fact, for anyone who can see, the arrow that killed Wademba was loosed even before the day he was born.' That is what my father says," concluded the child, looking at Ti Jean gently as if to apologize in advance for what he had to tell him.

"Then tell me, my young colt, when was the arrow loosed?"

At this the king's son shook his head gravely in homage to one who could understand, one who could sense that order and sequence in telling a story is part of the organization of the world itself. And with dilated nostrils, taking as deep a breath as possible, he began in a slow singsong like that of a schoolboy who has learned his lesson well:

"In truth, in truth, the arrow was loosed even before the day he was born: right at the start, the beginning of the beginning, when the egg that would produce the Sonanke still slept in the womb of the earth. . . ."

MAÏARI'S TALE, or
THE STORY OF THE ARROW THAT KILLED WADEMBA

Once upon a time, in a far, far country long years away from here on foot, there was a king who lost both eyes fighting an invader. So. His people, conquered in the same fight, had to run away. And a spirit appeared to the blind man in a dream, promising to lead them to a new country, a country which would be theirs and which the king would recognize by a certain smell which came out of the earth. What do you think of that?

And so they set off behind the blind man, driving their meager flock before them. And then one day the king began to stagger like a drunken man, and there they pitched their camp, and the people, guided by the king's sacred nostrils, marked out the boundaries of the kingdom the gods had bestowed on them. Season after season the children found their place in the sun there, until a new landless race came and knocked at the gates of this second kingdom. In the course of the battle it so happened that the old blind king, together with a few of his warriors, was entirely surrounded by the enemy. There were only a few arm's lengths between him and the barrier of spears. The enemy, sure of their prey, were already beating the drums of victory; they rent the air with their hissing and booing. The blind king sat down, and ordered his men to do the same. After a silence he arose and said, Come, kings are not slain like this. Then he advanced head high toward the barrier of spears, shouting: Make way, make way for my blood. And the enemy gave way, and he went through their ranks like a knife through butter and took refuge on top of a mountain, together with those of his people who survived and the remainder of their cattle.

So much for the beginning: the arrow was not loosed, but the strings of the bow began to be drawn.

A cow was sacrificed, and the soothsayers examined the entrails and said that only a new song could breathe new courage into the people. What do you think of that? The lute-maker set to work and carved a three-stringed cora. Then the oracle was revealed to the members of the king's family, and, led by the soothsayers, they were brought before the blind man that they might be sacrificed on the as yet virgin spirit of the cora. One after the other he took them by the hair, and one after the other he guided their life's current onto the wood of the cora. When it was the turn of his youngest son the boy was not to be found, and the king, who was very tired, said: Enough, that's enough for today. He picked up the cora, streaming with gore, and plucked a string, producing a wretched sound. And the king's councillors said: Enough is not enough. And toward the end of the day they thrust before the blind king his latest-born, who'd just been found in a bush. The life gushed out of his throat, and the cora, touched by the blood of the last-born and precious fruit of the king's loins, gave forth sounds of great beauty, and from the king's mouth issued strange words. The song told the story of the Heavenly Ones, a mysterious race who lived in the clouds and made war on human beings because it made them happy to see them suffer. Next day the blind king sang the song to his assembled people, and at the end the warriors shouted: Give us nations to devour, O king! At that moment the former people died, and a new one was born that took the name of Sonanke, which in the ancient tongue means the Devourers.

And the arrow rose into the air with a hiss that made all the neighboring tribes tremble. The Sonanke had been hunted like game, but now they were the hunters; kingdoms collapsed in their path, whole generations were buried under the earth. The blind king would touch the strings of his cora, his son's blood called for more and more blood, and the misery of men had no end. And it came about that after the king died the cora started to sing of its own accord, and the Sonanke continued straight ahead on their way like an army of locusts devouring all in their path. This went on for a thousand years, until the cora crumbled into dust. By the time that happened the Sonanke had reached the country where we are now, between the river Seetane and the great bend of the Niger. In those days the land was inhabited by a nation who had a name, who spoke their own language and had memories as old as the hills; and that nation was ours. The Sonanke had set out to devour us. But seeing that their course was run and the song of the cora reduced to dust, they set their heel on our neck, their customs became ours, and we forgot even our own name. And that is why, from long and long and longer still ago, we have been known merely as the Ba'Sonanke: the sons, the base offspring of the Sonanke. We remained on our own lands, but the produce of the earth belonged to them; the wombs of our wives belonged to them; and the arms of our young men defended their kingdom. Nowadays all that is but a dream; we threw off the yoke long ago. But it is their gods we worship, and we still build our huts on the models of theirs; for we have lost all memory of what we once were in the country where we are now. Children, can you hear the arrow flying through the sky?

"I can," murmured Ti Jean. "I can hear the arrow in the depths of my being. But I don't know what direction it's going in, and I feel as if I were going mad. Those men who enslaved you—they were black, weren't they?"

"Of course they were black," said the boy, frowning. "But what has the color of their skin got to do with it?"

"Mad, I'm really going mad, mad in my head and mad in

my bones," said Ti Jean. "I can see the arrow in the sky, but I don't understand its course at all. Alas, can the black man put himself in chains?"

"What is that strange expression?" asked Maïari, laying two fingers on the lobe of one ear. "It's not part of our language. It isn't used here."

"What expression do you mean?" asked Ti Jean in surprise.

" 'Black man,' " said Maïari.

Ti Jean gazed at him for a while, and seeing that he was not joking, answered at last:

"Brother, my little brother from across the water, forget what I said, and please go on with your story."

"Brother?" repeated the African incredulously. And he lowered his eyelids over the visible world and resumed his meek recitation in a slow and ceremonious voice which was at once his own and someone else's: that of the king, probably, speaking through his mouth.

Another thousand years went by. So. One generation after another found its place in the sun on the banks of the Seetane. But in the end every calabash gets broken, they go to the river and are broken, and so it was soon after the white man came to the Coast. What do you think of that?

Until then the Sonanke would from time to time sell some of us to traders who took the poor wretches by devious paths as far away as possible so that they could not find their way back to their villages. They sold those who had displeased them, those who gave them piercing looks and insulted them without opening their mouths. But with the coming of the white man, traders swarmed like locusts and whole strings of captives set off for the Coast, where they suddenly disappeared from sight as utterly as if they had gone down into the Kingdom of the Shades. It was then that the calabash broke.

On a certain day one of our young men was ordered to go and hunt antelope. Because he came back empty-handed his master flogged him and put him in fetters for the night. Next day the master unfettered his legs and told him to go and hunt antelope again, and the young man said mockingly, leaving his real meaning obscure: Today no doubt I shall kill, for I shall aim straight. That evening when he returned again empty-handed, his master came up to him with a whip. The young man aimed an arrow at him and he fell dead on the grass. Then the young man cried: So! And throwing down his bow, he said to the dead man's relatives, who had seized hold of him: Let me alone, I'm not a bird, I can't fly away. They put out his eyes and drove stakes up his nostrils, and those who saw it said, weeping: Today there is thunder over the earth, and heavy drops of rain. Now among those who watched there was a very old man called M'Pande, with white hair like the foam of the sea. When all was over with the young man he went away from the rest and revolved some wise thoughts. Inside his head many seeds fell, took root, and grew into a veritable garden. Then, having taken counsel with himself, he came back among his people and said:

"For whom do you weep? For whom do you fill your mouths with cries? We have forgotten our gods, we have forgotten our language, we have lost the very memory of our name. So from whom do you expect help?"

And the people answered:

"We expect no help. But we want to weep."

And M'Pande, he who was to become the first king of the Ba'Sonanke, said to them:

"I shall not weep with you today. For do you not see that what we have to do is dry up the source of tears and change our eyes?"

Someone smiled and said:

"Shouldn't we change our brains as well?"

"Yes," answered M'Pande.

"And our insides?"

"Yes," answered M'Pande.

"Our hearts?"

"Those too," answered M'Pande.

"And what will be left of us?"

"Nothing. Nothing will be left of us," answered M'Pande.

Then all the people rejoiced at the old man's words; they were weary of themselves, and rejoiced.

"Are you sure, old man?" they asked.

"Certain," said M'Pande. "For only two know the truth under heaven: he who strikes, and he who is struck."

At these words all tears vanished and the war began. The people without gods, without a language and without a name to their brow had reared up like a leopard, and soon the whole country smelled of human blood. In the intervals between battles, the relatives of the dead went to the two banks of the river and exchanged insults. And then the Shades themselves joined in. They came up through the underground passages and confronted one another in aerial combats even fiercer than those of the living, sending up whirling columns of dust over the plain. Great expanses were covered with skeletons whitening in the sun. The country was devouring its inhabitants, eating them up. And on either side of the river people began to murmur that it was time to start making men again.

The man who restored peace was one of supernatural height, such as is no longer seen. He belonged to the race of the Masters and had the power of changing himself into a crow, for he was the messenger of his king and did not owe this gift to witchcraft. One day he quietly put on his wings, flew across the river and alighted inside the hut of M'Pande, first king of the Ba'Sonanke. Then the dignitary resumed human form and sat by the entrance to the hut. When he appeared the king's guards held their breath and lifted their hands to their swords. They were just about to kill the former Master when the king came forward and offered him a glass of water. The man drank in silence, and the king cried: See, he has drunk of my water. Then he offered him a plate of meat, which he took and calmly ate. Then the king turned to his guards and said: See, he has drunk of my water and eaten under the roof of my hut. Today we must see whether we are men or Devourers. Then, addressing the visitor, he asked why he was there, and the Sonanke dignitary shrugged and said:

"What must we do, O king, for you to forgive us for a thousand years of servitude?"

The man with foam-white hair answered in surprise:

"Venus is always seen beside the moon, and that is why people think of her as its dog: but Venus is not the moon's dog. Allow me in turn to ask you, with due respect to you as a guest, what must we do, my son, for you to forgive us for no longer being your slaves?"

"You are right," said the stranger sadly. "There is nothing any of us can do, and we shall die to the last man."

"Who sent you?" the king asked gently.

"I am my own messenger."

"But at least you heard a voice?" said the king excitedly. And when the other shook his head, old M'Pande sat down opposite his guest and fell into a long reverie.

Then his face lit up. He ordered sixty two-year-old oxen to be brought, and went with his enemy to the banks of the river Seetane so that nothing should happen to him on the way. The man forded the river, the guards urged the oxen after him to the other side, and the king had not done him any harm. Thus ended the war between the Sonanke and their former slaves: without any word of peace being spoken. The only further incidents were due to "men in the bush," lone warriors who slipped across to the other side at night, striking at anyone living until they themselves were put to death. But all that was merely the tribute due to the lion, and such acts of madness did not end the truce, which lasted down to our own day.

Did I tell you that the name of the man who came as a crow was Gaor? After this adventure he was called N'Dasawagaor—I Am My Own Messenger. And his fame soon grew so great on both banks that it offended the throne. Then the king of the Sonanke had him killed by his sorcerer, who slowly ate his heart away. The king had all his family slain, and tore the flesh of his future, his only child, a boy of ten whom he sold to a caravan from the Coast. The child's name was Wademba, and he was sold a hundred and forty-five rains ago, some say it was more. Let us remember the father, yes, let us remember him, that his name may hover over this kingdom. But let us not forget the son, let us not forget him who wandered so long in the realm of the Shades, beneath the vastness of the sea, in order to find the way back to his village and to be shot there like a stinking beast. May the memory of the heroes live forever.

A shadow stretched out above the trees in the liquid and transparent air of dusk. It thrashed about like the ebb and flow of a tide or like a roller that hesitates, sending out a tongue and then withdrawing, then attacking the light again and again until it covered the whole sky with a dim sylvan veil. The world seemed to be waiting for a word to rise out of the darkness. Everything was in suspense. A bird skimmed over the water with frightened cries. And suddenly the silence gave way to the din of night's thousand voices, all awakened at once. Maïari's hands slipped from his face, revealing eyes swollen with sorrow, like transparent pigeon's eggs.

"The Sonanke say slavery is a leprosy of the blood," he said, "and if any of them is taken by the enemy, even if only for an hour, he cannot return to the tribe. For they say he is already defiled."

Then in a voice suddenly shrill again, with the charm and spontaneity of childhood, he asked:

"Are you going to cross the river?"

"Tomorrow—I will tell you tomorrow," said Ti Jean, falling forward onto the sand as if into the gulf that opened in the heart of the Beast.

Almost at once he saw Egea all slim and naked, a red fish in the palm of her hand. She was coming out of the Rivière-aux-Feuilles, advancing toward him smiling, but the distance between them stayed the same. Still she came toward him, murmuring indistinctly.

Suddenly a cool wind wafted her away like a straw and she vanished beyond the horizon. It was dawn.

4.

On the other side of the river an animal track wound into the wall of foliage. Ti Jean turned and waved to the boy, who was still on the boat of the gods. Maïari was dazzled by an oblique ray of sunlight. Shading his eyes with his hand, he kept repeating in a voice muffled by the wind, by fear and the wind:

"Farewell, cousin, farewell, and may those under the earth go with you."

At the same moment a human shape crept behind a tree trunk, and the first roll of the drum was heard.

After a long journey through the forest, where all the trees had eyes to see him and arms to catch him, Ti Jean emerged onto a plain like the one he had crossed the day before on the other side of the river. In the distance, among the blue clearings of a hill, stood the same round white huts thatched with straw. Wisps of smoke curled up from them, to be snatched at by the wind and dispersed like rockets exploding. But as he drew near, little stooping figures came out of the huts and disappeared among the tall grasses that surrounded them. And when he actually got there, Ti Jean was greeted by the bleating of a handful of goats straining at their tethers and trying to follow the inhabitants of the village.

Seen from close to, the huts were not all that much like Wademba's, which suddenly seemed to Ti Jean to have been a rather wretched affair. These were decorated like girls in their best, with freshly lime-washed walls and doors framed in carved columns. Each seemed finer and more elegant than its neighbor; it was as if they were about to set off for a ball, along streets lined with dwarf palms and so perfectly smooth and shiny you could have eaten your dinner off them. Ti Jean, wandering among all these wonders, couldn't help comparing them to the huts on the plateau Up Above, poor colorless bedraggled butterflies reduced to skeletons in their struggles against the briers of another world. Suddenly a familiar smell made his nostrils tingle. It came from an earthen pot standing on some still glowing embers under an awning. Two or three calabash bowls showed that the family had been about to begin their meal when they heard of the approaching stranger with a face like Wademba's. He took off the lid of the pot and recognized a dish of gumbos and salted tripe, with a bunch of herbs floating on top to flavor it, exactly the same as the people used to make in Fond-Zombi. Ti Jean sat down by the fire, poured some food into a bowl and began to eat. With each mouthful he choked back his heart and shook his head slowly, choking back his heart at what he had seen and heard the day before, and shaking his head because he still couldn't believe it. But in the middle of his meal he suddenly grew angry, and started pacing through the village shouting and bawling like a drunk:

"Listen, stop lurking in the grass like the snakes that you are, toads tossed out of your swamp! What you're going to see today is what you don't want to see, and what you don't want to hear is what I'm going to tell you: I am come to my own country, it is to my own country I am come, under my own roof! I am not a stranger, not a stranger. You sold me by auction, sold me and delivered me over to the whites from the Coast. But I am not, I am not a stranger, I tell you, you gang of crooks, you insatiable vultures!"

Suddenly his heart was calm again. He began to laugh at

his drunken insults, and made his way out of the village and onto a path that plunged right into the bowels of the Devourers' country. The next village greeted him with the same emptiness and absence, and so did the next. Here and there along the path there were all kinds of warning signs: hens with their throats cut, sticks stuck in the ground, little newly made clay figures with arms outstretched to stop him from going any farther. The earth was dry as tinder, but Ti Jean felt as if he were sinking into a swamp. It was like a great landslide: he went down and then up, and then the land slid again and he fell head over heels once more. The sun was now shining with all its might, and clouds of small butterflies rose high in the air in search of cool currents which whirled them abruptly round in billowing spirals. Even the animals sank into the afternoon lethargy. Only some red-ruffed monkeys ventured forth, leaping from branch to branch or hiding as best they could behind tree trunks, forgetting their long white tails still poking out. A group of three people appeared on the path, and Ti Jean halted. All three were tall, with short bodies on long skinny legs that made them look frail as storks. The two younger ones each wore an ox hide and carried an old-fashioned wide-barreled gun—not as old, though, as Ti Jean's musket. The third was an old man armed simply with a spear, with a cloth thrown over his shoulder and on his head the whitened skull of an owl, the beak covering part of his forehead. The old man's body was like stone and the lines of his face recalled those of a bird of prey, but in contrast to this austerity, as of something dead and petrified, his little round eyes were disturbingly reminiscent of the guileless glance of a partridge. It was he who spoke first.

"Who are you, and what do you hope to find among us?"

His voice was calm and amused and secretly full of relentless pride. It seemed to come from immeasurably far away, as if he were speaking from a star. Ti Jean realized that to this man's ears his own words would never be anything but a rush of air. Nevertheless he too spoke.

"I am looking for the village of Obanishe," he said.

"Obanishe is the first village, the one where you ate the gumbos and salt tripe. But I'm still waiting for the answer to my question: What are you doing, stranger, on this side of the river?"

"Not much really," said friend Ti Jean. "Not much. I am here just to repeat to you what my grandfather said the evening he died: 'If you ever go to the village of Obanishe on the bend of the Niger, you or your son or your grandson or one of your distant descendants down to the thousandth generation, just say you had an ancestor called Wademba and you will be welcomed like brothers.' Such were his words the evening he died, and it was in memory of them that I refused to believe how it is with you, men of the Sonanke."

A strange gleam flickered in the depths of the little pits of darkness, while the face itself remained impenetrable and smooth as stone.

"And now, it seems, the scales have fallen from your eyes?"

"My eyes are bare," said Ti Jean.

"Well, I am glad for you, for you know now what remains for you to do. Birds go with birds, as is well known, and furry animals go with their kind. The scales have fallen from your eyes and you have seen clearly. Go back to your own people."

"Am I not among my own people?"

"Among your own people? No. For us you are like the animals one sees sometimes in the bush, for which there is no name. For us your language is like the night, for us your words are like the hooting of an owl in the night. Listen, young man whose eyes have been opened, we have no wish to kill you, we do not want your ghost to come back and wander round our huts at night to poison us with its bitterness. We wish not for your death but for your life, and that is why we say to you again: Go. Go back to your own people."

"Is that what you said to Wademba before you shot him?"

"No, no—to each beast his own hole and his own snare. We have spoken to you in accordance with your nature, and to Wademba we spoke the exact words, the truth of his bones.

Unfortunately he was like his father, Gaor: a crow with a tough liver, a rheumy eye and an inexact mind."

"So what should he have understood?" asked Ti Jean quietly.

"That we are free men, and that there is no room here for those who are put in bonds."

This was said without anger, with a sort of cold and distant serenity as if uttered from up on a star. Ti Jean let the insult slowly sink in, first touching the memory of his ancestor Gaor, then flowing over Wademba, the lone old madman of the plateau, that marvelous scatterbrain, and then covering all the people of Fond-Zombi and their parents and grandparents in a choking salt and bitter wave reaching up to the shoulders of the first black man to set uncertain foot on the soil of Guadeloupe. Once again Ti Jean could not bridle his tongue.

"But wasn't it you who put him in bonds, you yourselves with your own hands?"

The old dignitary threw back his head and gave a short mirthless laugh, a dog's laugh that goes no farther than the teeth.

"Even though the sky lightens," he said, "a blind man's eyes are still in the dark. If your language was not like the night, if your words were not like the hooting of an owl in the night, you would know that Wademba was sold with the consent of the gods. Alas, how long will your madness last? And how many sons of nothingness will be born again among us, blinded by the desire to mingle their blood with ours?"

Up in the air a cloud of little white butterflies had lost height and scattered among the tall trees, torn and looted by a flight of sparrows who thrashed frenziedly about in all directions amid a haze of dust and broken wings. The cries of the birds seemed to come from the butterflies now in retreat, crashing among the branches and disappearing in the grass and undergrowth. The precise voice of the old man woke Ti Jean from his reverie. It was surprisingly gentle, with a sort of indulgence faintly tinged with regret.

"Is there any sacrifice we might make," he asked, "to appease you and those who come after you?"

"No need. We are at peace already."

"Would you like us to give you an ox for the journey?"

"No. My road stops here. All I want is to see what you're going to do," said Ti Jean, smiling.

The old dignitary waited a minute, an eternity, then a gleam crossed his guileless partridge eye—a flash of infinite sadness. And raising his weapon he aimed it calmly at Ti Jean, without haste or hurry, as if he knew that the young man whose eyes had been opened would not move. On the contrary, that he would square his shoulders and thrust out the middle of his body so that the spear should strike home.

5.

Dusk was falling when he regained consciousness. The three Sonanke had disappeared and he was lying in the middle of the path, gripping the shaft of the spear fiercely as if to prevent its going any deeper into his chest. The whispers and shrillings of night crowded in on him. Catching sight of the canopy of the sky, he felt as if a great hand were resting on the world, a hand which shifted gently, letting thousands of little lights shine through the spaces between the fingers.

He was lying on his back, the long shaft sticking straight up above him like the mast of a ship. The spear had gone through the bone, and he thought he could feel the tip in the pit of his thorax, a few centimeters deep. But this feeling was not accompanied by any pain, nor by any notion of burning or cold, and he realized at once that he was protected, surrounded by a magic which gave him the power to pull out the sign of death and go on his way. Intrigued, he took his fingers off the spear, and found that heat was coming from his belt, a fine intoxicating throb that radiated to the very marrow of his bones. At first, pleased with this discovery, he thought to himself: Well, the belt doesn't want me to die. But on reflection it didn't seem right to him to be alive in a world so close to dream, a world that was perhaps a vision of the Beast by the marsh, a world in which men like Wademba were shot. And so he continued to lie there on the path with the spear still sticking in his chest.

As the moon rose a slim form appeared amid the tall grasses. It was Maïari, looking all round him apprehensively, his javelin held straight out in front of him. Ti Jean could not help uttering a sigh, and the child came over to him, knelt down, and began to shed bitter tears that fell one by one on Ti Jean's cheeks. Our hero resolutely shut his eyes, for he had just decided that his sorrow was eternal. But after a moment, unawares, the little tears crept into the depths of his being like a soothing balm. And opening his eyes, he calmly sat up, much to the boy's astonishment, pulled the spear out of his chest and smiled. Hardly any blood flowed from the wound, which closed up as they looked at it and was already no more than two thin red lips. Ti Jean scraped up some earth, made it into a plaster, and carefully filled in the wound. The boy watched in silence, bemused at the sight of this magic. Then, tossing his head as if to get rid of a cloud of mosquitoes, he looked away from the miraculous cure and once more offered Ti Jean the hospitality of his village, either as the guest of the king, if the tribe agreed, or else as a captive. But in the latter case, he explained in a voice full of affection, he would himself be the prisoner of his friendship for Ti Jean.

Both plunged into the darkness, amid the dark ripple of tall grasses swept by the wind.

They avoided the beaten track, making wide detours around villages that Maïari named without even seeing them, just by looking up at the sky. Every so often, also, he would stop, snuff the air two or three times with his soft colt-like nostrils, then go on again with more confidence. He walked briskly, skipping along, the gold rings in his hair forming a halo which seemed to catch the moonbeams and give them forth again like a cloud of fireflies. Ti Jean had at first pretended to be tired, and leaned on his friend's shoulder. But after an hour or so he unobtrusively shifted his weight and began to walk quite ordinarily. The boy made no comment, and Ti Jean went on to relieve Maïari also of his gun, his powder horn and Ma Eloise's bag, all of which he had picked up when they started out. Then Maïari sighed, and without more ado carefully retailed the story Ti Jean must tell the people in the village if he didn't want to be stoned.

Until just now, he explained with an air of resignation, until he'd seen that terrible wound shut up like an eye, he hadn't really known whether Ti Jean was one of the dead or one of the living, and he didn't much care because he loved him with a true and tender friendship. But other people would not see things as he did. They hadn't been saved from the lion's mouth, he said, smiling. And that was why they must just be told that Ti Jean had risen from the realm of the dead to return to the tribe of his ancestors. Yes, that was the story that would flow most easily into their ears: the stranger came from afar, he had wandered for years in the nether regions, and when he came to the country of his grandfather he had first tried to rise from below via the womb of a woman of the Sonanke. But the Sonanke womb would not accept him, so he had come up through a cave in the mountains, two or three days' journey from where he had met Maïari. Above all he must not forget that the Sonanke had already sent him back underground long before they ever aimed their spears at him. So he was filled with violent hatred of the Sonanke, and ready to make war on them.

"War?"

"It's true the war is over, but sometimes a Sonanke chief is carried away when he hears the story of battles long ago, and crosses the river. We call it war, but very few lose their lives in it. It's only the pound of flesh we owe the lion."

"I'll make war, then," said Ti Jean.

"Stranger, do not mock, for your fate is still uncertain. We respect the traveler who sits under the palaver tree, but we put all sorcerers to death wherever they come from and whatever their disguise. That's why you must above all remember this: that you came up through a cave in the mountain, that you came to our country by human means and not by witchcraft."

"Is death a human means?" asked Ti Jean in surprise.

Ignoring this remark, which he seemed to regard as disingenuous, the boy threw back his head and dangled his arms wearily.

"Friend, I'm not talking just for the pleasure of hearing my own voice. We shall soon come before my father, and I don't want you to be killed."

"Why should they kill me today? I am of the blood of the Sonanke, and they killed me already yesterday."

"Don't laugh, don't laugh! You know very well what I mean. You didn't come here by human means, and when I saw you on the path the spear was buried deep in your chest. Tell me, to whom did you tell your pain? To a tree?"

"To the evening breeze."

"To the evening breeze?" exclaimed the child in amazement.

"To a star."

"Which one?"

"No, I told it to my belt," said the subject of the miracle, to put the record straight. "I told it to my belt, which came to me from my grandfather, a man gifted with great powers in his day."

"Pooh," said the boy skeptically. And he added, slightly condescendingly:

"My poor friend, it is wrong of you to jest on these matters. Perhaps they are unknown where you come from. But here, believe me, there is a threat that is more terrible than the Sonanke, for it is invisible. There are people living among us in human shape who are really bloodthirsty beasts. They kill people by magic and then change into hyenas, or vultures, or anything, at night, and go to the graveyard with the rest of their coven and eat their victims' flesh. The snake that bites your heel, the hen with her chicks who strays round the huts at dusk, the owl that perches on your roof, are all in reality evil spirits."

"And how can they be recognized?" asked Ti Jean, expressionless.

"Just by their power to change themselves into animals at night and go and drink up people's souls."

"And those who change themselves are sorcerers?"

"Yes, it's a sure sign, except for a very few cases like your ancestor Gaor, who received his wings from the gods. But there's

also their gift of insensibility. When they are captured they en-
trust their souls to a tree, and you have to hit the tree if you
want them to feel pain. That's why it would be best if you suffered
a bit more with your wound when we get to my village."

Maïari glanced slyly at his friend.

"Otherwise people might think you are one of those who
do not like millet and milk."

"These are strange matters," murmured Ti Jean, "and I've
never heard of them before. Beings thirsty for human blood?
How is such a horrible thing possible, brother? And where can
such a strange liking come from?"

The fugitives had come to a halt on a height overlooking
the plain. Not far off, beyond two or three sunken valleys, the
village of Obanishe could be recognized from its quincunx forma-
tions of huge bombax trees standing among the clutter of houses.
Maïari, disregarding this danger, scrutinized his friend and said
by way of introduction, his cheeks swelling with self-importance:

"Listen, great hunter. You've come a very long way to be
given lessons by a child. But after all, a dead man's business is
always odd, and if you want to live for a while under our sun,
the best thing is for me to tell you the whole story of the sorcerers
from the beginning."

"Yes, although you come from afar I'm rather surprised that
you don't know what happened in the beginning, at the start
of everything, when the earth had just been born of the imagination of Dawa, the divine thresher. At that time the Creator of
the world was dissatisfied with his labors, and every day redid
the work of the day before. And men went wandering through
the darkness, suffering and crying, and they entered villages, killing and wounding those they met and doing them all the harm
they could.

> Cold and death, death and cold
> Let me shut my ears
> Cold and death, death and cold
> Let me shut my ears.

"The sun had not yet been set on its course, so the song says. Only the moon traveled through the sky, and there was very little water on the earth, for the rivers did not yet exist, nor the springs. Everything that lived had to make do with rain, and the water from pools and ponds.

"One day, when a group of men and women were dying of thirst, they saw a little pool shining in the moonlight. They rushed toward it and drank their fill, and then they saw it was a pool of blood. All together, and unwittingly, it's true, they had committed the worst imaginable sin. Their insides were convulsed, they tasted again what it was to drink blood, and they went away uneasy, wondering what would become of them among the people of millet and milk. Then Dawa bent down to them and said: This being so, my children, I can no longer let you go among the people of millet and milk, unless I set two great horns on your brows so that men may recognize you and take care. But the unfortunates pleaded their cause, saying that it was thirst for water that had drawn them to the pool, thirst for water and not for blood; though that had come after, it's true. Dawa saw their point of view, and decided to create rivers and springs. As for the blood-drinkers and their descendants, he did not set a brand on them, but scattered them throughout the world so that evil should be the portion of all. And that is why sorcerers don't have horns on their foreheads, and nor do their descendants who still live among us, mingled with the people of millet and milk. But, as I told you, they can be recognized by certain signs—above all by their ability to change themselves into beasts at night, to go and drink up people's souls."

And Maïari added naively, with an uneasy laugh:

"I hope all this doesn't apply to you, my friend."

"Don't worry," said Ti Jean. "I have been endowed with certain gifts, but I don't use them in the service of evil. I am only a man under the sky, no one in particular."

"Might I inquire what those gifts are?" said the other suspiciously.

"Let's see how clever you are," said Ti Jean, smiling. "Let's see if you can guess things. My first gift—listen carefully to what I say—is something without either legs or wings, and yet it travels very fast and nothing can stop it, neither rivers nor cliffs nor even the thickest walls. What is it?"

"Have you got the eyes of a king?"

"The eyes of a king?"

"Yes," said Maïari. "The gift of seeing great distances even in the dark."

"I haven't got the eyes of a king," said Ti Jean.

"Do you see things in dreams?"

"No, it's not that," said Ti Jean.

The boy scratched his ear, forgetting all fears—the spirits of darkness, the wild beasts, the nearness of the Devourers. He was suddenly caught up in this strange game.

"Are you a soothsayer? Can you shoot an arrow without a bow? Or can you jump, all of a sudden, and be in two places at once? One of my ancestors could do that. It was very useful in battles. Is that what you can do—jump?"

"Alas," sighed Ti Jean, "my gift is much more modest, and I confess I am practicing it before your very eyes."

And as the boy stood and gazed at him out of his weird little round orbs, Ti Jean said imperturbably:

"The first gift nature bestowed on me was my voice. The human voice, my friend."

"Pooh," exclaimed the manikin. "I pity whoever has to do sentry duty in your mouth. I don't think I've ever heard such a liar. Can you tell me what your other gifts are, O great magician?"

"I have more gifts than there are stars, and each is more astonishing than the last. But we'll talk of them later, in a more comfortable place, if you don't mind. Otherwise I shall never have another chance to use them."

The boy laughed.

"You kill me, my friend. You slay me."

Dawn was still only an absence, a pale eddy rising out of the water as they reached the river. When they got to the other side, they dried themselves this time with parasite plants that Maïari got from the bark of a baobab tree and which had the slightly abrasive softness of sponge. The fruit of the baobab, which the boy called its eggs, provided them with pretty, edible seeds embedded in a white, downy pulp. The little black boy sat with his back against the smooth trunk, wagging his head, one cheek bulging with seeds and his hands pretending to hold in an overfull stomach. Both our fine fellows laughed in chorus, and Maïari, raising one sleepy eyelid, said gravely:

"My friend, we'll say the spear ricocheted off the bone."

"The spear ricocheted," said Ti Jean. "And didn't it ricochet?"

"You old fox. Oh, we mustn't forget the cave of the dead. If you insist on saying that you came on foot from the Coast, people will immediately see you with wings and stone you— they'll stone you, I assure you. No, you came up through a cave in the mountains, over there, two days from the tree where you saved my life."

"I came up in the cave," repeated Ti Jean.

"You'd been wandering for years and years in the Kingdom, for you could not find the village of your ancestors. And when you speak of the Kingdom of the Dead, just say . . . the sunless lands, or the abode of the blue cows. That will do. But above all don't forget to say that you were a slave in your own country, for we Sonanke still remember slavery."

"I wasn't a slave," said Ti Jean pensively, "but neither did I know freedom."

"It doesn't matter," the boy granted, "it doesn't matter that you weren't a slave. In fact, all things considered, it would be better if you didn't talk about your own country, for those who rise up from below never remember their former life."

"I won't talk about my own country," said Ti Jean.

6.

After falling asleep for a moment, the boy started awake and groaned with pleasure.

"Oh," he said, "I was asleep, and now I see the light again."

Then he yawned, sighed, stretched, scratched his head, and tugged at each tuft of hair in its ring of sun. He did all this in a measured and careful manner, as was right, so as not to disturb the sacred torpor of his blood: like one of our people getting ready to face another day of his time on earth. At last, having completed his performance, he loosened his throat in a burst of traditional laughter, and with a silent wink gave the sign for departure.

As they went along he let fly a volley of minute advice, detailed suggestions as to how Ti Jean should behave in the village, the words he should employ, the way he should kiss the king on the knee, the very old men on the shoulder, and all the men older than himself on the hand. Actually, he said, smiling, none of them would accept such homage, and all Ti Jean would need to do was make the gesture. But though King Emaniema liked the forms to be respected, he also wanted this done with good humor and grace. Otherwise, he used to say, he would end by being crushed by ceremonial. Thus one day, said Maïari, when his father was out on his ceremonial ox, it suddenly buckled at the knees and the noble passenger was thrown to the ground. A warrior was aiming his weapon at the sacrilegious animal when the old man stopped him, crying cleverly: Look at the foolish beast, my masters—you'd think the poor creatures couldn't recognize kings!

"Why did the king say 'my masters'?" asked Ti Jean, laughing.

"Because he is our servant," answered the manikin, looking at his friend in surprise. "Isn't it like that in your country?"

A path sprang up in front of them and the soil became like scorched earth, with little pale green shoots springing up out of the black ashes as if to storm the charred tree trunks. Farther on there were meadows, checkerboards of cultivated land with shady copses swelling out here and there in the wake of a tiny flat blue river that skimmed along level with the ground. A procession appeared on the opposite bank, led by a gaunt old man supporting himself on a spear. Behind him there came, in order, young men with weapons, women carrying heavy wooden trays on their heads, and then some marvelous little girls, smothered like their elders in dazzling veils but bearing only winds and dreams and reveries on their little round heads bristling with small black plaits. They all advanced like a line of sailing ships in fine weather, borne up by the folds of their many-colored robes, which at first looked like silk, but no—they were just raffia fibers, soft and polished, fined and colored as if by fairy fingers.

Ti Jean saw again in his mind's eye the tunic of Old Eusebius, which was also made of plant fibers, but all rough and gray and disintegrating like a badly cured goatskin. And Ti Jean's heart stirred, while the boy's eyes flew to a group of huts slumbering on a hill. They spiraled up from the plain to an enormous baobab tree, silvery, moss-grown, seeming to extend its protection over both earth and sky. At the entrance to the village two women were pounding grain in a wooden mortar, their rounded shoulders all lit up with sweat. Now they would sing in time with the pestle, now they would match the pestle to the varied rhythm of their singing in a sort of subtle airy dance—just like the dames of Fond-Zombi when they pounded coffee, cocoa or manioc flour, or dashed their washing against the white rocks in the river. And our hero's heart was moved, moved, by these familiar images, as if the two worlds had held out their hands to each other across the ocean without seeing each other, century after century.

Meanwhile children swarmed up from every direction, greeting the visitors' arrival with shrill cries; and heralded by an indescribable din, the pair proceeded up winding streets lined with dwarf palms, just like those in the villages on the other side of the river. The villagers, crowding up to the fences of their compounds, greeted the newcomers with a pat on the shoulder, commenting endlessly on Ti Jean's physique, finer than anything they'd seen for decades. That's what men were like in the old days, they said, in the days of the gods. And they put their hands over their mouths in admiration.

Right at the top of the hill there was an open space, round, smooth and shiny, in the middle of which stood the daddy of all baobab trees, which they had glimpsed from the plain. Maïari led his friend under its shade and sat him on a little bench which was rather like a beetle, with its jetty, insect-like back and short spindly legs. Then, with a gesture of reassurance, the boy left him and vanished into the crowd. All around Ti Jean were those cool white huts, white like cheese, spotless, each closed behind its painted door. And then there were all those men and women standing at a distance round the edge of the square, robed in rich fabrics both cheerful and suggesting majesty. After a moment's amusement at this pomp and luxuriance so reminiscent of the picture books, Ti Jean again remembered the little bench his grandfather had sat on on the night he died, and the beetle comparison that had occurred to him then. And his heart turned over for the third time that day; and there, before the astonished crowd, the son of Ma Eloise buried his face in his hands and could not suppress a sob.

At this point a murmur ran through the crowd, and a man came forward whom Ti Jean immediately recognized as the king, though there was no outward sign of the fact. He was an old man like the others, very thin, with white hairs on his cheeks, and leaning, like the rest, on a spear. But his eyes sparkled with strange wisdom, at once distant and familiar. A remote fire which he did not trouble to hide kept his eyes wide open, as if before a vision. Ti Jean, impressed by this look, bent forward to kiss his knee in homage, as the boy with gold rings in his hair had told him to. But the king, affably restraining him, sat down facing his guest, apparently waiting for him to speak. In vain. Then Ti Jean remembered, and said, not without a secret desire to laugh:

"O king, take me in and I will be your dog and bark for you every day."

"I see my son has instructed you well," said the old man fondly. "Don't worry, here you will be no one's dog, not even that of the king, for we Ba'Sonanke don't keep dogs with two legs. We know who you are, we have spoken to your grandfather on this very spot, and we know all about how brave you were with the lion." He smiled almost imperceptibly. "We also know what happened over there on the other side of the river, and that is why we invite you to live among us under the name of Ifu'umwami, which in the ancient tongue means 'He says yes to death and no to life.' Does that name suit you?"

"King," said our hero, smile for smile, "no one has ever chosen his own name, or the color of his entrails."

"Then you shall be Ifu'umwami, he who defies death but receives no answer, for death always hesitates to seize him. Will you make war for us?"

"I will make war," said Ti Jean.

"Will you respect our old men?"

"I will respect them," said Ti Jean.

"And will you give us sons of your blood?"

"I will give you sons," said Ti Jean.

"Then welcome," cried the king, kissing him first on one cheek then on the other, while the crowd surged forward enthusiastically around the palaver tree. A dance developed, lively and rhythmic like the handkerchief dance when the sugar cane season is over.

7.

Sitting on his little carved wooden bench, Ti Jean was offered gift after gift until evening, giving thanks for each in the traditional words: What a lovely present, my heart overflows. Then he would turn to Maïari, who would solemnly weigh in his hand the chicken or handful of maize or eternal basket of eggs, and then, shaking his gold rings merrily, cry with ever-renewed enthusiasm: Buried, that's what we are this time, buried with kindness.

Gradually, in the general euphoria, tongues loosened and people asked the stranger about his former life and what it was like before he went down into the realm of the Shades. Ti Jean, obeying orders, remembered nothing, and could only confirm the living in their own ideas about the Kingdom of the Dead, those sunless lands where blue cows grazed. But some questions bothered him: those about the white men on the Coast.

And he grew more uneasy about them with the passing of the days and weeks, the months and years: for they suggested a world where ships were still powered by sail, and guns fired iron balls, which ricocheted in all directions, "like flat stones on water," said the Ba'Sonanke.

These questions about another age confused Ti Jean, and he wondered what time he had fallen into since the gulf opened up in the heart of the apparition. And into what Africa.

The first signs of an answer came to him with his gray hairs, when he was about fifty. A few years before, a young boy had been stolen by strangers and put in a bag, like many another, to be sold to a passing caravan. But one fine day this boy, whose name was Likeleli, reappeared in the village, almost dying, and told a very strange and surprising story. He was skillful with the bow and had changed masters several times, ending up among the bodyguard of a great king by a river, a week's march from the Coast. The kings in those parts had always sold slaves to the white settlers who lived there in tall stone houses lapped by the waves of the sea. The traders in men left their homes only to stretch their legs at the express invitation of their hosts. But suddenly, two years after Likeleli's arrival at his last master's, the white men claimed the whole country and proclaimed themselves kings over it by right of the lion's claw. Then there was a cruel war, ending in the capture of the lawful king and the burning of his capital. Likeleli was sure that the fate of that kingdom, Dahomey, would soon be visited on every other country under heaven, and that was why, after many years of lonely wanderings, he at last made his way back to his own village. He had come to give them the evidence of his own eyes, and now he could join those who were buried in the earth. Which he did the day after his return, worn out by his long journey.

As well as the terrible light thrown by the slave's story as a whole, there was one detail which especially struck our hero. According to Likeleli, the white invasion had been supported by black troops in loose trousers and red caps with a tuft on top. And as he listened to the dying slave's careful and minute description, Ti Jean suddenly saw again in his mind's eye a yellowed photograph that used to be handed around by an old man in Fond-Zombi by the name of Bernus, an old rum-swiller who claimed to have taken part in his youth in the conquest of Africa. In Ti Jean's memory, the hand that held the photograph was itself worn to a thread. But there was no doubt, as everyone on Ma Vitaline's veranda had agreed, that the picture quite clearly showed Bernus standing to attention in the incredible splendor of his twenty years, and wearing the same showy uniform as the runaway slave now described.

Later on, by the time all these hints had converged, Ti Jean's gray hairs had become just one snowy thatch, one bush of cotton shining in the sun. And he wondered what would happen if the conquest reached as far as the kingdom of the Ba'Sonanke. Would he one day find himself face to face with the young man in the photograph? Would he recognize him in the midst of battle and try to speak to him? But what could he say to him? Wouldn't he be more likely to try to kill him? And then what would become of his memory of the old photograph he had once seen on Ma Vitaline's veranda? Would it fade from his mind, or would it still go on floating inside him, a piece of flotsam worn ever smoother and more transparent, no more than a breath, like everything else to do with Fond-Zombi?

BOOK FIVE

Which contains the life and adventures of Ti Jean in Africa
up to his descent into the Kingdom of the Shades:
a true and complete account, with many hitherto unknown
details about the loves of our hero,
his hates, his births and his bereavements,
his celebrations and his wars,
not forgetting his dreams of another world.

1.

His first few weeks in the tribe were as smooth and full and mysterious as an egg. Beneath the appearances of a natural kind of life, with no cares but those of birth, illness and death, the Ba'Sonanke concealed depths which were too subtle for a Negro from Guadeloupe. For them the earth was like a woman's womb: they were very careful about opening it and taking anything from it. Before felling a tree they would sacrifice a cock to the earth, and then pour a drop of palm wine on the cock's soul. As for their own living bodies, they regarded them as a kind of immortal seed, endlessly coming up from the Shade and going down into it again, so that everyone was at once his own grandfather and his own grandson. Most disturbing of all was their sleep, for they made no distinction between dreaming and waking, and thought nothing of calling you to account for your nocturnal doings. Thus a young girl dreamed that Ti Jean had made advances to her, and the next day there was a painful scene which might have ended badly if he had not been the king's guest. But fortunately, with rare exceptions, these people seemed to behave with the same discretion, discernment and scrupulous honesty asleep as awake.

Apart from such matters as the cock, and the palm wine on the soul of the cock, Ti Jean's life rather reminded him of the one he had led before in Fond-Zombi, divided between expeditions to the mountains and the peaceful, soothing, bustling life of the village.

The Ba'Sonanke were familiar with firearms, the "poupous," as they called the big metal tubes mounted on carved wooden carriages so beautifully worked they should have borne cannon of gold. True, they were dangerous weapons, and often exploded in the face of the gunner. But they were only used in time of drought, when they were fired into the air to bring rain. Ti Jean's musket made a great impression in comparison with all that old iron. Every morning the king's soothsayer would tell what game he had seen in his dreams, on what riverbank or in what wood or plain. Then, followed by a line of meat porters which varied in length according to the soothsayer's dream, Ti Jean would go on expeditions which themselves were like a dream, with the game seeming to wait for him in the appointed place.

The musket itself was enraged and mystified by its contact with African soil. All the ammunition was gone except for a last silver bullet, the very last, which Ti Jean kept carefully in memory of his grandfather. But even though he used any old ammunition, even iron nails or stones propelled by a wretched powder made from saltpeter which exploded with squeals like a pig, his shots went right into the elephant, pierced the plating of the rhinoceros, and even made their way through the invulnerable armor of the hippopotamus, which the Ba'Sonanke called the river horse. The meat was carried home to the sound of flutes, and torches were lit around the palaver tree. The feast would begin quietly, under the leaves, and then would suddenly spread its wings as the darkness crept up the mountain.

2.

The prettiest girls fluttered about the king's guest, attracted by the mystery of his origins and by all the promises which surround the unknown, the new, the rare and the inaccessible, and which would equally have stirred the heart of a girl in Fond-Zombi. In the heat of the dance the young man glittered like a sun, a ceremonial bull, they said, fit to give you three children at once in the wink of an eye, according to the old women who had given him a bath the day he arrived. The people in Fond-Zombi had said straight out that Ma Eloise's son had inherited a rod of gold: you could tell it even through his trousers, and that impressive statement was enough once and for all. But these folk on the other side of the water did not talk about a rod of gold.

In their eyes it was a sort of pyx, a tabernacle he carried between his thighs, the strapping young fellow, a high mass designed to fall on the whole kingdom like a rain of benedictions. But our hero had no intention of ringing the bell for that mass, and his ears only heard and heard again the cry of Egea, yonder, beyond times and worlds, under the banyan fig tree that had been an ark to them after the incident of the platform truck. No matter how he worked himself up or appealed to his desires or recalled the promise he had made to King Emaniema, it was no good. All he noticed in those charming young plants was a detail here or there, a breast, a hip, a turn of the neck, a convex brow bent in peaceful, happy reverie; they each reminded him a little of his lost love.

The only virtue of one of the girls was that her voice was like Egea's. It was her he chose to marry the day the king warned him that a rumor was growing up around the cooking pots which might spread beyond the women. This might be dangerous for him, for it is well known that solitude is the mother of witchcraft.

Everyone was rather surprised by his choice, for Onjali was not particularly pretty. She had a smooth, round flat face; hence the nickname, Little Bowl, which she had been called by since she was a child. Ti Jean met her in the village of the Hippopotamus on the banks of the river Niger during an excursion with the king's household. The huts stood slightly back from the river, looking down over a vast expanse of moving water dotted here and there with little islands that seemed suddenly to take flight as thousands of pink egrets flapped up into the air. Each hut was like a great clay bell, an enormous antheap rising out of the earth it stood on, with a little round opening on one side about the height of a child. They were like those frail and complicated constructions the youngsters never tired of building on the beach at La Ramée, and the sea never tired of destroying. But these were exquisitely cool inside, and several days went by in feasts so lavish they made the guests kneel and beg please to be let off. The men of this remote village never took their eyes off the king, and the girls marveled at Ti Jean's supernatural stature, his strength and beauty; a sun, they called him, behind the hedges. Then, spread by the everlasting voice of the cooking pots, the rumor arose that this star shone for another whom the stranger had known in his former life, his life before death, and whom he had not forgotten. And the young plants turned reluctantly away, to offer the scent of their youth to other nostrils which breathed only in this world.

One day, haunted by his dreams, Ti Jean left the village and went for a walk along the Niger. At the foot of a cliff a small stream flung itself into the river, and above the sound of the waterfall he heard the special laughter of girls at play. Lost in thought, he had forgotten to signal his approach, and was nobly withdrawing when he thought he recognized the voice of Egea. She was standing on the bank with her back to him, her body enveloped in a big patterned robe, red like the earth at Fond-Zombi, green like its hills and blue like its sky. Despite the bathers' indignant cries, Ti Jean went up to the girl, who turned toward him a face of dark night and surprise, and did not recognize him. He stood there dazzled, drinking in this stranger with lips darker than her skin and eyes darker still; the only lights were on the high, rather prominent cheekbones which stretched the skin like a drum. And he was just going to speak to her in Creole, when his lips unexpectedly uttered some words in African.

"It's I," he whispered. "Don't you know me?"

"Who's I?" she said, bewildered.

She was not really like Egea, except for a soft brightness like that of certain mangoes waiting in the shade, growing in damp and scented places. She glanced at him shyly, then said to her friends, now standing still, shining and plump, their hands modestly folded between their thighs:

"Who is this crank, sisters, this tall rascal, this gaping ox pining for the plains?" She spoke evenly, in the voice of old Kaya's daughter. "I don't remember seeing him in the meadows. Have any of you come across him by any chance, my little gazelles?"

One slender girl with an ingenuous look, standing up to

her waist in water, smote her cheeks merrily and said with the utmost seriousness:

"It's Ifu'umwami, the king's guest. But it's best not to gaze at him too long, for this fine young man does not shine for us. He's a soup simmering for another, one not of this world, apparently."

"A sad soup, from what I can see," replied the girl with the voice of Egea. "I'd been told of a young man glittering like the sun, a ceremonial bull fit to give you three children at once in the blink of an eye. But what do we see here, sisters?"

There was an insulting burst of laughter.

"Must we throw stones to drive you away, stranger?"

Then she softened, her cheeks colored, and her hand went to the hollow of her stomach, as if she had been naked. Her soul suddenly seemed to flood into her face, smooth and round as a bowl.

"Must we throw stones at you, eh?" she said.

"No, no need," answered Ti Jean.

"What are you waiting for, then?"

"For you to tell me your name," he stammered.

"My name, for you, will be Bleating Goat."

"Why so?"

"Because a goat that bleats is not thirsty."

That evening he saw her in the village square among the same group of girls as had been romping in the creek. And she was quite an ordinary child. True, her face was pleasantly smooth and round, but not especially striking despite her braids arranged in rows like millet stems, and the fine, sweet-smelling red dust on her cheeks, and the long white cotton panels that hung down her back to her heels in quivering, swirling fronds as they flew to the sound of the tom-tom. According to the king's son her name was Onjali, and she belonged to a good Hippopotamus family whose blood had flowed straight down from the earliest times and most distant generations. She had just come back from a visit a long way away, and that was why they hadn't seen her until today. Maïari said that her parents were both still alive; there was no doubt about it. And Ti Jean listened open-mouthed, wondering by what magic Egea, the daughter of old Kaya, could have been born of a woman of the Ba'Sonanke, with a face round as a bowl and eyes that did not recognize him. The boy, seeing his perplexity, offered to take her a present, together with a pressing invitation to a nocturnal rendezvous. But the ambassador came back looking very downcast.

"Alas, Onjali told me to tell you not to count on it. Her chickens don't peck in your direction."

On these disobliging words, Ti Jean went to bed. But he tossed and turned on his mat, unable to understand by what magic Egea, the daughter of old Kaya, could have been born of a woman of the Ba'Sonanke, with a face round as a bowl and eyes that did not recognize him. He felt like a raccoon caught in the teeth of a trap. He went up to her again on the days that followed, and said a few words in Creole at random in the hope of producing he knew not what, perhaps a shade in her eyes that went back to her former life. And every evening he nearly dislocated every muscle stretching himself tall as the stars in the ceremonial dance, in the vain hope of attracting her attention.

Maïari told him to take it easy, for too much haste makes a woman bear a child without a head. According to him and all his experience, the best wives liked to play hard to get, for the same reason as the best fruit is found at the top of the tree. And the boy was right: she was only biding her time, and a few months later she left the village of the Hippopotamus, with her red cheeks and her white fronds, to go and live in the hut Ti Jean had made her with his own hands. It was inside his compound, but separated from his warrior's dwelling by a narrow passage of closely woven withes, impenetrable to any eye.

3.

Egea never would recognize him. At first he hoped. He waited and waited for her to remember her true life, the time before the spell, before she came back up to earth born of a woman of the Ba'Sonanke. He often called her by her former name, Egea, Egea Kaya, as if in jest. Or else he let slip the name of a river at random, or of a plant or rock or bird, in the hope of taking her by surprise, of awakening a buried echo of Guadeloupe. But she would look at him round-eyed and frightened, especially at the name Egea, which he repeated again and again in a voice of despair. She saw it as the name of a woman he had had in his former life and was jealous, saying that the spirit of that creature was pursuing Ifu'umwami even beyond his death, preventing him from feeling about her as she would have wished, feeling about her with all the strength of a young man as beautiful as the sun.

She conceived in the first year of her marriage, which earned her the envied title of Happy Face with the Fertile Womb. Until then, though she hadn't really been ungenerous with her body, she had only given herself in the traditional position of the Ba'Sonanke, a position so common that the people of Fond-Zombi regarded it, disdainfully, as a pure waste of time. And then as soon as she knew she was pregnant she insisted on manifesting her gratitude acrobatically, standing on one leg with the other thrown boldly over Ti Jean's shoulder. She soon began to have fancies. For instance, they mustn't cough during their conjugal pleasures because the cough would go to the baby's chest; nor must they make love after sunrise, for that, she said fearfully, might cause all sorts of disasters, though she never explained what they were. She did agree to it sometimes, however, on certain flaming, magic afternoons, on condition that their bodies came together in the cooling waters of a stream. All this might have surprised Ti Jean or even worried him had it not been for the secret evidence of the girl's little shell, which expressed itself with exactly the same spirit and feeling as Egea's.

As her pregnancy progressed she complained that her stomach lifted her up in the air like a fish bladder, instead of weighing her down gently toward the earth. So on the high priest's advice they ballasted her by sewing stones into the hems of her skirts. Then, as the meteoric globe wafted her up to the ceiling, they had to hold her down by securing her with strings to the uprights of the hut. In the sixth month, when she had started to dream of things with a sharp point, she was stung by a bee in her sleep and awoke quite flat and deflated, a girl again. The night this happened a second hut rose up as if by some miracle in the compound allotted to Ti Jean in the middle of the village. And the next day, while the roof of the new hut was still green, one of Onjali's little sisters appeared there, a child siren with breasts scarce in bud, whom the elder girl presented to Ti Jean as his second wife.

"Is it really you saying that?", said Ti Jean, amazed. "You yourself actually ask me to . . . ?"

"Yes," answered Onjali gravely. "You must be nourished by her as well as by me. It is fitting for a man of your rank."

These words completely unnerved Ma Eloise's son, who looked at Onjali without recognizing her. For the first time he wondered whether his African wife really was Egea, despite the fact that she had the same complexion and the same liquid voice whose sounds stirred his soul as if they had traveled through layer on layer of water before coming to the surface again under the African sky. As years went by, a third and yet a fourth wife came to add to his perplexity. New huts went up near that of Ti Jean, around which his wives went back and forth, merged now into one great anonymous wheel that never stopped turning, never leaving him a moment's rest, a real moment to himself in which to open his nostrils to the passing of time.

Onjali ruled over this world with a firm hand and a voice that brooked no contradiction. And she spoke of the host of children who tumbled about in the compound as if they were her own, sprung from her own womb, with a look of gentle pride on her round bowl of a face which greatly surprised Ti Jean. But now there were wrinkles about her eyes and mouth, her temples showed threads of silver, and she didn't know what to do with herself on the nights when it was her turn to receive the lord and master of the house. There was both an impulse in her and a resistance, like water when you go against the stream, simultaneously offering and withholding itself in one enveloping flow. She found true fulfillment now only in sleep. Every time, just before dozing off, she would turn to Ti Jean and whisper an apprehensive and anxious farewell, because her soul was setting out on an uncertain journey from which, her mother had told her, the traveler does not always return. And then she would disappear deep into peaceful waters in which her features shifted, re-formed, and suddenly recaptured the sparkle and soft glow of youth. Ti Jean was always intrigued by this magic. And sometimes, leaning over her face as if over an abyss, he had a sort of delusion, and he thought the depths stirred and the old wife's features were swept away like foam, gently giving way to the face of Egea.

One night when she was wearing the other's face, Ti Jean could bear it no longer and gave her a sharp pinch on the shoulder. The sleeping woman shuddered. Then she opened her eyes, but they were blank, still turned toward her dream, so she couldn't find the way back to her village. But her people knew how to bring a soul back home however far it had strayed in its nocturnal journey. And on the eighth day, after they had danced, sung, implored those who go under the trees, and washed her whole body with a decoction of caiman's eyes (caimans are supposed to be able to see hidden things), her own eyes moved in their sockets, she awoke, and told them about her journey. She remembered dimly that she had been living in a strange country, a strip of land surrounded by water that never saw the sun. And there she was pregnant with a real child who drank her blood from afar and prevented her from giving birth in this world. She was weeping as she finished her story.

Never again did Ti Jean pinch her while she was asleep. He just gazed at her, whole nights through, leaning over the waters where every so often an absent face appeared. And when she woke, touched by the influence and physical pressure of his glance, her handsome aging face lit up, and the arms she stretched out toward him were as round and fresh as on that first day, over there by the waterfall, the waterfall that flows into the Niger.

After other promises which all ended in nothing, the queen of the compound wore a face that was sometimes peaceful and full of distant serenity, and sometimes darkened by a cloud of melancholy which hollowed her temples and veiled the brightness of her eyes. More little sisters had come to live around her, each with her own hut and "visiting" day, and all equally eager to compensate for the shortcomings of the eldest. When stocks were exhausted, Onjali hesitated for several years before she brought one of her cousins to be covered by Ti Jean. She'd chosen a very ugly girl who looked like a marooned mongoose, badly made and not quite cooked. But as soon as Onjali had thrust the girl into a hut with the thatch still green, she mysteriously became mortally jealous of her. She nagged her and gave her hell, and when her turn for bed came, used to kneel till dawn by the outer wall to follow her taking off and losing her breath and the way she grew wings in Ti Jean's arms; but Onjali was a woman of intelligence and experience, and no one ever knew. For her part, the cousin, instead of modestly taking her place in the great wheel of the compound, immediately distinguished herself by the cries of triumph she let out beneath Ti Jean before he'd even touched her. True, the song of the womb was not unknown to the Ba'Sonanke. On the contrary, they believed it had a very beneficial influence on the millet; the oldest among them remembered bumper harvests that had grown in a single night because of a woman drunk with joy and spreading her honey and savor over all the world. Unfortunately the cousin's cries would not grow a single grain of millet; the whole hill knew this at once, and so did the clouds, and the furthest trees on the plain. For the cries came not from her entrails but from a little head cracked with envy and with a craving to dethrone the queen of the compound.

One night Ti Jean was with this piece of the wrath of God, whose turn for bed it was according to the strict order established by Onjali, when he thought he heard a faint sob. Rising noiselessly, he went out of the hut and found the great queen kneeling outside, her eyes shut and one ear pressed to the wall. She was half naked and her rounded manatee shoulders shone in the moonlight, which lent a dazzling whiteness to her aged hair. Ti Jean went quietly back inside, making no sound for fear of wounding the ears of Onjali, whom he still sensed to be near, sobbing, sinking under the weight of her age. But the cousin, her suspicions aroused by all this, left the hut in her turn, and approaching the old wife stealthily, gave her a great blow on the head with a stone. Onjali fell forward, not even knowing what was happening.

There hadn't been such a scandal for generations. No matter how vehemently the mongoose defended herself, saying she had thought it was an envoy of darkness, some beast of evil, she was solemnly ordered to go back to the village of the Hippopotamus. The same sentence acknowledged that all Onjali's joy was to make Ti Jean's millet grow, to enlarge his flocks, and to give him children, even if it was through other wombs than her own. In truth, said the Ancients, she had always been a cool refreshing gourd to Ti Jean, a roof that never lets one drop through, a woman for all weathers. The clouds knew it, and the trees on the plain were not ignorant of it. And that is why they kept her in the village, with old Ifu'umwami, despite the dreadful shame to which she, the queen of the compound, had exposed herself by publicly showing her jealousy.

Life went on, the old wife's wounds healed. And everything seemed to have returned to normal, to the old peace, when Onjali felt a strange difficulty in breathing. All her bones hurt, and soon she complained that there was a red cock inside her. Then everyone went wild, for they had recognized her illness. Every night, at the slightest animal cry, the women set up a wail to drive away the envoy of darkness, the sorcerer who was slowly gnawing at Onjali's soul. And the men, carrying torches and armed as if for war, slaughtered everything that crept or crawled or fluttered in the air, right down to the most harmless insects. But these were only living creatures, holy creatures born, like men, of the earth, and the patient's condition did not improve. But one evening Ti Jean, who had posted himself under the thatch of his own hut, saw an owl flapping heavily round his old wife's roof. He shot at it. A direct hit. The owl gave a hoot which ended in an infinitely sad groan, and a woman's body crashed down on the edge of the compound. It was the little wife he had repudiated, half of her face still recognizable. They dragged her toward the place of stoning, but she died on the way, so they consigned her to the river Seetane tied to a tree trunk, for the sweet water to carry her to the sea, whence none returns.

Onjali did not long survive her. Ti Jean, lying by the dying woman, forgot what was seemly and cried his heart out, while a murmur of disapproval rose from the crowd gathered round the hut. At last, when he thought she was already gone, she came back long enough to give a faint smile, tinged with coquetry, and in a voice that seemed to have crossed stretch after stretch of water to reach her lips she murmured apologetically:

"Life is a capricious woman, and as I'm a woman and a half I have been even more capricious than life. But who were you, my comrade, my fine ceremonial bull? Who were you, my dear?"

Apart from those tears at the end, there was nothing tangible with which to reproach the king's guest. He had always followed the path of magnanimity, accepting the concubines the queen had brought him and treating them absolutely equally, without any sign of according the slightest precedence to any of them, without the slightest favoritism. But there emanated from the whole affair something excessive, suspect, a whiff of extravagance, of a frontier having been passed between man and woman. Such was the rumor that started in Ti Jean's compound and spread all round the village, whispered by the busy tongues of the millet pounders and returning considerably magnified to its point of departure. Then Onjali's little sisters were seized with fear, and went back to their native village, taking with them cows and clay pots, together with the children they had had from the seed of the king's guest and then placed in the lap of the dead woman.

Ti Jean suddenly realized that his hands had been empty, desperately empty, since the day he arrived among the Ba'Sonanke. No matter how great the king's goodwill, which had granted him possession of the compound, and despite even the friendship of the king's son, the kind and faithful Maïari, not an inch of land could belong to him, doomed to remain a stranger and own not a stalk of the thatch under which he slept, not a drop of the blood that flowed in the veins of his sons. The only thing he had ever possessed, under the sun of this world so close to dream, was the heart of Onjali. And perhaps that had never existed.

4.

Every year at the time of the millet harvest the Ba'Sonanke went and offered the first fruits to the dead, in the cave in the mountains that the king's son had told Ti Jean about on the boat of the gods, the day after he had fallen into the African sky. Processions wound through the scrub and joined together near the cave, where the living sang and danced with the dead for three nights, offering them food in consecrated clay pots. When the Shades came out of the cave they were all wrapped in the same kind of indigo cloth, which merged into the night and seemed a part of the living, indeterminate darkness. Ti Jean knew that none of the Shades would recognize him, for they remember only their own lineage, mortals of their own clan and blood. But regularly every year he awaited the apparition of Onjali, and was pleased to see her move around gracefully in her mantle of darkness, hear the news of the past year like the rest, and then go and sit opposite a relative of hers from Hippopotamus, and talk with him as she helped herself daintily from the dish set down between them. Her eyes were two half-circles of silver reflected in still water, and when she went out of the cave they darted from one living person to another, gay and shining with childlike intensity, but never lingering on the face of Ifu'umwami.

But our hero finally tired of this glance that passed over him without recognition, and stopped going to the cave of the dead. He lived alone now, in a hut on the outskirts of the village, a sort of ajoupa built of lime-washed withes after the old fashion of Fond-Zombi.

In those days he wore only fifty years on his body, a living body that looked as if it had come straight from the foundry, a brand-new bronze cannon. But there by the cave, waiting for a glance from Onjali, he had acquired some gray locks. Life seemed a light thing, and his feet were no longer firmly on that dream earth. War roused him out of this torpor. It began with a rumor, a vague prophecy that promised the Devourers another thousand years of conquest. Then independent groups of warriors crossed the river, "jungle men," who advanced straight before them attacking everything alive until they were stopped by a spear thrust. Then King Emaniema had himself carried to the banks of the Seetane and harangued those on the other side as follows:

"Neighbors and noble warriors, hear the voice of my gray hairs."

A sarcastic reply came from across the river:

"We'll listen if you wrap an old woman's skirt around you."

"Neighbors," cried the old king faintly, "I tell you it is better to thresh your millet than to sharpen your sword. For war is the victory of the dead, the caldron of the seven sorrows, and if ever the white cloud that comes from the Coast—"

He was interrupted by an arrow, and they bore him into the shelter of a tree. There, as insults were being flung back and forth across the river, he murmured something in Maïari's ear and quietly expired. What he had said was this:

"My son, he makes the world better who does not take revenge."

But his words were immediately swept away, gone with the wind of a furious and pitiless attack, more cruel than anything Ti Jean could have imagined, despite all the stories he'd been told. He himself lost all sense of moderation, and his name was soon surrounded by a halo of legend. A song described him as

Swift as the hyena and like him tearing his prey to pieces,
Seizing the most skillful runners by the hip
And throwing them down.

Several times the musket charged with scrap iron pierced the enemy ranks surrounding the new king, his faithful and affectionate Maïari. But the Devourers had excellent preparation on their side, and their skillful ferocity gradually spread consternation among the former slaves, who fled in disorder toward the river Niger. One night Ti Jean dreamed he was swooping down on the enemy with beak and claws. Opening his eyes, he found he was changed into a crow, his great wings outspread over the young king, who was sleeping beside him in the tent they shared. Then he summoned up a man's body, and afterward went back again to that of a crow, and so on four or five times, until he was sure he could metamorphose himself from one to the other at will. Bursting suddenly with rage, his feathers bristling, he left the king's tent and flew to the enemy camp, where he dealt destruction with beak and claws until dawn. When he resumed human form back near the tent again, his whole body was covered as if with a butcher's red apron. He bathed in a stream and then went silently back to bed near his friend. He repeated all this the next night, and the next, and all the other nights, until a wind of madness began to blow through the camp of the former masters.

Then another rumor went through the sky of the Devourers, proclaiming the emptiness of the prophecy. And when this second rumor had triumphed, when the last enemy had crossed the river Seetane and plunged back into the wall of vegetation at the very place where the threat had once burst through, the Ba'Sonanke looked for the bones of King Emaniema and buried them in a grave beside an aged lion, for he had been the supreme chief. After that they organized a great feast in honor of all the departed, and the witch doctor urged them to mount through their wives' wombs as soon as possible so as to produce new lives beneath the sun. Then he sang lengthy praises of the deeds of Ifu'umwami, the well-named, and the new king thrust girls before him, little sirens like those Onjali used to bring him. But Ti Jean only smiled, and they let him go back alone to his hut of withes, according to his heart's desire.

He now worked on the land, like the women, on a little plot of millet and sorghum and sweet potatoes, for he had completely lost his passion for hunting, which reminded him of his arms being red with human blood. When the day's work was over he would sit in front of his ajoupa in the shade of a parasol which shifted slowly round, hour by hour, following the course of the sun. He liked the sudden onset of the African night, like the dropping of a curtain. His eyes fixed on all that vagueness and change and wandering, he listened to the peaceful rustle falling in a sweet rain from the stars, and every day nearer; and to the sound of the human beings on the hill, every day more distant.

Sometimes the king would come to see him in the evening, there in his deserted compound. The child with the gold rings in his hair was now much changed, and the crown of his ancestor M'Pande rested on a bald head. His frail lanky body shook with convulsive tremors. As for his soft colt-like eyes, they had given place to great hollow sockets with the tired look of a broken-down hack which keeps straining and straining at the harness. And what Maïari was hauling along thus, with his immense weakness, was a whole people.

The king always came alone, leaning on a spear in place of a stick. He would push open the gate into the compound and sit down silently opposite his friend, and they would look at each other without speaking, unless one of them lighted a pipe or took a pinch of snuff. Then the other would say, "Save my life, friend," and they would exchange the pipe or the tobacco pouch, just for the pleasure of the exchange. And that was all their conversation under the stars. They knew, knew well, that there was everything between them, separating them: the living, the dead, the gods themselves—all was an abyss, save friendship, and that was why they each kept their words to themselves. Sometimes Ti Jean longed to forewarn Maïari, to tell him, to put at his service the scant knowledge he himself had of the white men, whose real strength did not lie in guns, despite what one might think, but in that which one day would follow the guns. And images would float up in his mind, photographs from old newspapers or magazines in Fond-Zombi, absurd and sinister visions to which he'd paid no attention as a child, being solely preoccupied with the Africa of his dreams. He longed but he was silent, thinking that everything that was to come was already accomplished; not really in the future, the genuine future, but well and truly past, dead. He longed and fretted, and finally sealed his lips, for there was no place for such words in his friend's mind. Then, when both had been assiduously silent, the king would put his hand on Ifu'umwami's shoulder and say with a smile:

"A good conversation strengthens the ear, as they say. And now we have told each other all, come and let us climb the hill together, old comrade. But whatever you do, don't stay here, don't stay here counting the stars."

Ti Jean would always start at the words "counting the stars," because that was what the people of Fond-Zombi used to say about anyone who had capsized into solitude and darkness. Then he would get up and go with the king to the village square, under the palaver baobab, where the people's conversation would immediately give place to dancing. Every time Ti Jean promised himself to stick to the traditional figures of the Ba'Sonanke, but the voice of the drum bemused him, swept him insidiously toward another time, another place, another inner music. And he started to flail out at space, slicing the darkness with eloquent gestures that sang of the worlds and the worlds beyond the worlds, of the woods beyond the woods, of earthquakes and landslides and falls.

And the circle widened, and fell silent around this dancer who seemed to get lighter with age, to fly up into the branches of the baobab, where his head became a dazzling white bush, a cotton bush tossing in the wind.

When the king didn't come, Ti Jean would sit on in the compound until all the sounds of the village died away, first the tom-tom of the evening gathering, then the last murmurs in the huts and the last growls of the dogs in their sleep. Then he would take long breaths of the salubrious night air, and smiling already at the great spaces, he would murmur, in a clumsy, hesitant Creole that would have made the people of Fond-Zombi roar with laughter:

> "Over the eyelids of men
> Over the leaves
> Over the muzzle of the lion
> I spread my black wings."

Then he would take a few steps across the compound and, with a faint silky sound, rise up very swiftly and very high into the darkness, borne up by a rapture which gradually subsided as the huts of the village turned into little white pebbles set out in a snail-like spiral as if in a children's game. He loved the air currents, the invisible paths that crisscrossed in the plains of heaven just as they did on earth. And he would sometimes let himself be borne along at random, in the void, a grain of pollen, free, until a pallor on the horizon told him to return to the village. But usually he chose a wind that blew toward the land of the Hippopotami, above the bend of the Niger; he admired the calm, majestic course of the river, as of a god who advances without a gesture, enveloped in his own immobility. And there, somersaulting in the sky, the exile would dive down toward that great ribbon of silver and perch on a tree or an overhanging rock on those man-forsaken banks.

None of the animals took any notice of him. They were linked together by a pact as old as the world, these creatures coming to drink, each species with its own beach or creek or inland lake. From these unspeaking bodies there emanated a soothing truth, in which Ti Jean used to steep himself before winging home. But sometimes he would hesitate just before taking off, and dream of going to the Coast to solve the mystery of Bernus, in his loose trousers and his red cap with a tuft. With a bit of luck he might perhaps manage to get onto a boat that would take him back to Guadeloupe, long ago, even before Ma Eloise was born. He laughed at this idea and enjoyed looking at it from every point of view, for he knew very well, deep down inside, that he would never resign himself to leaving Egea in the past, beneath the earth of the Ba'Sonanke. But was Onjali really Egea, he sometimes asked himself jokingly. Perhaps, by dreaming about the one, he had attracted the other into his dream. Perhaps he had merely snared in a dream that girl on the banks of the Niger, with long white plumes hanging down from a head-band to her heels.

Other strange ideas had come to him lately, twining up round his mind like parasite plants that he could not always get rid of. What increasingly intrigued him was whether it was really by accident that he had fallen into this Africa of another age. Perhaps he had fallen exactly where he was destined to, because the Beast had only dispatched him into his own dream, into the very country and time that flowed in the depths of their blood. Perhaps, if he had loved little Guadeloupe as he ought, if he hadn't carried this worm hidden within him, this strange treason, he might have fallen among the heroes of the past: Ako, Mindumu, N'Deconde, Djuka the Great and the rest? But why had Wademba spoken so eloquently to him about his village on the night of his death, unwittingly sending him to his precipice? Had he too dreamed too much of Africa, the old green conger curled up there on his rock, and let himself be carried away by his dream?

Thus all sorts of visions arose in Ti Jean, sending up rank weeds that he didn't even try to cut down. Ah, ideas, he sighed down his beak, at dawn, before winging home. Ideas, ideas: there's nothing grows up more quickly, ladies and gentlemen.

Up he flew, wistfully, sorry to have to return among men. And when he arrived over the sleeping village he descended in ever-narrowing circles, his flight deadened and almost painful in its silence; and he landed like a shadow in the middle of the compound.

Once a faint pink mist was rising in the east when he was getting ready to quit the banks of the Niger. He felt weary at the thought of going back, and as soon as he'd taken to the air a strange stiffness stopped him from making up for lost time. Then his joints started to feel painful, and his wings increasingly heavy and uncoordinated, with the result that the sun was almost up when he came within sight of the king's village. By a supreme effort he flew over a few roofs and alighted at the entrance to his own ajoupa, took a few crow steps in the dark, then resumed human form. At that moment a number of hands started at him out of the shadows, and the voice of Maïari, tinged with a distant, twilight sadness, was heard:

"Friend, what have you got to say to us?"

Our hero thought for a moment, feeling how frail this universe was that could vanish like a bubble at the lightest breath. Then, rather than destroy the dream of the Ba'Sonanke, he followed for the last time in the steps of the dreamers, and made himself smile.

"Good king," he said, "I found myself face to face with a lion, and fear lent me wings."

5.

There was soon a trial, under the still damp and sparkling leaves of the palaver baobab, and the king pleaded for a long time, while the crowd remained obstinately silent. In ringing phrases he recalled the story of Ifu'umwami's ancestor, he who had changed himself into a crow in order to enter his enemy's tent. As far as he knew, no one had accused that hero of witchcraft: they had simply said that his clan were allied to the crows. But, cried the king in his aged voice, was not Ifu'umwami his descendant, and could he not have inherited this gift without being an eater of souls?

Ti Jean, who was tied by the ankle to prevent him from flying away again, could smell in the morning breeze the scent of approaching death. At last, without saying anything, the people took him to the place of stoning, where he dug a hole that came up to his waist. There he stood, his hands free, looking at the old dignitaries, his friends, who were standing facing him in a single row with heaps of sharp stones at their feet. They had removed all the ropes binding the drinker of souls, because he was helpless in daylight, like a crocodile out of its pond. And Ti Jean breathed in the dawn, wondering what stopped him from suddenly spreading his wings and starting a new life; what prevented him from flying to the Coast, for example, whence he might perhaps be able to make his way to Guadeloupe, as he had often dreamed of doing at night on the banks of the Niger. Meanwhile the king seemed unable to bring himself to give the signal. His little left eye was no more than a thread, like a child's when the sun is too strong. Then a tear ran down his old white whiskers, and seeing it Ti Jean smiled and said:

"Maïari, old cloud swallower, what in heaven's name is someone like you doing here on earth? It's a place of ricochets and zigzags, twists and turns, and so where are you if you can't laugh instead of crying, dance instead of walking? Eh, where are you?"

Then, with a faint sob, old King Maïari threw the first stone, and the others followed in an ever-increasing shower. When one of them hit Ti Jean on the head, knocking him over backward, he dimly remembered what Wademba had said about his future of sadness, solitude, obscurity and blood. He got up, but was felled again by a second stone, and a third. He could no longer see, and it was very difficult to get to his feet and find the direction of the crowd so as to face it as duty required, on his legs, like a man. Then suddenly the effort to stand up seemed extraordinarily easy. He felt light, nonexistent, like a floating wisp of mist in the dawn sun. And then, with some astonishment, he wondered whether it was his body or his spirit that was confronting the crowd.

Standing there in the faint light of dawn, Ti Jean felt a sort of wound, a wave of fire, the well-known effect of light upon the dead. At once he crouched down under the heap of earth and lay low in his remains, awaiting the Shade's permission. Through a halo he could see human shapes piling more rocks on him, hastily, before running away as fast as they could. Then the hours went by, and the sun stood over his grave, a patch of brightness surrounded by gray. And the smoke of day gradually shredded away, eaten by the teeth of night, and the sound of singing came intermittently from far away, mingled with the dull thud of the tom-tom.

There was a melancholy moon shining when he climbed out of the grave and set off for the village. He had left his corpse under the stones as a snake abandons its old skin. Sometimes his feet came down above the surface of the ground, and sometimes beneath it, up to the ankles, according to the strength he put into his long, graying legs. Then he got used to his new state and could walk quite ordinarily, and even make the grass bend under his feet if he felt like it.

At the foot of the king's hill there was a cow, but though

its eyes were wide open it did not see him, which touched the dead one with a certain sadness. Then, inside the village, he stopped beside a young couple courting in the dark, and when their eyes didn't see him either, his sadness increased. A big crowd was gathered in the square, around the palaver baobab. The singing was over; only a drum beat softly. As Ti Jean marveled at this softness, he saw that the skin of the drum was covered with a cloth to deaden the sound. He was intrigued by all this. He had expected to find rejoicing, and all he saw was solemn, troubled faces, as if at a bereavement. A fire was flickering in the middle of the square, under the whispering fronds of the palaver tree. Beyond the flames, his back resting against the trunk, his friend Maïari sat on a ceremonial chair, his eyes closed and a look of meditation on his face. Suddenly tears flowed down the king's cheeks, and without opening his eyes he started to sing the song Ti Jean had heard from his grave. It was not a song of rejoicing, as he had thought, but a sad, slow, peaceful funeral dirge, the same the boy with gold rings in his hair had murmured fifty years before, to the stranger with a spear within his breast:

> An animal is born, passes and dies
> Then comes the great cold
> The great cold of the night, the dark
> A bird passes, flies, dies
> Then comes the great cold
> The great cold of the night, the dark
> A fish flees, passes . . .

One after the other, the various living forms paraded through the song, greeted by the quiet beat of the drum, until it was the turn of man to be born at the hands of the god, and then to pass and die. Then a great peace fell, and Maïari, gazing into the flames, wept without restraint. The crowd were all watching him, and every time his chest rose and fell they too heaved a sigh, as if joined by a thread to the king's sorrow. Thus, no longer in fear of the sorcerer, the Ba'Sonanke mourned the man they had known and loved and one day even extolled to the skies, although he did not belong to them or their blood. And this was very sweet to the departed, as he went down the other side of the hill to his compound, where he found all his possessions unharmed, and not profaned as he had feared all day in his grave. They were all there, the musket, the powder horn, the bag, the ring of knowledge and the belt—the buckle glinted in the moonlight as he fastened it round his waist. At that moment a neighboring dog sat down on his hindquarters, lifted his muzzle to the moon and let out the special howl that animals make when they scent the presence of a Shade. Then there was a single uproar, a single tumult echoing like gunfire over the king's hill.

"Leave them in peace! Leave the living in peace!"

The shout rose up from every direction.

Driven away by the clamor, Ti Jean strode from his compound to the plain, the domain of the beasts of the night. He was allowed three days in which to revisit the places where he had found his sun, before he had to go and look upon the hidden face of the earth. But the cries of the living had touched and hurt him, like a new kind of stoning. So, shaking off the dust of this world, the hero set forth straight away for the cave of the dead. He arrived at early dawn, just before the flame of the sun.

At the back of the cave there were steps worn by the ebb and flow of generations, which spiraled down to the depths of the earth in ever more palpable darkness, a sort of black porridge that forced itself through your lips like mud. A few hundred yards farther down, the stairs merged into another cave exactly the same as the one above, with a similar porch opening onto similar lofty vaults, a kind of hidden church buried like a womb in the rock. Outside there was the same ledge halfway up the mountain, except that a rocky ceiling stretched over the forked baobabs, ageless twin trees which according to the Ba'Sonanke dated from the separation of heaven and earth. A mild gray light suggested, deadened as through a veil, the usual colors of things.

It was infinitely lighter than the gray night of Guadeloupe, the night that fell in the past or in the future, he didn't know anymore, when the moon and the stars disappeared. Ti Jean, puzzled, plucked a handful of grass and found it as soft as the foliage overhead. Smiling in spite of himself, he went down to the foot of the mountain and set out along the path that led to the king's village. Some blue cows were grazing at the entrance to the village, not far from the pool where the women drew water, and he recognized without surprise this or that tree or slope in the ground, the look of a wood on the right, and farther on the outlines of the first houses with their carved wooden doors. The Ancients had always said that the world below was an exact replica of the world above, except that it was wrapped in the mists of eternity.

BOOK SIX

Which tells how Ti Jean entered the Kingdom of the Dead,
and how he left it again; which, as you know,
my children, is always more difficult.

1.

At the foot of the hill, hanging on the lower branches of a fig tree like washing out to dry, were a number of robes all made of the indigo blue material used for shrouds. The largest seemed to have belonged to someone who died a very long time ago, for its color had faded away almost entirely, worn and erased speck by speck by the invisible hand of time. Ti Jean put it on and went into the village of the dead, where the first person he met was a young man who had been killed by a lance thrust twenty years before, during the war against the Devourers. The dead man was sitting in front of a hut with his head in his hands, apparently deep in reverie. Sensing that someone was there, he ponderously raised a head like that of a wild sheep, with eyes bulging with darkness and ecstasy, their whites covered with a fine silver film.

"Hello," he said in an absent voice. "Greetings to one who is not of this place."

"Hello," breathed Ti Jean.

"Why do you look at me like that, stranger? Did we perchance meet among the living?"

"I held you on my knee," said Ti Jean.

"And what is your name, stranger?"

"I knew your father and your father's father," said Ti Jean, "and I held you on my knee, and danced at your wedding, and walked in your funeral procession."

"I am sorry, for you have a kind face and the sound of your voice is true. But if my eyes saw you up above, and if my ears heard you, I have not brought the memory of it here below. So continue on your way and forgive me, stranger."

Ti Jean took leave of the young man and walked along streets full of Shades all sunk in perpetual reverie: warriors with expressionless faces, dreaming lions, does and snakes and field mice all huddling close in the same silence, hunters and their former

183

prey all deep in the same absence of desire. There were some unknown faces, the dead of a different vintage, but others to which he could give a name and a story, like that of King Emaniema, whose frail form lay on the ground across the path, his face, like all the rest, turned up toward the stony sky. But all, whether their faces were known or unknown, whether dead recently or long ago, first quivered at his approach and then resumed their former position, with eyes upturned to the sky like puppets manipulated by strings leading to the village up above, on the lighted side of the earth. Ti Jean, somewhat taken aback, wondered if these really were the mighty dead who commanded the living, the great protecting Shades people prayed to, loved, and worshiped even in their dreams, and without whom nothing was ever done under the sun.

He paused only before Onjali, whose face looked suddenly empty, like a cage from which the bird had flown. Then, shrugging his shoulders, he crossed the little square with the baobab tree and went down the other side of the hill, where he set out for the country of the Devourers.

There, on the banks of the Seetane, the wall of green opened and stones were thrown at him.

Ti Jean, driven away by his ancestors, withdrew into an icaco bush and coolly summed up his situation as a shipwrecked mariner without a compass, lost under a starless sky on a limitless sea. In this world, which he had fallen into like a tuft of kapok, life was not life and death was not death; time itself was suspect, a good century late, like an old alarm clock asleep on a shelf.

On the third day it occurred to him that if the Kingdom of the Dead stretched all the way under the earth, as the Ba'Sonanke believed, perhaps it went as far as Guadeloupe, small as Guadeloupe was and invisible on the map of the living. And perhaps the dead of Fond-Zombi, who had always spoken of heaven and hell, were now under the hills and valleys and mountains of the island, carrying on as usual in the dark, without worrying too much about the absence of the sun or the crazy shadows that reigned above. And why should they have bothered about the world, those children of slavery who, as they had always said, really had sprung from nowhere, fallen from the hand of God in bad luck and bad weather like a startled shower of flying ants?

Yes, he suddenly decided, that was where he belonged, under some mound of red earth open to the wind, with dead men who would recognize him and not say, Where do you come from, stranger?

2.

Eternities went by in the vain search for a path, a track, a sign of an underground way leading to Guadeloupe. None of the dead had ever heard of that speck of a country, and while they might know that there was an ocean somewhere, no one could point out exactly in what direction it lay. Gradually Ti Jean grew resigned, and the eternities merged into one long flow, a sort of vague sea occasionally broken by waves which immediately faded away into nothingness. One strange wave was the period during which Ti Jean resolved to exploit all the sensual resources of the Kingdom of the Dead. The women lent themselves wholeheartedly to his metamorphosis, but even in the heights of pleasure they remained vaguely remote, and Ti Jean gradually wearied of this dance without music which always ended in a charade. Then he began to see the Kingdom of Darkness as the kingdom of boredom, as the Ancients on the hill had always called it, the old men of the old days, the tired and the toothless, decrepit and dreading the last hour, those who could only see the sun now with the dim eye of deep-sea fish. Admittedly the Kingdom was a reflection of the worlds up above, but in water that was gray and cold and tasteless.

Thousands of times the sun crossed the stony sky, traveling through the dull and colorless silence of the Kingdom like a drop of water crossing the surface of a pond. And Ti Jean saw thousands of villages, perched on cliffs or hollowed out of caves, sheltered behind ramparts or standing on tall colonnades of terra cotta, with luxurious huts painted like palaces; villages built on piles or like birds' nests on the tops of tall trees, with ladders made of vines that the inhabitants pulled up after them at night in remembrance of surprises they had had under the sun, the real sun, the one that drives away the darkness.

Everywhere he saw the same blue robes he had met with in the village of the king, and everywhere the same abandoned attitudes, the same eyes turned upward to the worlds that are lit, waiting for a sign or a message from the living, for a drop of palm wine poured out for them. The dead knew no rest, and their hearts rustled louder than a nest of bees. In the daytime, when the drop of water showed that it was day, they echoed the action of their village, going with a sister to the pool, with a son to the river to fish, or with another relative to hunt, or to work in the fields, or even to war, in which too they came to the aid of the living. And when night came they entered the sleeping heads of dreamers to impart a remedy or a piece of advice, or above all to remind them to keep the ancient customs, of which they were the fierce and uncompromising defenders. Whatever their memories of life, and even if they had experienced the deepest misfortune, to them the world above seemed decked in the brightest colors, and their only wish was to go up there again forthwith to spend another season in the sun. The shrewdest among them studied the matter carefully, including the circumstances of the period, the respective advantages of different branches of a family and the character of their future mother, before abandoning their great blue robes to the darkness, like caterpillars shedding their chrysalis. But most were not so particular, and struggled like madmen as soon as they opened their eyes on the Kingdom of the Dark, eagerly watching the women up above from dawn onward as they went to fetch water, so as to slip into the first womb that was ajar.

Their only pleasure was that of love, but it was a fairy-tale love, without limits or bounds, no longer confined by the parsimonious laws of earth. When they grew tired of watching time go by, the men would fill their members with an imaginary breath that made them flame up to prodigious proportions and reach the depths of their beloved's heart; and then both of them would stay like that for hours, perhaps days or weeks, only emerging from their lethargy to utter a brief word or take an enchanting draft of milk from the blue cows.

But the older dead no longer found the same delight in love, and when newcomers exclaimed at this they would cry bitterly: "Friends, what use to us are these members of gold, of dream and of legend, if they have no seed in them, nothing with which to make children to rejoice our hearts?"

And Ti Jean laughed in his heart at the thought of the magic that those in the king's village attributed to the dead, seeing them as formidable spirits without whom nothing was done under the sun, not even the sprouting of the millet, which the Shades were supposed to cause by breathing gently on the roots. Alas, all that useless talk, when all that the dead ruled over was just the dreams of the living.

All in all, they were only an insignificant crowd of fish stranded on the beach, feebly straining their gills toward the waves in the pale hope of a tide. They greeted the stranger politely, and from one end of the Kingdom to the other the children curtseyed and the girls bared a shoulder as a mark of respect to his gray hairs. But on the whole Ti Jean now preferred the company of the Wanderers, who like him had died far from the house where they were born and who tried to find its trace or echo or path under the stony sky of the Kingdom. They were of all sorts, slaves and free men, merry or taciturn, daring or prudent; there were sages and contemplatives, jesters and fools, people beyond the pale and aristocrats manqués. Even the children looked at you peacefully, without astonishment or fear, with deep in their innocent eyes the same wild yearning to return. Many had been carried off in wars, taken away in the baggage of the invaders; others were the victims of spells, others again were sorcerers and swallowers, drinkers of souls whose heads had rolled to the bottom of the sea. Yet others were dreamers in faraway countries who had been suddenly woken and left to solitude and exile. There were some, too, who had come back from the Coast, wild-eyed and bearing strange rumors about the whites which made even the most hardened shudder. Ordinary Wanderers were quite willing to swap stories, summoning one another from all over the plain to exchange reminiscences around a camp, stories so vivid with the longing for life that they were more living than life itself. But those who had returned from the Coast did not linger: a few monosyllables and they were off, harassed by the need to transmit the message, there beyond this grayness, to the sleeping heads in their native land.

Neither the ordinary dead nor the Wanderers had ever heard of Guadeloupe. As for those who had come back from the Coast, they had forgotten the way, and their fingers always pointed it out in random and contradictory directions.

Some of the Wanderers even said that everyone was lost, and none could ever find their own village and live in the sun again except by the remotest of chances. Yes, everyone simply went round in the same circle century after century, they said, returning to their point of departure. Then they consoled themselves with a story told by the oldest among them, the veterans of Darkness, those who no longer mattered in the accumulated circles of Time.

"In the beginning, when the sun had not yet been launched and the night crossed the sky alone, Dawa took his drum and beat on it softly, softly, with fingers as light as a moonbeam. Leaves, charmed by the divine drummer, detached themselves from the trees and flocked to him from every corner of the earth. And lo! they turned into a man and a woman, a man who was a woman and a woman who was a man, the two united with one another in the same sinews and skin. But no sooner had they been given life, this man in woman and woman in man, than each wanted to go in a different direction. And as they fell heavily to earth, flinging their arms and legs all over the place, the following song issued from their single mouth:

> Yeh oh yeh
> The man to the left, the woman to the right
> Yeh oh yeh
> A man is a man
> A woman is a woman
> Each at home, each in their own home.

"Then Dawa was overcome with a great anger, and he said in his heart: Oh shameless little man, oh shameless little woman. And he blew and blew, and the leaves scattered all over the earth, and each leaf became a man, and each became a woman, and they formed villages such as we know today, with a chief, and laws, and the dead to make the laws obeyed. Then the sun and the moon were launched too, each for himself in the sky.

"Such is the story of the great anger of Dawa, the divine drummer; but we know that it will not be forever, we know that perhaps tomorrow, perhaps today, all the leaves in the world will be gathered together again in one sinews and skin, as at the beginning. And so we contain ourselves in patience, we the Ancients who know the moon and the stars and the great tree of the world. Patience, patience, until Dawa takes up his drum again."

3.

Patience, patience; but even asses die of too much of it. So, setting aside this fine story, our hero set resolutely about making his way through the Kingdom, a way that would take him across the seas to beneath a certain tuft of wild grasses. But however energetically he came and went, searching and ferreting and turning over one patch of darkness after another, he never came across the slightest sign or dying echo of Guadeloupe. Sometimes he thought that while he was about it, wandering at random without any track to follow, he might as well lie down and rest until death itself dissolved and fell to dust, like the cora of the Devourers. But all the same he did not stop, but went on walking and walking, stooping when the burden grew too heavy, but walking still.

After eternities that merged into a single endless flow, he one day met the lostest of the lost, a young woman with lips distended by two wooden disks, who didn't want to see the sun again. She said she was from a distant country on the edge of a huge desert inhabited by people who neither plowed nor sowed, and knew only pillage, profanation and blood. Her people were the pond where those of the desert came to fish for slaves. So the little girls had rounds of wood, a larger one every year, inserted in their lips, to make them unfit for the raiders' purposes. One day she herself had jumped into the river in the hope that her face would be different in the kingdom of the dead. But her infirmity had followed her, and ever since she had wandered through the underground worlds, through countries where there was no danger of meeting with a mouth like her own. It gave her a strange satisfaction to see people smile as she passed. Despite herself, she explained to Ti Jean, she had need of these smiles; they slaked a kind of thirst in her heart. But she wasn't altogether disillusioned, only withdrawn, she concluded, turning her head away modestly, suddenly delightful in her simple night-blue tunic, with her round head and upward-slanting eyes, suggesting the mischievous charm of a little ornamental duck.

When he began to speak to her she listened as he had listened to her, with interest, honor and respect, without showing the slightest surprise, so that the life of Ti Jean, told simply like that, became like any other story, no more foolish than all those he had heard himself. And as he went on, Ti Jean thought, smiling and not smiling, then smiling again, that it wasn't until he met the lostest of the lost that he had dared to unburden himself of the wild folly and extravagance that he was obliged to call his life, and that someone had listened to it without laughing. They were sitting by a fire in the middle of a plain stretching in waves as far as the eye could see. All around them animals lurked in endless idleness, snakes that did not bite, buffaloes that did not bellow and clove only empty air with their great carved horns. When he stopped, the fire was only a heap of ashes, and the young woman remained pensive for a while, a finger on her brow, showing that the words were flowing now through her bones. Then, opening the blades of her lips, she murmured, in a voice suggesting faint surprise:

"That cow that swallowed the sun—I think I've heard of it."

"From a Wanderer?" asked Ti Jean anxiously.

"No," she said. "It wasn't among the Shades I heard the story. They used to tell it in the evenings in my village when I was a child. But perhaps it wasn't the same Beast, because ours was big, so big that the most farsighted eyes couldn't see from one end of its body to the other. And when it had swallowed up everything, sun, moon, and stars, human beings and animals, all that was left on earth was a woman and her son, a little boy called Losiko-Siko, which in my village means 'he who says yes to death.' "

"Are you sure about the name?" interrupted Ti Jean.

"As sure as I am of myself, but not more," answered the young woman, smiling.

"Perhaps you heard it somewhere else?"

The young woman turned a moist eye upon Ti Jean, and said in a faint murmur which scarcely parted those strange flat lips:

"Forgive me. I can see that name disappoints you, so I shall not speak it again. To make my story brief, let us say that one day, after a thousand adventures, the hero took a knife, made his way inside the monster and began to cut up its innards. When he reached its heart the Beast let out a terrible bellow and fell to its knees, its bones broken, actually broken, by its own weight. The hero now hewed his way through the flesh, swish, swish, and as he pierced the great stomach the point of his knife made the thousands of creatures imprisoned with him cry out: Take care, you're cutting us! Finally his knife reached the beast's hide and made a great slit in it, whee-ee-ee. And out of that slit poured all the nations of the earth, one by one. Then came the turn of the sun, moon and stars, which meekly resumed their places in the sky. And that was the story they used to tell the children in my village," she ended, wiping away the beginning of a tear which had appeared right at the end of her tale. "It's only an old tale, you see."

"At least it has a happy ending," murmured Ti Jean, thoughtfully.

"My dear old man," she said, "all our tales have a happy ending, unlike our lives. Otherwise, what would be the good of telling them? But truthfully, I must confess I abridged the end of my story, because all sorts of other things happened to . . . him whose name I shall not speak." She gave a sudden laugh as she said this.

"What things? I beg you to tell me!"

"Well, not to keep anything from you, it came about that men started to hate him just because he had saved them from the Beast. And then one day when he was being pursued by his enemies, the hero came to the banks of a deep river and changed into a little flat stone—you know, the sort that seem to have wings, they're so nice to throw. And one of his enemies, annoyed at his disappearance, picked up the little stone and hurled it onto the opposite bank, shouting: 'There, that's just how I'd crack his skull if I saw him.' "

"And then?" begged Ti Jean.

"And then the stone turned into a man again."

"And after that?"

"And then my story is over," said the young woman, with a sort of merry trill, like the musical sound of a pea in a whistle. Then she shook her head incredulously, as if for the first time astonished by her interlocutor.

"What!" she exclaimed. "A man with white hair asking for stories? My dear good man, don't you think you should be on your way again if you want to get home?"

"Way? Have I got a way?"

"Listen," she said earnestly. "No one has ever heard me out to the end, and you've been like a soothing balm to me, like water to a thirsty throat. I have long been a Shade, and for ages and ages I have wandered beneath the earth. I have visited very strange places, and several times I have heard of a witch who knows all the paths in the Kingdom, and even the secret ways out of it. It is said that some Shades have consulted her, and that two or three have been given the answer they sought. But it is very hard to approach her. Very hard."

"And her name? Do you know her name?" cried Ti Jean eagerly.

"Old man," she said, smiling, "you too have probably traveled far, but I see you haven't forgotten the impatience of your youth. Her name? They say she has no name, because she was born of a spirit and a woman, and so is recorded nowhere. But I have always heard her referred to as the Queen with Long Breasts, and I think she is to be found on the other side of the mountains over there—and then beyond more and more mountains still, as many as the waves of the sea or the hairs on the head of a child."

The young woman stood up, putting her hand before her mouth in an instinctive gesture of modesty. And then, on tiptoe, she solemnly pointed to an inky black strip on the horizon, beyond the uniform gray of the plain.

Standing up she appeared to him even younger—slim and graceful, with her long, supple, duck-like neck. She seemed suddenly animated by the old man's presence, making eyes, going to and fro, twirling around on one toe, happy to bask in the light of someone's eyes. Then she stood still, embarrassed, and resuming her place by the fire, gravely raised one eyebrow and told what she knew of the Queen with Long Breasts, a magician and genuine soothsayer who knew all the paths in the Kingdom.

Few were the Wanderers who knocked at her door, and fewer still those who found favor with her, for her mouth watered for her favorite food, which was human blood. However, one has to make up one's mind what one wants: a mouse that leaves its hole runs the risk of being caught in a trap.

"And the mouse that stays in its hole runs the risk of starving," Ti Jean agreed eagerly. "Thank you for this word, friend. I shall cling to it as a child clings to its mother's skirts. But you, my little heap of flowers, won't you take this path too, so that we can knock at the door together?"

"No, no," she said, drawing back as if afraid. "I want nothing to do with any door or any path."

"Are you as tired as that?"

"No—I've already told you," she said with strange insistence. "I'm withdrawn, but not at all disillusioned. Probably the day will come when I'll feel like finding the sun again, and perhaps there'll be another spring with watermelons and cucumbers for me, little wild goat that I am. Who knows?"

"The day will come," repeated Ti Jean gloomily, "but meanwhile, what will you do all alone in the midst of the darkness?"

"Meanwhile," she said, "meanwhile, everything that happens must be beautiful."

4.

There were always eternities after eternities, mountains beyond mountains, and an endless succession of different peoples as infinite as the waves of the sea. Ti Jean went on and on under the stony sky, and the peoples slipped through his fingers like dust; human beings became for him like grains of sand, indistinguishable from one another, yet each shining mysteriously in the shadow and still somehow unique. He went on and on, but the eternities were no longer a torment for he had something to greet them with, to make a place for them within him, since he had met the young woman with the beak of a duck, the lost one who no longer tried to find her way, who might perhaps wander till the end of time, refusing right to the end to be disillusioned.

The memory of this creature lit him up like a sun, and when his mind foundered in the fog and merged with eternities past, present and to come, he had only to summon up her sweet, mischievous face to be transported immediately to Guadeloupe, to find the way back to Fond-Zombi, where he now knew every stone and tree and face better than he had known them when he was alive.

One day, as the young woman had said, he found himself confronted by a range of mountains whose peaks curved back over the stony sky, closing the Kingdom of the Dead in upon itself. After ages and ages, and searches lasting another eternity, Ti Jean finally found the gap leading to the outside slope of the Kingdom. The descent ended in low half-crumbled cliffs, covered with thorn bushes and plants with great limp, weary flowers like tufts of graying hair. In the midst of this desolation there was a path. It led to a cave deep in the cliff; inside the cave the light was brighter than outside. Then the cave dwindled to a narrow gorge opening suddenly onto a huge hall lit by a wood fire. By the fire sat an old woman, naked, incredibly thin, a real skeleton of black bones with long breasts hanging right down over her belly like dry tobacco leaves. She was using both hands to stir a big earthen pot with a stick; clouds of flies swarmed round her, and legions of lice promenaded over her forehead and came and went on her cheeks and jaws, before quickly seeking shelter in her dirty, tangled hair. At Ti Jean's approach she lifted her pointed chin, and whined:

"Aah, the poor black man, aah, aah, what's this man doing here at the edge of the universe? Doesn't he know that if you stick your arm up an elephant's behind you run a lot of risks? If it stands up, for example, you're left hanging from its rear."

Then, after wagging her head backward and forward and from side to side as if in pity of the terrible fate awaiting her visitor, she went on:

"And doesn't he know that to set foot in my Kingdom is to lose forever the hope of leaving it again?"

Meanwhile our hero respectfully bared one shoulder and said, calm as a jar of oil, and with a gay and affectionate smile:

"Queen, for a long while this black man hasn't known anything at all. Yes, for a long time he has been wandering through the vast world looking for a way, a path, a sign that will take him back home. If he knew his way, would he have come here, to the edge of the universe?"

"True." The old woman laughed. "If he knew his way he would have taken care not to cross the last mountain. Who are you and what is your name, you who gambol over the plains?" she added, suddenly looking at him indulgently.

"My name is Ti Jean, and I'm just anybody, anybody under the clouds."

"And your country?"

"It was called Guadeloupe," said the exile.

"I fear I've never . . ."

"Queen, queen, don't apologize," said Ti Jean with a laugh. "My country's so small that no one's heard of it, and my people are so weak that they scarcely believe in their own existence."

The old woman gazed at him for a moment, then stretched her arms out to the fire, shaking her head at length as if Ti Jean's answer had fulfilled some secret requirement. Then, with a gloomy sigh, she resumed in a tone that was cold and insinuating, with a tinge of menace.

"Child of man, you address me by my title and I thank you. But tell me: aren't you surprised to see a queen got up like this, with a face like mine and a head crawling with vermin?"

"Why should I be surprised?" said Ti Jean gently.

"Are you sure there's nothing surprising about it? Nothing at all?" asked the old woman, with sudden suspicion and a kind of veiled sadness.

"Nothing," said Ti Jean thoughtfully. "Ever since I started wandering through the vast world, the only thing I've found really surprising is myself. Why did someone like me come into the world? That's what I don't understand, and what surprises me more than anything else. And I can admit it to you, for there is no disgrace in a man's opening his heart: more and more often, when I look at myself, I laugh."

The old woman let her jaw drop, and her eyes began to glow.

"I don't see what there is about you to laugh at," she said in surprise. "You may not be very young anymore, but your face is all there and your skin shines . . . shines like a new snuffbox."

She had a strange air as she said this, and then went on with an embarrassed laugh, her voice trembling and her eyes lit up like a drunken glowworm flitting crazily through the dusk.

"You are a worthy fellow," she said, smiling, "even though you're not short of oil for greasing other people's hair. Here, take this, and see if you can oil my back as well as you have done my soul."

With this she handed him a little green flask, and twisting round on her stool exposed a long hairy spine from which the bones stood out like knife blades. Ti Jean took the flask without comment, and his hands started to bleed as they touched the sharp ribs. Soon it even seemed to him that the smell of his blood excited the witch, who every so often turned a foaming, hyena-like muzzle toward him, with huge yellow fangs bared as if to bite. Suddenly her spine started to writhe voluptuously.

"Well, worthy fellow, which is the softer, my back or the flesh on your hands?"

"Your back," said Ti Jean.

At the same instant he saw before him a beautiful back with round, firm shoulders and hips like a terra-cotta jar. Then she turned round. It was dazzling. Beauty seemed to spring out of the darkness itself, smooth, soft and scented, with nails and teeth sparkling like stars, and the whites of her eyes so bright they looked blue. The girl dipped her neck coyly, and raising one leg skyward, allowed Ti Jean to admire the shapeliest shell he had ever seen; except Egea's, he quickly corrected himself in his heart. Thereupon, as if she had divined his thoughts, she asked in a voice full of anxiety:

"Which of us two is the more beautiful?"

Then Ti Jean burst out laughing, put his arms around her, and embraced her with all the strength inspired in him by terror, desire and the cruel seduction of the moment. As he did so, he whispered slyly in her ear:

"The most beautiful, queen, is the one I hold in my arms."

When he awoke, the beautiful girl had gone, and Ti Jean saw that he was lying on a hide in a sort of rocky hollow at the back of the cave. A few yards away the old black skeleton seemed to be dreaming over the dead fire, her elbows on her knees and her hands bashfully covering her face. Suddenly she turned on him a look that was both languishing and cold.

"Well, worthy fellow, aren't you surprised to see me like this?" she asked.

"Queen, I should lie if I said I'm not disappointed. Yes, I'd be lying. But why surprised—why should I be surprised? Haven't you the right to live as you like, to come and go, to give and take back again as you please?"

"Don't be sad," she said. "I act not according to my whim, but according to a law that is as harsh for me as it is for you. My real body is the one you held in your arms, and what you see here is just a castoff, a shirt of sorrow. Alas, I can stay young only for a few hours; after that I turn back into this heap of bones and this old head full of lice. That is the role assigned to me by the gods. It is not the result of my whim, I assure you."

"Queen," said Ti Jean, with emotion, "as I have told you, I know nothing, nothing at all, and who may be forgiven for their mistakes if not those who walk in darkness?"

That unclean creature dropped a melancholy jaw.

"Worthy, worthy fellow," she said, "I see your eyes are beginning to open, and to look at things in the right light. Go, leave me now, let my body go into action, for so far today it has been too idle."

Then she hurried to the entrance of the cave, where, bending backward and raising her shift up to her hips, with her legs slightly apart, she began to strike little double blows on the skin of her belly, as if on a drum. As she did so, she sang a refrain:

Kacoutou Kacoutou Kacoutou
Kacoutou Gangala.

As she drummed, a number of little colorless imps came out of her navel and went and ranged themselves in front of her like soldiers awaiting orders. Ti Jean had counted twenty-two of them when the old woman let fall her shift and began to talk to them in a sharp and domineering voice. At once the little creatures got moving, some gathering wood for the fire while others dashed out of the cave with all kinds of miniature tools over their shoulders—picks, cutlasses, hoes and digging sticks. They looked vaguely human, with red tufts on top of their sugar-loaf heads and little string aprons down to their ankles. When they had all gone, the old woman came back to the fire and stretched her arms out over the flame, her bones trembling violently. She had completely forgotten her visitor, and was wandering in dream through places unknown to ordinary mortals.

Three days went by like this, in deathly silence, before she changed again into a marvelous young woman the whites of whose eyes were so white they were blue. But afterward, when she became a skeleton once more, Ti Jean was surprised not to feel his former disgust at what the Queen with Long Breasts called her castoff body. He seemed to see beyond her hideous appearance. And although her smell was still disagreeable and her voice still grated on his ears, he was even able to cover that wretched skin with the vision that lurked in the depths, awaiting and fearing his male glance. Sometimes she guessed the secret, and would say, touched:

"They are really beginning to open, those eyes of yours, those that are inside your head, and their eyelids are just being raised for the first time since you were born."

And as soon as she was restored to her body of glory, her tenderness for her lover was redoubled. She literally melted in his arms, with words so passionate that Ti Jean, he knew not why, was uncomfortable on account of the old woman.

She began to confide in him, recalling her early days when she lived with a spirit and a mortal woman. According to her, her true body was the one Ti Jean held in his arms, and the living sepulcher, the old woman's castoff, was completely alien to her and even filled her with horror. She refused to accept the injustice by which she was doomed for eternity to the cave, while the ordinary dead could go up on earth again and find the sun via the womb of a woman of their blood. Sometimes she would cry as she spoke of the other's crimes, her perfidy and the rumors she spread to attract the Wanderers of the Kingdom so that she might devour them. And that was why she would allow Ti Jean only fruit and water; every other kind of food made his flesh smell too tasty in the old woman's nostrils. To confuse the old woman and deceive her sense of smell, she would make Ti Jean drink drops of her blood or bake a special bread that would perfume his sweat. She would anoint her lovely body with honey, spread grain on the floor, and roll back and forth in it like a rolling pin. Then, plucking off the grains one by one and grinding them into flour, she would bake a fine golden loaf which he had to eat at once in order to catch its smell. Ti Jean teased her, saying that the bread was only a love charm, designed to make him return at once to the table of her body.

And so eternities passed away between these two creatures who were but one and yet who seemed to have no link between them except in the memory, ever dimmer and more confused, of our hero. The old woman dreamed by the fire, always perished with cold, and the imps bustled around her; and the young woman was as fresh and new still as on the very first day. Time passed like a deep river, like a great everlasting tide, and the traveler began to understand what one of the queens had told him about his inner eyes, which according to her were just about taking their second look.

Now, one day when he was sporting with the young woman, the image of the old one interposed for the first time between him and the scrap of black night he held in his arms. At once the charming creature froze, and let out a cry that she soon stifled. Then she gently laid her fingertips on Ti Jean's lips as if to prevent him from making any pretense or protestation which would only make things worse.

"Worthy fellow," she said, "it is time for us to part. No, don't say anything. Remember that the word that loves you stays in your mouth."

Ti Jean looked at her, not understanding, and began to weep, for the image of the old woman had faded and all that was before him now was a fresh young woman as moist as a fish sprung out of the wave. She tried to console him, drawing the old man's head to her breast, rocking him like an infant and saying in her soft clear voice:

"Thank you, worthy fellow, thank you for the tears you shed on me. Did you think it was all eternal, and that I'd keep you forever? It is time for you to go, for you to accomplish that for which you came to my cave some years ago, do you remember? I shall help you; I shall clear the stones from your path, as I decided to do the first day I saw you. But I can only take you halfway home, for there my power ends. After that, alas . . ."

"After that?" said Ti Jean, surprised to see her so calm and kind, a great peaceful lake in the forest, despite the child-like wave that trembled beneath the even surface of her glance.

"After that," she said, "you will have to start wandering again, and searching as you did before, and perhaps getting lost."

Leaving him for a moment, the queen went to the back of the cave and came back with Ti Jean's old gun and bag. Her cheeks were dry, her smooth face expressed not a trace of sorrow; everything was in her eyes, which sparkled like diamonds. Seeing her thus, Ti Jean mastered his own feelings and agreed to put on the blue robe fringed with gold which she had woven for him. She clapped her hands, and immediately a little imp appeared. She showed him to Ti Jean, smiling with an air of distant majesty, then said with a sigh:

"Follow my servant to the river where a boat has been waiting for you for years. Follow the current, and stop where you please; that is all I can do for you. But remember this: your voyage will end on the first shore, for the boat will sink into the water, it will sink, I say, as soon as you set foot on dry land."

Ti Jean scarcely heard what she was saying. Tears rose to his eyes, hot with a pain that would not be comforted.

"Is that all?" he asked. "Have you really nothing else to say to me after all these long years?"

A breeze of merriment rippled the flat lake of her eyes, lighting them with a delicate irony.

"My heart was at peace," she said, "and I looked for something for it to torment itself with."

The young queen appeared to shrink, to curl up in the dark, her mouth closed gently over the brightness of her teeth. In that gracious countenance, with its simple beauty, each feature seemed to have been formed one after the other to form a total harmony, and the eyes were two intermittent sources of light, so that one never quite knew whether she was shy or just keeping her thoughts apart in a realm known only to herself. She moved backward slowly, without taking her eyes off Ti Jean. Then she made a sign with her hand to show there was nothing more to be said, and turning her head away reluctantly, told him:

"Just one more thing, mortal. Forget me."

The imp had difficulty matching his pace to that of Ti Jean, whose legs were too slow for the other's swift little limbs, always leading him on ahead until he suddenly disappeared among the grasses as if swallowed down a trapdoor. Then he would retrace his steps as if puzzled by the mystery of those long human legs, and seething anew with impatience, run off in front again, soon to be engulfed once more by a mound of earth, a tuft of grass or a big stone. His attitude was disconcerting: he was always making sarcastic remarks about Ti Jean, calling him the Patient Man, "the man whose patience would cook a stone and make soup out of it." These nicknames he would repeat over and over, with a special meaning that escaped their victim. Every so often, driven by the devilry in his blood, he would dance about Ti Jean in an absurd manner, cutting capers, thumbing his nose, turning toward his companion a little face like a shriveled, over-ripe tamarind, and warbling in a strident, emphatic voice:

"I'm telling you
  You, gamboler of the Kingdom
  You're heading for deepest darkness
  You're going woefully astray
  You gamboler
  Gamboler of the Kindgom!"

After three weeks they caught sight of the river from the top of a hill. The land sloped gently down to a steep bank covered with shining rocks. The water flowed along with a kind of brash tranquillity between huge trees with sharp bare branches pointing up almost to the stony sky. A canoe lay in an inlet, just a small fishing boat with two tholepins in the stern for a pole. But the imp, following Ti Jean's gaze, told him that he wouldn't need to paddle, for the canoe had good legs and knew its own way. He would have to careful, though, very very careful, for this joker of a river was full of snags.

At the last moment, when Ti Jean had got into the boat, his guide started to dance up and down with impatience, and suddenly, with an expression of great anxiety, squeaked out that the gamboler wasn't to be surprised if the image of the queen stayed with him. True, she had said "Forget me," but did she really want him to? The imp had a secret to tell him: the young queen had cast a spell on him, and he must forgive her, mustn't he? For, he added with the wink of a connoisseur of the female heart, it was only the result of her extreme affection.

"On the contrary," said Ti Jean. "I hope the spell will last forever."

"Don't make fun of me, Patient Man," said the other. "And allow a tiny creature to tell you that even the greatest spells are not eternal, but wear out someday. The only thing that doesn't wear out is the heart of men, which is made of cheese, as everyone knows."

"As everyone knows," agreed Ti Jean.

5.

The boat had been hollowed out of a tree trunk, like the gum trees whose soul the Guadeloupe fishermen remove with fire and iron. But this boat bore no trace of adze or ember; the only marks to be seen were millions of little nail marks from the hands of countless little servitors.

Ti Jean, sitting in the boat with his back propped against the poop, waved a friendly hand at the imp, who had frozen in a sort of epileptic trance on the bank after he had told the queen's secret. He returned Ti Jean's salute, then, skimming the earth like a spider, flew up the hill and disappeared in the gray haze. Whereupon the boat freed itself of its supernatural moorings, floated to the middle of the stream, and calmly offered itself up to the current.

Just at that moment the image of the young queen overwhelmed Ti Jean swift as the wind, and he felt as if he were enveloped in a wrapping of fire. He felt like laughing and crying at the same time, and as he splashed water over his body he thought of the girl in the cave, and also of the old woman, who whatever the young one had said was after all a good sort of creature, yes, a poor woman incapable of malice, incapable even of lighting a candle to bring misfortune on someone. The young woman especially stayed with him, pursuing him over long distances, emerging from the water, from the deserted riverbanks, and from the stony sky stretching out as he went along like a black arch without any definite bounds. Ti Jean kept pouring water over his face and chest and over his member, that root of the Kingdom of the Dead, which seemed now to want to tear itself away from him like a flaming spear.

With the days and weeks the spell wore off gradually and was reduced to long shining tresses swirling inside his head or brushing against his cheeks. Ti Jean, opening his eyes at last, gazed in surprise at the immensity of the world in which he now found himself alone, without either friend or enemy; and his long patience abandoned him. He was filled with the desire to land, to land anywhere, despite what the queen had told him; to set foot on dry land and leave behind this cursed canoe that floated along like a piece of dead wood taking him the devil only knew where. He spoke to his own body, keeping himself company with long speeches punctuated with shouts which echoed back to him from the sky. Or else he would start to laugh at the chain of events which had brought him here to this senseless river that seemed, like himself, to be going round in circles. And his laughter was a mockery of the life which so mocked him, and in the depths of it he found the strength not to land. And when even laughter failed him, Ti Jean would console himself by bellowing out the song of the river, an amusing refrain which he had made up himself, words and music. He stood up on his mortal legs in the middle of the boat and bawled it out to the stony sky:

"Zig zag zog
At Mr. Chon's
They make corks
To stop all mouths
To stop all cries."

One day as he was carrying on like this, a vaguely human head approached the boat, its mouth half open over the dark water. It had greenish scales, big sea-green eyes with transparent lids, and little sharp teeth from which emerged a musical sound like that produced by a skillful flautist. After Ti Jean had had his turn they looked at each other in silence, not as from one species to another, man to fish or fish to man, but like two beings who profoundly understood one another and knew exactly how both felt about their solitude in a world that was hostile, incomprehensible and frightening. Then, lowering its eyelids knowingly, the thing gave a kind of smile and sank down into the water. And Ti Jean smiled inside himself, thinking: I am as old as the hills, but I shall never say that there is nothing worth going on for. Everything is still intact. The mystery remains.

Tufts of grass tossed here and there in the current, snagged sometimes on rocky outcrops which Ti Jean avoided by a stroke of the pole. There were forks and branches in the river between which the boat seemed to hesitate, drifting round uncertainly until it appeared to be carried off along one alternative by chance. In the end the river flowed under a low vault that seemed within hand's reach, with sides plunging deep down in the river and enclosing it in a rocky tunnel. Ti Jean recalled a rumor or legend about how certain rivers in the Kingdom took you to the ends of the earth, while others hurled you into the mouth of a god. He shouted now without stopping, and when he slept he shouted in his dreams. Once the nightmare gave way to a beautiful dream of space and light. Above him there floated a silken dome of dizzy height, with two or three stars twinkling under a crescent moon. In front of the boat was a sandbank covered with a crowd of waterfowl whose plumage ruffled up in a snowy foam. Ti Jean, waiting for the dream to end, feasted on the moon and stars, on the river and its suddenly sparkling waters, and on the trees and birds that he would never see again.

Some ibises flew up from the sandbank, their cries piercing his ears, together with all the other sounds of the African night. Then the boat turned round on itself and set off in a new direction. It went through a sheltered backwater, then rejoined the main course of the river farther on, where it gathered together the tributaries from all over the valley.

Suddenly, as if by a squall of wind, the whole sky veiled over and began to descend in a gray fleecy layer which gradually covered the river and the trees. But it was neither the light gray haze of the Kingdom nor the mist that fell sometimes over the sunny lands of the Ba'Sonanke at the start of the rainy season. No, it was the thick darkness, blind and merciless, which had fallen slowly over Fond-Zombi, over Guadeloupe and the world, on that far-off day when the Beast swallowed the sun.

BOOK SEVEN

How Ti Jean crossed the three seas and the four kingdoms
and came to the cold and arid lands of France.
And how in the end he traversed Death itself.
No, gentlemen, I'm not joking.

1.

And then there was a next day, and a next day still, with real moonlight and real stars. The banks now showed signs of human life, but of a life that seemed to have been wiped out long ago: there were canoes lying gutted by the water, ruined villages with broken walls blackened by fire. Ti Jean's brain seethed and tossed in all directions as if it wanted to start out of his head, while the boat from the Kingdom of the Dead sailed peacefully between high cliffs echoing with the cries of the animals above. The old man was borne quietly along, dreaming, trying to put his thoughts in order. But cliff followed cliff, and questions were succeeded by fresh questions, and so he traveled on from mystery to mystery, seeing as dimly within himself as without, in the uncertain light of the stars. Suddenly his breast was pierced by an idea. However was it that this world had not faded away altogether, since it was centuries ago that the sun had disappeared? And why this activity on the riverbanks, this throbbing of insects and birds, this luxuriant vegetation, when everything ought to be resting beneath layers of cold and silence?

One day, as he stood in the bow of the boat, the sound of a shot came from the bank and he saw a group of wild-looking men, some of them on horseback and brandishing guns, and others rushing toward boats that were bristling with spears, throwing-knives and clubs. Suddenly there was a shower of arrows, and some shafts stuck quivering in his chest. As he showed no particular reaction to this, a warrior stood up in one of the assault craft and pointed to him in terror, shouting:

"Look, brothers, a spirit of the dead is on the river!"

Ti Jean, seeing them retiring in disorder, some rowing for the shore, others jumping into the water to escape the apparition, brought his boat abeam and called out imploringly:

"Oh, don't run away, don't run away!"

Then, when no answer came:

"At least tell me—what time is this? What century are we in? What century? What century?"

Left alone, the traveler of the dark looked in astonishment at his body, stuck like a pincushion. The arrows had entered it painlessly and he knew they would leave it likewise. And as he plucked them out of his body—dead or living, he no longer knew which, probably both—he laughed at the good turn that the queen's jealousy had done him. Being alive and dead at the same time, he belonged to both worlds yet was to both a stranger, as incongruous and out of place on earth as if he had fallen down from a star.

The rest of the journey went by in a state of enormous torpor which crushed Ti Jean and slackened his blood. Standing there in the middle of the river, not hungry, not thirsty, nothing, he was fascinated by this infernal canoe which kept fending off obstacles—islets, floating tree trunks, hidden rocks just under the surface like bones. Once he thought he saw in the distance a modern city alight with electricity. A squall was blowing, and the boat was gusting forward when he caught sight of a group of buildings, their fronts all dotted with lights. But the current was swift, the reflections were broken up into sparks by the water, and as soon as the momentary brightness was over, all he could remember was a dream, a spell born of the lightning.

A few days later the curtain of fog rose on the estuary of the river, a huge delta where the stream was divided up by countless spits of sand. Some branches of the delta were covered with a layer of ice, and under a livid low sky a flaccid moon rolled its great paunch close over the broken mirror of the water. On the horizon a great foaming roller growled like a forest on the march. Just as it was about to plunge into it, the boat jibbed, rose horizontally into the air and flew over the snowy crest to land on the sea on the other side. Then it clove through the waves toward the open sea as if driven by an invisible propeller.

Crystal infinities glittered on the surface, and Ti Jean's skin was covered with white frost, mingled with glassily glowing specks of salt. He grew worried, and thought of changing into a bird and flying back to Africa. A beak grew out from his cheeks, his eyes shifted up toward his temples, and thousands of black feathers sprouted out of his chest in great vulture's wings. But human arms still hung in front of the wings, and the whole lower part of his body was still a man's, its member protruding vaguely from among down and feathers. Then the metamorphosis ebbed away again, and a few seconds later all that remained were two little spikes in his side, which came away painlessly when he plucked them out.

Ti Jean now went through periods of slight delirium. Sometimes he dreamed he was a fish, and sometimes he thought he heard a murmur from another world, speaking with the voice of an old Negro from Guadeloupe and incessantly repeating: "Ho, how goes life with you, little one?"

In places the crystals gathered into hills, floating mountains which stopped the boat and forced it to make a wide detour. On them sported great troops of unknown animals, dragging themselves ponderously along on flippers. They roared like lions as the intruder went by, shaking their heads angrily, angrily, as if they couldn't understand such impertinence. Then the sea became human, scoured by high-decked ships whose sirens never stopped hooting through the fog, uttering long wails until the first star appeared. In the distance, coasts appeared which were nothing like those of Africa. There were wharves and sheds and hundreds and thousands of lights, some of them almost pricking the sky. And suddenly you could see heaps of shining, blackened ruins, the corpses of cities gripped in a hard frost and reflecting back the light of the stars. One day the boat trembled from end to end, approached land, and went straight up the estuary of a river. It was an animated scene, a frenzy, a bacchanalia of ships leaving and entering, some with shares tossing aside heaps of ice and throwing them onto the banks in tall silvery cliffs. Then there came a sort of halt, and white men crowded in increasing numbers by the rails to point at the absurd little boat making its way among the giants of the sea, with an old black man perched on its poop as on a throne of ice, carefully and solemnly holding a sort of popgun between his knees.

Suddenly the boat broke down, pointing first left then right, as if uncertain of its prey. Then it made for a row of searchlights, a wall of them that almost hid the whole town. The only thing that showed above the band of light was the outline of a belfry merging into the transparent blue of the sky. Ti Jean threw the musket over his shoulder, and as he jumped ashore the little boat gave a long animal shudder; then, turning on itself in a kind of playful farewell, it deliberately dived down and fled through the waves like a shark, probably in a hurry to get back to its place in the inlet, under the stony sky of the Kingdom.

Ti Jean ran recklessly through the docks, past heaps of bales and packing cases and with a frenzied crowd of the living at his heels. Suddenly he found himself confronted by a tall metal fence stretching out as far as the eye could see. He didn't know how, but he was immediately seized by the image of a bird. At the same moment a wind of panic lifted him into the air, and he became one with the powerful frame of his wings. Meanwhile his arms, still human, clasped the bag and the musket to his chest. His wingspread wasn't far short of a dozen feet, but however madly he whirled and shook his pinions, they weren't strong enough to hold him firmly in the sky. He fell down on the pavement on the other side of the fence, made one, two, three bounces of several yards like a rubber ball, rose again to a height of two or three stories, came gently down between the houses, and took off again in a light and airy leap. The white men cried out and made way for the black angel bouncing through the city.

2.

As he loped, half man, half bird, toward the tops of the buildings, it never occurred to him that his great sails of wings might suddenly let him down, as they had on the coast of Africa. Hungry for information, he read the name on a shopfront, and was greatly astonished. Well, I never, he thought. Here I am in France. Then came a succession of smelly mean old streets where white men vegetated, white men of a kind Ti Jean had never seen before, mere ghosts of white men, gaunt, wretched and in rags. And our hero's eyes blinked before the incredible. Well, I never, he thought. Just look at those whites. There were some soldiers on sentry duty at an intersection, and one of them nervously let off a few rounds of machine-gun fire which went through Ti Jean's nonexistent body. Then Ti Jean flew over the blockhouse and was in another, larger town. Ruins stretched out as far as the eye could see. Here too they were blackened and stained by the smoke of fires.

Now our traveler found a strange refuge, a mere stretch of wall holding up an elevator shaft as high as the second story, where a bedroom was suspended in the void. He used to venture out of it to see the people, the age, just at dawn, when the stars were driving away the last shreds of a milk-white mist that drenched you to the skin. It was out of the heart of this mist that he rose every morning, having learned to leap up high with his body held straight and his arms assisting his wings. All he did was alight on some roof, where, if he hadn't been detected in flight, he would lie down near the gutter to watch the people, the age, as he called it.

The upper part of the town was surrounded by soldiers in uniform, just like those in the garrison in Basse-Terre. The houses here were fine and large, the streets clean and wide, worthy of the idea people in Fond-Zombi had always had of France. Ti

Jean would usually arrive at daybreak. And suddenly the street lamps would light up like glowworms, the shutters would open and patches of yellow appear in the windows. Now there were people moving about under the crescent moon. Shopwindows lit up, cafés breathed out marvelous warm steam every time their glass doors opened and closed, a marvelous bright cloud iridescent like a soap bubble. But it was not the same, no, nothing like, when Ti Jean landed on a roof in the lower part of the town, above the dark evil-smelling streets that went down to the sea. And when he saw that crowd of ragamuffins slinking along, so thin you could scarcely believe they were white, his first astonishment would return, and he would say to himself, as on the first day, Well, I never, just look at those whites. Sometimes, leaning over his gutter, he would mysteriously forget to see them as whites and grow angry all over. His head would be angry, and his heart too, not to mention his liver leaping about inside, unable to bear some of the things that happen on earth. Then he would return to the upper part of the town, where many tanks awaited him at the intersections and invisible wires were strung across some streets in the hope of ensnaring him. And he would go back in triumph in the evening through the alleys of the poor quarters, where all the people waited for him at their windows to greet and even applaud him discreetly from inside their houses.

This went on for three weeks, then his wings started to perish and he stopped going up to throw a scare into high society. Gradually he ceased all his excursions, whether in the upper or the lower part of the town; his bones had grown heavy, and he couldn't leap as high as a flea. He stayed in his lonely refuge, huddled up under his clothes like a blind octopus with his bag of black ink clutched to his heart. One day he found specks of mold on his cheeks like patches of green lichen: death had got to work again. Probably it had never left him since he left the Kingdom; only given him a bit more rope, that's all.

The work of death accelerated. The lichen covered the whole surface of his cheeks and attacked his plumage, which left great green streaks on the wall. He perspired invisibly, like a bird, under the feathers and down. A few steps away was a tap, where he drank or pretended to drink a mouthful of water or washed away the green fluid that burned the corners of his eyes. Then came the black abyss he fell into as soon as he lay down again. And he was always haunted by the same dream. There was no village or town or city, no place that was inhabited. The world was just one huge forest and he stood motionless in the middle of it, staring at the dark in the hope of finding a clearing. All around him the trees soared to dizzy heights; they were strong and gnarled, with deep roots, and he looked on them as brothers because of their beautiful green color. Then a voice would arise out of the darkness, like the voice of an old Guadeloupe Negro, like an order from afar, almost inaudible, the same as he had heard in the middle of the sea. He would be filled with hope, and set off eagerly through the tree trunks. But after he had taken just a few steps the trunks would start to sway where they stood and fall on him one after the other, turning into a pungent dust or mold amid which he struggled and shouted, uttering cries for help that were absurd because there was only the sky above and the delusive forest: the earth was deserted.

When he awoke the air would taste of ashes, and he felt encumbered with himself, encumbered with his body, just encumbered pure and simple. And he remembered with gratitude the friendly voice that had hailed him in the middle of the forest, a voice that grew more urgent every night, and now conjured up around itself the familiar halo of a face—the little wrinkled nut-face of Old Eusebius. Once, as he was opening his eyes, Ti Jean saw that the trees were still crashing down. Then the whole forest vanished, and listening more carefully, Ti Jean thought he could hear knocking at the door, knocking that was light but imperious and accompanied by the murmur of a human voice. At last, as if being hauled out of a ravine, Ti Jean got up and tottered toward the door, flapping his wings whenever his legs started to give. Then there were three more little knocks, and a voice whispered quite distinctly, in Creole: "Hey, what crab's nest have you got yourself into now, eh, boy?"

The voice was the same as he'd heard in the middle of the sea, and then in the middle of the forest—at once grave and sweet and with the tinge of solemnity peculiar to the old men of Fond-Zombi: their own blend of coquetry. Ti Jean opened the door quietly, and the moonlight fell on the shoulders of a very old Negro with completely white hair and a face as lined as a cashew nut. He was dressed in the old style, in canvas tunic and drawers, with a big raw leather bag on his hip and the eternal straw hat flopping over his shoulders like the last time, centuries ago, among the broken-down houses on the plateau Up Above. His feet, bitten all over by jiggers, were bare, and the wrapping of skin that held his bones together still had all the color and appearance of life.

Ti Jean, taught by long experience, could see at once that the other was not standing on the landing. No, he was in another world, probably inside his, Ti Jean's, own mind. He contemplated the mirage for a moment, then, with a sigh, lifted a reproving finger and said to himself, smiling at his own foolishness:

"Well, Old Eusebius, old weasel that you are, everlasting old weasel—so you've ferreted your way into my dream, have you?"

3.

The apparition glided lightly into the room and Ti Jean, afraid he might vanish in smoke, made haste to close the door. He remembered his first impression, as a child, of the other, as a sort of spirit hovering between heaven and earth, forever undecided about exactly where to set his ghostly, transparent foot. For a moment Eusebius looked at him apprehensively, as if recognizing and yet not recognizing him. Then he turned his eyes away, looked at the room abandoned to dust and cobwebs, and said ironically:

"Why didn't you open the door to me? Ah, youth, youth—no respect at all for my white hairs."

"Youth?" cried Ti Jean bitterly.

At this the apparition turned to Ti Jean and gazed at him pensively, with surprise and yet with indulgence, as if still seeing in him the lad of other days, the boy with smooth limbs and the grace of a young elephant. Then, raising its icy hand, the vision brushed our hero's gray temples and said in a deep, reproachful voice:

"Child, child, how old do you think you are?"

Eusebius's face softened at this indirect reference to the past, and he really seemed to see a child in the old man in front of him. Then suddenly his expression changed. He frowned, his dark nostrils twitched suspiciously, his face became watchful, and he said coldly:

"Isn't there a smell of death about you?"

Ti Jean smiled at this pretense.

"Nothing surprising about that, Old One, in a dead man."

"Dead? Are you sure?"

Ti Jean just burst out laughing, but the apparition went on, completely unmoved by what should have shattered it and sent it packing:

"I'm prepared to believe you, but perhaps you only say it out of ignorance, my son, because you don't know anything about either life or death."

"What do you call someone who goes down under the earth, then? A spark gone to a dance?"

"Listen, I don't mean to flatter you, but I've never seen a dead man as resplendent as you. And though I can smell that confounded smell, I can also smell a smell of life, of skins still green underneath. So I'd like to know which smell to believe, if you'd be kind enough to enlighten me."

"First answer one little question, and then I'll tell you all I know. Saving your presence, Old One, are you anything but a fancy inside my head?"

A flicker of amusement lit up his sorcerer's eyes, and once again Ti Jean was amazed to find himself being treated not as an aged man but as the youth he used to be ages and ages ago, before he arrived in the great starry night of Africa.

"Mad as you are," said Eusebius, "if you want to take me for a fancy I'm afraid nothing will stop you. You know," he went on, his voice suddenly breaking, "we'd lost all hope, when a few weeks ago we heard your voice."

"My voice?" said Ti Jean in amazement.

"Perhaps you call it singing? Well, let's say we heard a song coming from far away, in the middle of a great river somewhere in the heart of Africa. The voice was weak and moved about, coming sometimes from sweet water and sometimes from salt, until one day we heard it very distinctly, coming from the land of France. So then I set out to find you, and that took me to Paris first, and do you know what that is like?"

"It's a city," said Ti Jean. "A big city, a capital."

"No," said the other, "it's a heap of stones, a heap of stones as big as Guadeloupe, but only a heap of stones. And you weren't in the middle of those stones, and I strained my ears until I heard your cries again. Haven't you got anything to say now?"

"So you heard my cries," said Ti Jean politely.

"Yes," agreed the other, smiling. "But they were different, very different, from those I'd heard from Guadeloupe. Now they were thin and sharp, like a bird singing. And when I got here they were so strong they shattered everything in my head. Almost at once people told me about you and your big black angel's wings, and I said to myself: That's my lad. But to tell the truth, I didn't expect to see you wallowing in a bath of death and calamity like this. The more I look at you, the more I wonder whether I can help you much. I'm a man of knowledge, true, and I've cut my eyes as they cut crystal, so that they can see things visible and invisible. But I'm afraid what you need is a tough, thick-skinned old chap like Wademba was, with big teeth just right for tearing apart the Powers of darkness. Tell me, how is it with you really? Are you really one of the dead, or do you ever feel some green skin underneath?"

"This will make you laugh," said Ti Jean. "I walked and

walked, and finally I came up from out of the Kingdom, but for nothing."

"And what else?"

"It will make you laugh," said Ti Jean. "But as you see me now, I don't belong either to the living or to the dead. I don't belong to any world."

"What do you belong to, then?"

"I belong to the room," said Ti Jean.

For some time now Eusebius had been hopping from one foot to the other making little clicks with his throat, quick impatient noises, while his big straw hat flapped like the wings of a mosquito trying to sting someone. Suddenly, slipping his hat down over his back, he uncovered a strange ferrety muzzle which he poked at every part of Ti Jean's body, as if seeking a sign or signal buried deep in his blood or bones. Finally, gripping his member between two fingers, he lifted it up and passed his nose under it carefully, saying:

"Death is here, in the hollow of your seed. This is the first time I've found it in such a place. Usually it settles in people's eyes, or runs in their veins, or sits inside their throats and prevents them from breathing."

A furrow appeared on his brow, and he spoke dreamily, obviously to himself.

"I ought to have known, to have realized it would install itself at the very seat of life, the cradle of all things. For the Ancients used to say that its name is Rebirth."

Then, silencing Ti Jean with a peremptory gesture, he went on in a voice heavy with apprehension:

"No, be quiet, for our old friend is listening, and at the slightest word she might wipe you out from the worlds, if she hasn't done so already. As you know, she has sharp ears and a jealous heart. So pay attention to what I'm going to tell you, my son; think, and don't speak unless it's absolutely necessary. You must tell me nothing, though I have to understand everything. So, are you surprised that the smell comes from there?"

"No," murmured Ti Jean, "I'm not surprised."

"Everyone knows that the dead eat and drink," said the other, "and some say they enjoy themselves as we do. Why shouldn't they?"

"Why shouldn't they enjoy themselves?" said Ti Jean indifferently, as if merely repeating the sorcerer's words. The sorcerer gave a pleased little laugh.

"The leaf that falls from the tree never falls far from its roots. But the seed flies far, and it's the seed that carries the tree's secret. People also say that the seed knows it carries the tree's secret. But does it?"

"The seed probably knows of the secret inside it."

"But is it certain?"

"The seed knows its secret," said Ti Jean.

At these words the man with the face of a spirit froze; only his straw hat waved above him, like a kite hovering in the sky. He seemed to be out of time and space, out of darkness and cold and death, but all his features were so clearly defined that it was hard to see him as a fancy, a figure out of a dream. Suddenly he came back into the world, and putting one hand on a bird shoulder, carefully parted the down until he touched human flesh. Every trace of irony had disappeared from his eyes, which now held only the warmth, the veiled radiance of an old lantern, of the gaze of an old Negro.

"To tell the truth, boy, what do you really know?" he asked.

"What about?" said Ti Jean calmly.

"About spirits and gods, and powers of all kinds. Didn't they teach you anything over in Africa?"

"They told me nothing," said Ti Jean after a pause. "They kept me out of everything. I know, I know that the Force is at work everywhere, mysterious, smiling or terrible, right down to the quivering of a mosquito's wing. And I know too that there are forests behind the forests, worlds behind the worlds, and all sorts of unknown powers. Is that what interests you, maître?"

"Unfortunately no," said Old Eusebius. "I was wondering

whether you'd picked up some enlightenment along the way, but I see that suffering has only cleaned out your ears a bit. I must warn you: if you agree, this room will shortly become the scene of an unequal fight which you have little chance of winning. Assuming that you are not altogether a Shade, the death which is in your body will not let itself be driven out easily. It will employ all its tricks and appeal to its allies throughout the world, and chiefly the one that is in you."

"And what is this ally of death?"

"Fear," said Old Eusebius.

"And what must I do in its presence? Can you tell me, maître?"

"Nothing," said Eusebius. "All you have to do is keep your innards quiet, and become like a rat in the dark."

"I shall be a rat in the dark," said Ti Jean.

Eusebius made him lie down on his back, and taking a chalk from his satchel he carefully drew a line around him, enclosing the traveler of death in a sort of little boat. Then he placed in his arms the musket and Ma Eloise's bag, examining its contents one by one: the knife, the powder horn, the flint and its mate the tinder, a last coil of wire for snares, and the last silver bullet, which Ti Jean had looked after like the apple of his eye. Eusebius hopped from one foot to the other, moved by a mysterious inner mirth which found expression in furtive little clicks of the throat. Holding on to his straw hat, which was flapping as if about to take flight, he cried merrily:

"Dear me, just look at that: Ti Jean setting off for the zoo of the worlds with a birdcage in his hand."

He then began to contemplate the various tools and ingredients—flasks, leather pouches, little bunches of herbs—which he had arranged on the floor as carefully and systematically as a housewife. After that he bared his chest and drove the point of a short dagger into the base of his heart.

He collected the blood in a bowl and added some powder from a shriveled green leather pouch. Then, using his little finger as a brush, he touched Ti Jean's eyelids, hands and feet with the blood, together with the frames of the door and windows. The blood stopped flowing from his chest, and he was suddenly enveloped in vapors, exhalations that rose up from his cheeks and shoulders as if he'd just stepped out of a bath. He added some more powder to the bowl, and the liquid stirred, each drop creating a transparency around itself until all the blood had turned into clear water. Then he sat beside the little chalk boat and said, his black mouth emitting a faint bluish smoke:

"I have seen to the four corners of the room and closed it to all influences, and I have arranged some threads of light over your body. In a moment you will drink, slowly, this water of blood. But let me tell you this: others have told you that there are forests behind forests, and that is true. But I tell you that there are also forests inside the forests. So in this room around us there are several worlds, and in each of them there are forces waiting to strike. All that's needed is a chink. That is what happened with the Beast, and that is what will happen shortly when you jerk about like a rabbit being slit open in the dark."

"What should I do?" asked Ti Jean.

"Nothing. Do absolutely nothing, and the forces will halt at the frontiers of your heart. But if you make the slightest movement it will be a sort of opening through which they will enter and destroy everything."

"And death?" said Ti Jean. "What should I do about that?"

"Nothing," said the other.

And he held the brew to Ti Jean's lips. He was surprised at how perfectly clear it was, and at its taste: it was like slightly brackish water in which some sarsaparilla roots had been steeped.

Ti Jean's first reaction was a feeling of cold, which increased and intensified until snow and frost and splinters of ice were flowing through his veins. Then the feeling turned into equally extreme heat. A red veil descended before his eyes, enveloping everything except Eusebius's face, which had gone quite blue, like a cloth dipped in lamprey water, with two lighter patches in the angles of the jaws. Suddenly Ti Jean thought he heard a window fly open somewhere, admitting a violent wind which swirled around him, at once freezing cold and hot as a live ember. Lifting an apprehensive elbow, he turned to Old Eusebius and said:

"Shouldn't we shut the window, maître?"

The sorcerer gently put the elbow back in its place.

"Hush," he said. "It's the Powers."

Then, as Ti Jean, open-mouthed with astonishment, showed signs of going on:

"The window is in your breast," said Eusebius in a scarcely audible voice as the wind in the room grew more violent, with occasional howls fit to blow down the walls.

A chink opened in the middle of Ti Jean's belly and was slowly made wider by the claws of the wind. After an infinity, he closed the rent with his hands and said:

"Maître, I can't bear any more."

"So you surrender," said Eusebius.

"Maître, the wind has got inside me and it's going to blow me away. Throw me a rope so that I can hold on to the earth."

Eusebius's voice grew fainter and dimmer still, almost drowned by the furious assaults of the wind.

"There is no rope to hold on to," he said. "None but in your own mind. Keep holding on to that, my son, and whatever you do, don't utter a complaint—not even in your heart, like some people who squeal like piglets and are heard to the ends of the earth. Only, if you feel you must, you may just whisper a few words."

"Which?" Ti Jean implored.

"It doesn't matter which, so long as you say them to me, calmly, as if you were throwing me a mooring rope. But whatever you do, don't shout."

"Maître," said Ti Jean, "I am far gone, and I can't find words."

"Take a little breath, then, and say with me, slowly, without making one word more emphatic than another:

> Spirit of earth
> Vast vast vast
> I speak to you
> And you will understand
>
> Bird that passes in the night
> And speaks the language of men
> I speak to you
> And you will understand."

From the incantation there arose a serene music, and with it there mingled the veiled beat of tom-toms, borne on the breeze weaving its way through the tall grasses on Bartholomew Hill. Ti Jean was just about to pluck a leaf of lady-grass when it happened. He at once set down Ma Eloise's pannier and kept still, trying to hear the song as it went through the already darkening valley. In the distance, the red wooden disk of the plateau Up Above sparkled like a mirror in the setting sun, to the last notes of a song full of glory and sadness, opening its child's heart irrevocably to other worlds. Then the voice died away, the beat of the tom-toms melted into the evening, and the play of the sunlight shrank to a thread of light on a hilltop, between two huge gates in the sky. Our hero, amazed, saw the shape of Old Eusebius sitting cross-legged on the other side of the chalk boat. The room was now filled with a great silence, which seemed to frighten Eusebius. He clutched Ti Jean's hand convulsively as he lay there.

"I can't do any more for you now," he said. A huge shadow suddenly rose up on the horizon.

One of its jaws reached the clouds above the town, while the other crawled along at street level ready to swallow up everything in its path. Its eyes were veiled, covered with a whitish film, and its huge teeth were transparent as rock crystal. Ti Jean snatched up the musket, threw the bag over his shoulder, and fled precipitately through the streets of the deserted city with the jaw of Death at his heels. His wings flapped and scraped on the pavement. He ran from one house to another, shouting, "I'm Ti Jean—why don't you open the door to me?" But the doors remained obstinately shut, and he set off again, harassed by the enormous draft which attacked his ribs and sent forth a vortex of wind and stinging sand as cold as ice. When he reached the edge of the sea he saw a black woman standing in the water a few paces from the shore, stretching out toward him arms of which the mere sight was a caress. There were vapors rising from her cheeks, hiding the contours of her face. But something tender and familiar emanated from her black perfection, and heavy tresses wound themselves about her belly as if to protect the crop of children dreaming inside her under the translucent skin, five or six of them, perhaps even a dozen, silent, tangled up together, waiting to be given life. There was the shadow of a smile on her lips, the smile of a woman who knows herself beloved, desired, pursued right to the end of underground galleries. And tears sprang into Ti Jean's eyes, and he rushed into the waves, weeping like a child: "Why did you leave me, abandoned under the banyan?"

At once, without a word, she took him in her arms and led him to the depths of the sea, from one level to another, ever deeper, darker and colder, until she brought him beneath a rocky ceiling stretching out as far as the eye could see, like the stony sky of the Kingdom. She laughed, and her teeth showed crystal; her hair tumbled like seaweed to the ocean floor. Ti Jean fought and struggled in vain to escape her hold. He was filled with a cloud of fury, and his member stood up like a sword because Death had dared to borrow Egea's smile, the smile of Egea Kaya, who was waiting for him on the riverbank with a crop of children in her belly, five or six of them, perhaps even a dozen, their lips closed, waiting to be given life. He clawed at the creature's scaly back with his fingernails, and it repulsed him now, terrified, and writhing underneath him like an eel. Suddenly he gave a vicious thrust with his sword, and Death uttered a loud cry. Then came an ebb and flow, a strange silence spread over the world, and Ti Jean saw the form of Old Eusebius, sitting beside the chalk barque.

The ebb and flow made itself felt again. Everything seemed to merge in a moving light emanating from within objects. Eusebius's face was a black sun. Ti Jean had never seen a countenance so beautiful, so mysterious, or so incredibly new: the old man's features seemed to be born every moment from some strange mold. Sounds reached Ti Jean as if through a layer of water. Recovering, he saw that they really came from Eusebius's lips, which twitched continually in the middle of his face as he repeated in an imploring voice:

> "Spirit of earth
> Vast vast vast ... "

4.

Every time Ti Jean opened his eyes he found himself inside a bubble on the surface of which there was a magnified image of Old Eusebius. An enormous hand would burst the bubble, and he would feel a splash of water on his tongue, or be given a bit of food on the tip of a finger, the way a newborn child is taught to take milk. He remained in the bubble for several days, hovering between life and death as if he hadn't quite made up his mind. Then he was better, and Eusebius turned himself into a crow to make incursions into the fashionable parts of the town, from which he brought back good food and wine for the convalescent and something light for his own gullet. One evening the sorcerer expressed surprise at Ti Jean's mass of gray hair, which should have dropped off at the same time as his wings. But he thought that some skin had stayed green underneath, and it bothered him not to be able to distinguish the green from the gray.

What he wondered was, had Ti Jean, in the place he came from, really lived a man's life in all its length and weight?

"A man's life is just what I lived," said Ti Jean.

"Are you sure?"

"Sure as sorrel," said Ti Jean with a smile.

"Ah, it's a nuisance, that sort of thing," said the sorcerer, wagging an anxious brow.

"But why? Aren't I Ti Jean anymore with this hair?"

"Only you know what you are, but you're certainly not the one Wademba told us about. I can tell you now: a few days before he died the old man revealed that a child would warm up the sun again. And as we teased him about that strange notion, not seeing how a little human could relight the great lamp if ever it should go out, and saying that it was more a man's work, and not just any man either, he looked us straight in the eye and said: 'My little baboons, don't be misled by the three faces you know how to make, for the only thing in the world that surpasses the knowledge of the wisest is the ignorance of a child.' "

"So you thought my gray hair was going to fall off?" Ti Jean smiled.

"Alas, yes; I hoped that old age would vanish with Death, and here it is hanging on more tenaciously than the other—which you drove away so nicely, I must admit, like a real cock of darkness. But after all, perhaps one shouldn't go by either your hair or your words. Especially the words, my boy, for more than one person has been known to think he was drowned just through drinking a cup of them. So it seems to me the time has come for you to tell me your story from the beginning—from the day you set foot in the mouth of the Beast, two years ago."

"Two years for you"—Ti Jean smiled tremulously—"but more than forty years for me, Old One. You might even put a few eternities in the scale too."

And as he hesitated, already trying to summon up air from his lungs, Eusebius urged him on like one who knows things, anticipates your most secret thoughts, and will spill his own blood with you, drop by drop, as the words fall from your lips.

"And a few eternities in the scale too. Yes, very well, old warrior," Eusebius said.

Ti Jean leaned his back against the wall, and the other turned his head away, showing the storyteller only his profile as if not to embarrass him with his sad little gimlet eyes. Eusebius listened with all his might, with all the sinews in his living body; and yet it was as if he had already heard a version of the story, as if Ti Jean's words had already dropped into the hollow of his brain in another age, perhaps another world. His eye only really lit up for the bird perching in the Beast's ear, and about that he insisted and insisted on hearing everything. But each of his questions contained its own answer. Did the creature have this kind of plumage, or beak, or eyes, he asked with growing excitement, not realizing that he was running with the hare and hunting with the hounds, and forcing Ti Jean to accept Eusebius's own indirect but lengthy and detailed portrait of the pelican.

After that the mesmerizer's eye suddenly lost its gleam and Ti Jean went on, unreeling his little story without haste, as he had done before to the girl with the duck's beak, and as she herself had done to begin with, detaching each word one by one like grapes until her bunch of woes was completely exhausted. Eusebius just nodded his head gravely as if he had known all this for a long time, and was hearing of a country where he had lived for many years. Neither the fall into Africa nor the meeting with the boy with rings in his hair made his eyes light up again, and Ti Jean felt like a schoolboy being examined by an elderly teacher who knew much more than he did himself. He grew tired, and his mouth started to hurry forward lightly; he passed swiftly over what happened to Wademba, and was preparing to gallop straight on, without any twirls or flourishes, when something mysterious brought his tongue to a halt. Eusebius suddenly froze. His cheeks slowly changed color and became like the fruit of certain vines—wrinkled and slack, entirely hollowed out by hummingbirds. At that moment the old man, noticing that Ti Jean was looking at him, quickly turned his back, placed his hands flat on his head in sign of mourning, and murmured bitterly to himself:

"Water and fire . . . True, everywhere there is water and fire, but the earth is not the same everywhere. Ah, water and fire, and you'd like to hide the sky with your hands, but will it let itself be hidden, and is the palm of a human hand big enough? No, everything overlaps on all sides, everything overlaps, the sky and the life of man, and the shadow of man which follows his every step. And so they shot Wademba, they shot Wademba. And what shall we do now, I ask you, if our mother Africa casts us from her bosom?"

Ti Jean was struck with consternation at the anguish of this Negro of Knowledge, a master man if ever there was one, and no mere cork tossed about by the wind. But after a moment Eusebius swung round, holding his hat down over his face as if to conceal his troubled expression, and said wryly:

"Ah, well, crying won't mend a broken pot, so do me the favor of going on with your little story, boy. Only," he added with a strange short laugh, "don't go galloping along as you did just now. The tongue should be used in a proper manner, and words are sometimes surprising."

Then his shoulders shook as though with inner laughter, and he fell quite silent and distant, showing no reaction either to the spear thrust into Ti Jean's chest, or to his long stay in the king's village, or to the final stoning. But when Ti Jean came to his arrival in the Kingdom of the Dead, and the ancestors' rejection of him, he thought he saw Eusebius's lower lip tremble slightly; the old man had now let go of the brim of his hat. But Eusebius didn't say a word, and Ti Jean went on. The other now seemed scarcely to be listening at all; sometimes he would nod his head dreamily, far away, and now and then there would be a little gleam in the corner of his eye, though it immediately vanished. Ti Jean kept talking, but like someone dancing in front of a blind man, and he relived alone the underground galleries, the river, the sea and all the rest. And when at last he was silent, he wasn't surprised to hear the old man murmur, as if nothing had been said in the interval:

"And didn't you ever hear anything about Wademba in the galleries of the Kingdom?"

"No; no one mentioned him."

"Don't you think he might be on the way, on the way to Guadeloupe?"

"No, I don't," said Ti Jean after a pause. "I think he's wandering through the galleries, not even thinking about returning."

"Ah, I see," said the old man softly. "He's ashamed."

"Ashamed," said Ti Jean.

5.

After that, several gloomy days went by up in that little niche in the void, stuck up there on the front of the building amid the expanse of ruins. At dawn Eusebius would make himself invisible, to go raiding in the fashionable districts. Like a thieving magpie he would bring back all sorts of bizarre objects which had caught his eye: hats, doorknobs, and old alarm clocks which he would set ringing avidly. Then, sitting in a corner with a bottle of rum, he would giggle and shake his shoulders up and down like a child showing off, until suddenly drunkenness wafted him up to the ceiling and banged his head against what was absolutely and definitely solid, when he had thought he was under the stars.

On one such morning Ti Jean saw the mesmerizer sitting on his pallet with his hat flapping over his head and his bag firmly over his shoulder, just as he had been when he first appeared a few weeks earlier. His eyes shone bright and sharp again, diamonds cut by Knowledge, and Ti Jean realized that the old man was moving once more into the irrevocable. Ti Jean slipped out of bed and silently went and squatted in front of him, waiting until the man from Up Above should be ready to speak. They looked at each other for a long time, and then the old man said ironically:

"Old warrior, I'm not going to chew the fat with you. You have spoken, I have listened, and indeed you have lived a whole human life since you left Guadeloupe. So I ask you: Are you still determined to follow that path, even though it is no longer your own?"

"A fine question for a rainy day," said Ti Jean.

"Right," replied the other. "Well, I've got you a passage, a sort of passage, on a kind of cargo boat that sails this evening. But you'll have to stay a crow until you get to Guadeloupe, for you'll have to travel in the port lifeboat and it's a bit cramped."

"And of course you're not coming with me," said Ti Jean.

"Of course not," said Eusebius.

"So you think you're going to find Wademba?"

Eusebius started. "I see you're becoming intelligent," he observed.

"I don't know anything about it," said Ti Jean, "but isn't the Kingdom of the Dead rather large?"

"Old warrior, it is bigger than you think, for you only skimmed its surface. But there are many other floors underneath, not to mention the halls reserved for the gods, about which we know very little."

"I don't know anything about it," said Ti Jean again, "but I don't think you'll find Wademba unless he wants you to."

"True, true, but I've always heard it said that when the leopard dies its colors die with it. And I have lived under your grandfather's colors. Do you see?"

"I don't know anything about it, but it seems to me that the Beast—"

"My friend, whether you like it or not, the fate of the world is a matter of indifference to me if Wademba has to wander through those galleries alone with a bag of bitterness on his heart."

"I like that," said Ti Jean gently.

"Then all is as it should be, and it is time for us to part. Give me the belt and the ring so that I can put them on the boat, and let us bid each other farewell like the old fools we are, incorrigible old fools who have always liked hopeless tasks. Well," he added, smiling pitifully, "this old duffer of a Eusebius has decided to play the lunatic, but it's been proved that the world can be more lunatic than the human heart. So if ever I should meet Wademba at the end of my foolishness, have you got a message for him, a good word or two?"

Ti Jean smiled at the incredible fantasy concealed in that poor old brain, beneath the appearances of knowledge and reason.

"The only word I know," he murmured at last, "is that the soil of Guadeloupe was generous once, before the sun disappeared. If you cut a branch off a tree and just stuck it in the ground, and if the virtue of the branch was still intact, it always sent out its own roots in the end. Tell him that."

"Old warrior," said Old Eusebius, "I'll tell him about the branch."

"Tell him," went on Ti Jean with a pang, "tell him that perhaps we are the branch cut from the tree, a branch swept away by the wind and forgotten. But perhaps in the end it will send out roots, then a trunk, and new branches with leaves and fruit. Fruit that will be like no others, tell him."

Eusebius's eyes scrutinized him, trying in vain to understand the story of the branch. After a while he heaved a friendly sigh, and lightly touching his companion's gray temples as if they were those of the boy of old, he said:

"One good foolishness deserves another, so here's one for you: If ever you come across the Beast again, remember that its strength is not in itself, but in the bird that nests in its ear."

6.

Ti Jean fell twisting round and round toward the ground, until, becoming aware again of Eusebius, whose great wings were already disappearing in the distance, he rose with one bound to the top of the building, avoided a row of electric cables stretching over the street, and reached the open sky.

The lights of the town teemed like a mass of foliage amid the darkness. But the higher Ti Jean flew, the nearer the clouds, the more the tracery of silver threads fell into a new order, like the vague outline of a face, which suddenly revealed its secret just before the harbor. The estuary, enclosed and confined within the city itself, now seemed at one and the same time to leap toward the sea and to capture its immensity and hold it. An icebreaker sang its way through the fog, followed by a line of ships trying to leave the port. The sea was that dark expanse beyond the lights, and the two crows flew calmly toward it as to a tree covered with berries, with a sort of happy peace due to their feeling of being completely alone somewhere in the forests of the night. Eusebius examined his companion with an attentiveness that disturbed Ti Jean. His beak was open, showing a bit of flat tongue which twitched curiously, as if both friendly and sarcastic, as if to demonstrate what he felt about their present situation. Suddenly he shook himself and glided downward, followed by Ti Jean, his wings flapping ponderously, stiff with cold and melancholy.

When they reached the ship, just at the entrance to the estuary, the icebreaker was swinging round toward the town. There was nothing ahead of the freighter but the immensity of the night. Eusebius, skimming the waves, alighted on the edge of a lifeboat attached to the side of the ship. Under the tarpaulin, waiting, were Ti Jean's gun, his belt of power, his bracelet, his bag, and a little pouch of seeds. Eusebius gave Ti Jean a tap on the head with his beak, plucked at the little feathers on the nape of his neck, then, with a last silent laugh, spread his big black wings and launched himself over the sea, toward the Unknown.

BOOK EIGHT

How our hero brought back the sun. And what he saw
that day in the mirror of the waters.

1.

Ti Jean got under the tarpaulin, sank his aerial body onto a bed of cordage, and then stayed there with his head under his wing. His daily ration consisted of a few grains of wheat and a few drops of dew. Every so often he would do some physical jerks in the hull of the boat to stir up the blood that was freezing in his veins, full of invisible ice crystals. Then he would go to sleep, only to wake again with the same feeling that his wings were as brittle as glass and would break at the slightest movement.

There were all the usual shipboard noises: the panting of the engines, the creaking of pulleys and winches, and the shrill clatter of doors shaken by the blast. But something indefinable was missing. No shouts echoed over the deck. And several times, looking out from a ventilation shaft, Ti Jean was surprised at the silence in which the crew, composed almost entirely of Negroes from Guadeloupe, went about its business. It was like a strange new kind of clockwork: the masters made signs, and the slaves obeyed with a sort of mournful, detached acquiescence. The whip was used rarely, and even then only in the void, so to speak, the lash curling back on itself in the air as if merely to stir the blood of animals perfectly trained.

Afterward, when Ti Jean took his beak back under the tarpaulin, the inhumanity of the silence would give rise to strange thoughts. Sometimes, even, his down would bristle with dread, and he wondered whether the whole ship was not operated by Shades.

After five or six weeks the wind grew soft, pleasing, consoling, and the ice floes all disappeared from the water. Small groups of gulls came, wheeling and turning in front of the ship as if to show the way to land, now felt to be near and about to emerge from the waves at any moment. The blue of the sea deepened. There was no longer a single splinter of ice, and the wind bore whiffs of pepper, stagnant water and sulfur, mingled with a distant murmur seeming to rise from thousands of breasts. One day shouts did echo over the deck, black shouts and white, of slaves and of masters, strangely united in one familiar truce. Then there appeared the bare slopes of La Désirade, with its plateau looking as if it had been leveled with a trowel; Marie-Galante in the distance, resting smooth and flat on the sea; and at last, under a bright yellow quarter of moon that seemed to remember the sun, the first promontories of a land Ti Jean didn't dare name, a land that suddenly seemed charged with a vaster mystery than that which fell from the stars.

The siren hooted, and the ship, slowing its engines, entered the channel that lies between the coast and Brumant island, whose guns command the entrance to the harbor. Ti Jean, the belt and the ring hung safely round his neck, gripped the worn cord of the bag in his beak and took off toward the coast, thus exposing himself suddenly to the revolving lights that sweep to and fro over the waters of La Pointe. There was a little beach of black sand just before the promontory, and Ti Jean, dropping his treasures by the water in full flight, went back to extract the musket from the lifeboat, using his beak and claws as best he could to get it free of the tarpaulin. A cry arose from the deck, and a white hand pointed at the bird as it flew off holding the strap of the musket in its claws. Every wingbeat was an agony. Just as he was nearing a stretch of darkness, a tiny target flickering in the lights of the harbor, there was a volley of shots and he saw some feathers flying past his beak.

The butt of the musket was dragging on the crest of the waves when he reached the shore, the little cove of black sand behind the promontory. There he dragged his belongings into a clump of trees, crept under the roots of a mangrove, and crouched there, suddenly turned to stone. Only his legs moved beneath his body, going back and forth and gently scratching at the damp soft sand, his native sand, in a never-ending caress.

The last star slid into the sea and a thick gray quilt covered all Guadeloupe. Ti Jean, still perched under his mangrove, stretched out his beak in all directions through the darkness, trying to catch some scents through the pungent smell of the seaweed. First he noticed the sour aroma of some nearby grape trees; then the gentler odors of sea-loving trees, almonds and acacias, sandboxes and manchineels, with their sharp, irritating stench like the sigh of a bug. Then there was the surprising perfume of a bashful crab, come to wave its pincers over his shelter. And lastly the warm and brotherly fragrance of a bird, which he tried in vain to recognize and name, until he fell into a dark hole which had just opened under his refuge. It went down into the depths of the earth, with lighted openings giving onto landscapes which he brushed by in his fall, but without being able to catch hold. He passed little round huts like those of the plateau Up Above, standing out strangely against the endless plain of the Ba'Sonanke; anthills like the village of the Hippopotamus; tall cliffs with peepholes; and then the city of the white men was already disappearing over his head, vanishing in smoke as he fell flat, arms outflung, cheeks touched by a cool black breeze, into the abyss that awaited him in the heart of the Beast.

2.

When Ti Jean awoke, shreds of mist were still wreathing round the roots of the mangroves, but a multitude of stars dotted a sky that was all round and smooth and bright, with milky gleams as in old china. Extricating himself from the tangle of roots, Ti Jean advanced a few steps over the damp sand and was delighted at the sight of a pink crab which looked as if it were running to meet its doom as human beings do, its little beady eyes looking back in the opposite direction. Ti Jean's throat let out a croak— a laugh: no sooner had he been saved from drowning than, fool that he was, he threw himself at the top of a coco palm, and now here he was, risen from the dead, only to land for the second time in the innards of the Beast, not even knowing why.

A ship hooted beyond the promontory. Coming back to the present, Ti Jean thought the time had now come to put on human skin and go to meet the new story that awaited him, the most extraordinary and preposterous of all, nonsensical, because it wasn't even his. Uncertain what to do, he hopped toward the bush where he had left the musket, the belt and the ring of Knowledge. But as he approached he was seized by another fit of laughter, and the idea struck him of making a youthful trip over Guadeloupe to see how the country had changed since he last saw it. He wondered, one leg poised in the air, how to find out what he really wanted. Then, borne up by laughter, he soared straight over the line of mangroves.

A group of Negresses were going in single file along the main road to Pointe-à-Pitre, each underneath a heavy tray of fruit and vegetables. Although there was no one supervising them they advanced silently and evenly, stopping only to urinate standing up, legs wide apart under an incredible mass of rags, sacking and shreds of blanket that they kept over their shoulders as best they could with hands bundled up in mittens. Ti Jean, seized by an obscure dread that reminded him of what he had felt in the lifeboat, watching the mysterious interplay of masters and slaves, flew over a donkey, then a team of bullocks, then a group of slaves on their way to work with their hoes over their shoulders, apparently free as air. Soon after, he had a vision of a real old-fashioned carriage, a gold coach like the ones in picture books, jolting along the road and driven by an old black coachman in livery and top hat. Two slaves gleaming with sweat ran in front of the horses holding up lighted lanterns, and Ti Jean felt dizzy at the sight: had he fallen into another time, another Guadeloupe, just as, before, he'd fallen into a bygone and forgotten Africa?

Ti Jean's brain was seething, and when a damp gust blew him past the road he noticed that the rain, as it touched his feathers, changed into flakes of frost, transparent like splinters of glass. Soon he was only a tiny ball of fear wheeling at random from one hill to another, ceaselessly astonished at the sight of whole villages reduced to ashes, and ruined, foul-smelling sugar mills surrounded by the skeletons of cattle lying with their ivory hooves in the air. Swooping like a whirlwind over the Rivière

Salée, the Salt River, he saw at last the first living, or surviving, plantations, with their hordes of slaves swarming in the fields like dense clouds of mosquitoes over pools of stagnant water. But everywhere there was the same deathly silence, the same piles of sacking beneath which the people moved like fortresses. The cold had made a fantastic attack, piercing through everything: human flesh, dying trees, and a sky where chill gray clouds briefly formed only to vanish again. Suddenly a thread of music rose to greet him from long rows of people who were digging a slope white with frost. No searchlight shone on them; there was no cracking of whips, no trained dogs to catch runaways. Just two or three overseers some distance away on blanketed horses, while a strange singing came from the men bent to the earth, a song without hope or pain, weariness or boredom, as empty as space:

> "Bone of my knee, work
> Bone
> Bend, bone of my knee
> Bone
> Bend right down to earth."

Immediately it was as if the song had caught Ti Jean's heart and hurled it, scattered and squandered it into the sky. Oh, let me go, friends, let me go; an old crab at the bottom of the sea, an old crab was what he wanted to be; so said Ti Jean to himself, panting, failing, while a wind blew him roughly to the other side of the hill. The crowing of a cock came from the right, a dozen yards or so from the wood where he alighted. Parting the leaves, he saw an old man, a cripple, weeding a garden not far from a single-roomed hut. With one hand the old man supported himself with a crutch; with the other he gently maneuvered a little hoe like a child's toy. As he weeded his plot of yams he spoke to his own body with little interjections meant to give himself courage, like such of the old people as, long ago, wouldn't give up working in their bit of land. A bloodwort hedge separated him from the world, and Ti Jean, reassured by the hedge and by the old man's inoffensive appearance, flew to the edge of the wood and took on human form again.

Having flapped his wings in the meanwhile, he found himself naked in the grass, his arms hanging at some distance from his shivering body. At once the cold covered him with a suit of frost. And then his hands were running over his skin, following the shape of his limbs to see that they were as they should be. Everything was all right, it seemed: arms, legs and the rest, including the deep scar from the spear wound in his chest. But there was a drop of blood on his left wrist, and putting his hands behind him, he got hold of a little feather still in his shoulder blade: a discreet warning from the gods, he said to himself, smiling. Then he left the wood altogether, and the old man looked up, examined him closely, and said quietly:

"Stand over there by the bloodwort hedge or they'll be able to see you from the hill."

He put down his hoe, limped over to Ti Jean and scrutinized him at length with his shrewd little eyes, like slits in a countenance of wood.

"You're not in your first youth either," he said, "and it looks to me as if you need to sit down."

He pointed to a big stone beside the hedge. Then he added, strangely:

"Don't kill me—I'm just going into the house for a moment."

Still navigating with the aid of his crutch, he returned with a bowl of cold vegetables which he held out to Ti Jean. Again he asked his visitor not to kill him, then hobbled back to his hut, returning this time with an old horse blanket.

"Put this around you," he said, "so that we can talk to one another like Christians, with all due respect."

When Ti Jean had emptied the bowl, the old man stuck his crutch in the ground and sat carefully down on the grass. Stretching his neck out avidly and already breathing heavily as a furnace, he cast a glance around him and whispered:

"And now tell, tell!"

He turned his slits of eyes upward, like an old dodderer addressing the empty air, and went on in a plaintive, ingratiating voice:

"Look, I haven't too much to complain of. My carcass doesn't let water, and as well as this hut I have my little garden and my fowls. People leave me in peace, except when it comes to looking after and layering the trees, for I've got the knack, and it'll be a long time before anyone takes my place. I've grafted trees all my life. Yes, I've always worked on other people's land, and I still do—I don't see the difference. The only thing that's wrong is that there aren't so many good stories now. In the old days there was always something happening to someone; there were always some good stories. But now nothing happens anymore. Everyone carries on soberly like a rat on a rope, and to tell you the truth I'm bored—I long for a nice little story. And so, my lad—I've hidden you behind my hedge, and fed you, and covered your shame; so now haven't I got the right to say, Tell?"

"You helped me," said Ti Jean, "and I didn't break your crutch over your shoulders. In my view we're quits."

The old man was startled at first, but seeing Ti Jean smiling, and smiling as one should do at an old fool, he started to laugh at himself too for a while, to wipe out all traces of misunderstanding. Then he leaned forward and said in the same imploring voice:

"Now that we understand one another, I can tell you that it's a long time since we've seen a man of the woods around here. And before you appeared just now, I thought there wasn't a single one left in the whole of our fine Guadeloupe, and that the last one had been done in three months ago over by La Soufrière. But there you are, so I suppose there must be at least one, though it looks to me as if you've had a narrow escape, with nothing but your old hide by way of shirt and trousers. Are you sure you haven't anything to tell me?"

And as Ti Jean looked at him with red and absent eyes, he seemed afraid and added hastily:

"But never mind, friend; I've only got to look at you and it's like hearing a good story. So little happens, you see, that I miss the taste of life in my mouth. The soldiers have gone, the masters have settled down, and powder their hair and ride in their carriages, and the black man can say he's happy every day—oh, yes, he can say that, so long as he behaves himself. The last time the crack of a whip was heard here was more than six months ago, because of that . . . well, some people called him accursed, a runaway pig, but I suppose I really oughtn't to talk like that about a lad the masters ended up by well and truly hanging, after torturing him good and proper first. Yes, you could say they really tickled him up."

Ti Jean suddenly realized what world it was he had just fallen into, and his voice broke:

"What had he done, this . . . accursed one?"

"Ah, you've made up your mind to speak at last! My little story interests you and you're showing the color of your teeth. You're all the same, you black men of the woods. That's the sort of thing that makes you prick your ears up. But I don't hold it against you, and I tell you, if that Negro was gingered up it was because he took it into his head to stir us up against the masters, no less. It was the same as the famous Young Man Chased in Vain that we had for a few weeks in the plantation last year, and he sang us the same tune. Don't you ever talk about anything else, you black men of the woods? Just liberty, dear liberty? I've seen a lot of things in my life, and the one thing that's sure and certain is that the very bird that flies in the sky is not free. No, sir, he is not free."

"You speak like an angel," said Ti Jean, "but what a strange name that is you just said—so strange that I'm not sure I heard it right. Did you say the Young Man Chased in Vain?"

"Yes," said the old man calmly. "He was under a spell, and when he came to the plantations no one took any notice at first; people immediately thought he'd always been there. That was because of the spell, and people firmly believed it. And then he started to laugh, at us of course, to make fun of our various weaknesses, until one day he came right out and tried to make us rise against the masters. Then the spell didn't work anymore, and everyone saw that he was the Young Man Chased in Vain. He was killed twenty times, but he always reappeared in some plantation. He was burned in a charcoal oven and his ashes were scattered in the sea. They did everything you can imagine to him. I can't tell you how many times he was cut up in pieces and scattered all over the place so that the pieces couldn't come together again. But you can't pierce the wind, and a good spell will always be stronger than the hand of man, and no later than yesterday he was recognized at the Hennequin plantation."

"The fields that belong to the distillery over at Petit-Bourg?" Ti Jean asked mechanically.

"That's right—halfway to the heights of Montebello," agreed the old slave.

Then he added slyly, his eyes suddenly shut and as if swollen with waiting:

"I hid you under my hedge, I gave you my vegetables to eat and I clothed your shame. I've even just told you the best story we've heard in the plantation since the sun died. All I ask of you is a few words, my friend, a nice little story about what happened to you in the woods, something to make me laugh, or cry, or both at once, as used to happen so often in the old days. Just a few words, if you're not in the habit, my friend, just a few words for this evening, so that I can go to bed with the taste of life in my mouth."

"I don't know any stories," said Ti Jean. Then he added in a ringing voice:

"No, nothing that I've seen on earth deserves to be called a story in comparison to what you've just told me."

"Thank you," said the other, wiping away a tear of satisfaction.

Ti Jean couldn't help smiling, disarmed by so much innocence and foolishness.

"Listen," he said at last. "If the sight of me is a story in itself for you, then I can tell you a story and a half. Only there is a condition: you mustn't be afraid, not for a mere tale that won't even harm the shadow of a hair on your head."

"You're not playing a trick on me, are you?"

"No," said Ti Jean, changing back out of human shape.

For a few moments the old man hesitated between dread and delight. Then he bent upon the bird a long look that was placid and childlike, the look of a born believer, and Ti Jean bowed to him, uttering little waggish caws. Then with a single flap of his wings he was up above the hut and the bloodwort hedge and the amazed old man, who now clapped with both hands as they used to do on certain evenings in Fond-Zombi when the storyteller had done his work well—had spoken with a mouth so clear that you saw beyond his words, until you didn't see anything anymore.

3.

He alighted by the inlet and took a few steps in the dark black sand, followed by a bright trail that flowed from the open wound on the tip of his wing. When he resumed human form, blood was flowing freely from his left wrist. He made a makeshift tourniquet with a vine, and threw on his belt. A damp wind had sprung up, scattering icy droplets all over his body; but as he buckled his belt a great warmth spread from his loins and the blood stopped flowing. His skin became covered with a strange film, a kind of transparent carapace like glass, which deflected everything before it could touch him. Ti Jean, intrigued, put the ring of divination round his arm, and a string snapped somewhere in the depths of the dark, and he knew that after eternities of silence the ring was coming to his aid, and was telling him the sign, and the path, and the way.

He put on his old wandering garb and set off, listening to the voice of the ring. It wasn't exactly a human voice. It was like branches seeking him in the dark, finding him then losing him again, then sending out fresh tendrils which wound about his breast so as to drag him in the right direction. Drawn by these threads, he crossed the line of mangroves which he had recently flown over as a bird. When he got to the main road, the roar of an engine made him dive into the grass, and a truck swept by, with a searchlight on top which probed back and forth from one end to the other of the horizon. Then our hero took refuge in the fields, following the main road at a distance and making a wide detour whenever he came to an open space where he might be picked up by a beam of light.

One by one the gray night stole away the stars, and Ti Jean went forward slowly to give his eyes time to make out the shapes crouching in the mist. Strangely, he could see the distant ones more clearly than the others, those that were near his eyes of flesh and blood. Then he realized that this was because of the ring, and after a while he lowered the lids over those imperfect organs, so as to be guided by his inner vision alone. With eyes shut he moved forward into a Guadeloupe that was dead beneath its shroud of fog. The roads were deserted. The villages he went through were only masses of shadow. There was no singing, no whirring of insects, no sound of animals running away at his approach. When he got near Pointe-à-Pitre there were a few bright patches like melons hanging at the intersections: street lamps that lit up nothing and attracted no moths. And by the bridge over the Gabarre, under the harsh cone of a floodlight, stood an abandoned guardhouse, its doors and windows closed on darkness. Ti Jean obediently crossed the empty bridge and followed the main road as far as Petit-Bourg, where the ring drew him toward the mountains and the heights of Montebello. There he went along a path through the sugar cane which girdled a hill and came out on a sort of plateau, in the middle of which some long buildings stood arranged in a horseshoe. A little farther on, the wheel of a distillery was turning sluggishly, worked by a stream diverted from the river Onze-Heures, or Eleven O'clock. The plateau was enclosed by a fence, ending in a tall wrought-iron gate. This was the Hennequin plantation, which the old man had mentioned and which was now to witness a new act in the story of the Eternal Young Man.

For some time Ti Jean had been wondering why the ring was drawing him toward the places the old man had spoken of. When he saw the gate, he experienced again the feeling he'd had several times since he fell into the starry sky of Africa, the feeling of being led through the worlds like an animal hauled along by the nose. And he didn't really see, our hero, why he should be dragged along like this in the dark like a beast. But still, his job was to keep walking and not to understand why, to walk through the dark with his belly full of dark: that had been his job since the day he was born, and to be sure, he'd acquired a talent for it. He smiled, opened the door onto an empty courtyard and went past a platform by which stood tip trucks full of lengths of cane. Farther on, the rather sickly smell of cane juice gave way to the aroma arising from a shed in which dozens of slaves were crammed, lying side by side in damp straw that had never seen the sun. Ti Jean went round the building to an inner courtyard with a mango tree. There was a small island of light in the surrounding shell of fog. It was a wood fire with two armed slaves dreaming beside it, one standing and leaning on the barrel of a gun while the other crouched near the flames trying to roast a few sweet potatoes in the embers. The first guard was looking up at a human shape hanging from one of the main branches of the tree. He let out an awkward, disagreeable laugh.

"A fine sight you are now," he said. "Strung up like a side of mutton. And to think he wanted to make everyone tremble."

"Don't talk about mutton," begged his companion. "Just hearing the word reminds me of those mutton stews we used to have, with boucoussou peas that melted in your mouth. Remember?"

"Yes," agreed the other ecstatically. "Boucoussou peas soaked in a good hot sauce with onion and green lime, leave them to marinate the time it takes to smoke a pipe, and then add some pimento and three cloves of garlic, four if you prefer, cover the pot again for a bit to cool down the pimento, then take it off the fire and add the marinade. Ooh, when I think of all that, I can't believe I've ever actually eaten such a marvel. And you, my friend," he added, looking up again at the hanged man, "do you think a little stew with hot gravy would do you good now?"

"What he really needs is a chair, a nice little chair to sit on and stretch his poor legs. But still, he'll soon be stretching them for good, those backwoodsman's legs of his."

"Until the next time, you mean. Ah, boy, I don't like to hear you making fun of that poor wretch on his branch. If you want to know what I think, he may remember it the next time he comes back on earth."

"I'd be surprised," said the other after a pause. "I'd be surprised if the Young Man went and remembered a little word said like that, without thinking. It would surprise me greatly, if you want to know."

But he had been seized with a certain uneasiness, and, dimly aware of a wickedness beyond his understanding and surrounding him on all sides, he added, to the shape now swinging in the wind:

"Whoever you are, lad, don't be cross about an innocent little play on words, with no offense intended. Forget it, comrade. Think of it as a draft which went in one of your ears, and send it out the other side as quick as you can. And don't hold it against us that we leave you there on your branch. We may joke, but we'd like to be able to undo the rope and bring you down to sit by the fire."

"Yes, warm you up a bit, let you rest before tomorrow morning. But you know as well as we do, Young Man Under a Spell, that what the poor have to do is bend the way the wind blows, be flexible. Right?"

The youth was hung simply by the wrists, but as his arms were behind his back, his chest thrust forward and his shoulders stuck out; all the bones were dislocated. Ti Jean, petrified, looked at that face risen from his childhood, and some images floated up from a past that he had thought buried forever: Anancy discoursing mournfully about the soul of the black man, then uttering inflammatory words by the gate of the sugar factory, and carried shoulder-high by the strikers, like a Roman emperor. Then later, talking about man's degradation outside old Kaya's hut when all Fond-Zombi went meekly down to collect their flour and paraffin. Lastly his mysterious smile before he climbed up on the platform surrounded by soldiers; as if he were already inspired by the resolve that was to lead him one day to swing on the branch of a mango tree like a side of dead meat.

Ti Jean made up his mind at last and entered the circle of light. The guards smiled unbelievingly, stupefied at the sight of this fantastic shape with eyes closed like the dead. Ti Jean took them both by the neck and started to bang their heads together, not to smash them like coconuts, no, but to stir up the water a bit inside their skulls and send them to sleep. Then he laid them down carefully side by side on their backs, murmuring gently:

"Go well, brothers, with bright eyes and red blood—that's all that's wished you by a Negro here present who is on his way to death."

He went over to the mango tree, let down the rope, and laid the body of his friend down by the fire. The bonds round the wrists were so tight he had to cut them with a knife. The shoulder joints, suddenly released, clicked back into place with a sound like that of wet cloth, and Anancy's eyes moved slowly and slantingly like streams not completely overcome and dried up by drought, and which emit a trickle or two before starting to flow again.

Then, swiftly, Ti Jean snatched up everything he could from around the fire—the gun and its cartridge belt, a machete, a gourd, and some clothes, in which he quickly dressed Anancy. Then he rolled him in a blanket and lifted him gently over his shoulder.

The burden seemed extraordinarily light. And as he set off again through the fog, he stopped to wipe away the tears that were blinding him, impeding his view beneath his closed lids with a flood that reached up to heaven.

4.

The Young Man was still sleeping when they reached the Brade-fort falls. At the foot of the cliff the old log cabin was still intact; no one had come this way since the death of the sun. Ti Jean put his friend down on the bed of branches and took from his bag the humble ingredients of fire: the piece of wood with a hole in it, its mate of tinder, and a few scraps of tow that had survived the journey. Outside he found the huge basin into which fell a stream of water more than thirty yards high. A strange emotion filled him at this evidence of the immutability of things in the midst of darkness. The trees went on growing up to the edge of the cliff, from which the vines fell in a shower, covering the rock with a close mantle that outlined its every variation. And the roar of the falls was the same as he'd heard forty or fifty years before, with a few eternities thrown in, when he used to rove the forest. When he reached the water's edge he bent over a big siguina leaf and kissed its soft smooth surface as he might have kissed a woman's lips. Then he stood on tiptoe and dived into the seething water, letting himself be carried against the side, as in the past, looking for the holes that sheltered mullet and cat-mouthed crabs. A little later, with his fish wrapped up in a vine leaf, he wandered slowly round, looking for the medicines he used to gather for Ma Eloise. He also found the little plot of vegetables and the two or three wild banana trees still growing in a clearing that were the last of a man called Sainte-Croix. He had taken refuge and lived there alone and completely naked a few years before Ti Jean was born. While some fish and bananas were cooking slowly in the embers, Ti Jean crushed a few aloe leaves between his hands and bent over his friend's suffering body. He rubbed it from head to foot, sinew by sinew, muscle by muscle, trying to vibrate every centimeter of skin and to follow the inmost blood vessel, as Ma Eloise used to do to cure mortals, her skillful fingers green with anoli. After a while, bright moonlight came in through the open door and Anancy slowly opened his eyes. His swollen lips parted in an ambiguous smile, both ruse and hope, a crazy anticipation like that of someone who suspects a practical joke but is still trustful—fairly trustful—nevertheless.

"Father," he said, "will you tell me where I am?"

"You're at Bradefort falls," said Ti Jean.

"Falls? What falls? Aren't I in the other world?"

"No," said Ti Jean soothingly. "You're in the land of the living."

The other gave an enigmatic laugh. His mind seemed to be roving the sky again, far away from the hut, and he murmured to himself with an expression of surprise and disappointment, like a child seeing a bubble burst:

"I was beginning to feel comfortable at the end of that rope. I could see a big hole at my feet and I was falling into it gently, gently, as into the depths of a river."

Suddenly Anancy fell asleep, but his eyes of affliction went on gazing at the old man through sleep, through madness and death, as if to speak to him of victory in the heart of darkness, and of an inexhaustible patience longer than all future defeats. Ti Jean continued rubbing in the balm, concentrating especially on the arms, which he raised from time to time as if he hoped to restore life to the stretched ligaments. Soon he too fell asleep, and it was as if he dived swiftly into the pool under the falls, where multitudes of leeches swirled round his face. One drove itself like a nail into his left temple, and he thought: I must have some bad blood there that it's draining away. Then he started, and awoke in the cabin beside Anancy, with the feeling that there was an invisible cupping glass stuck to the vein, trying to draw away some unknown substance.

The next day, after washing the lad's arms and legs and giving him food and drink with his own hands, Ti Jean suddenly realized the state his friend was in. In every feature Anancy's face was as it had used to be. But a sort of torpor rested there, and his senses reacted slowly, as if images and sounds had to travel a long way to reach his brain. He spoke slowly too, without much effort to answer, to link what he said to what he had just heard. And Ti Jean pondered, and wondered how he must seem in the eyes of the youth, who looked without surprise at him, this huge man standing in the cabin as bare as a tree and with a little blue-black feather sticking out of his side. The Young Man Chased in Vain hadn't even asked his name, but addressed him as someone old and venerable, saying just "Father" in the old Fond-Zombi manner. Sometimes he would be visited by memories which he called daydreams, unable to distinguish very well between the inventions of his own mind and the fantasmagoria that dwelt in the heart of the world. He mentioned the Beast, which he'd seen several times at a distance, and related certain conversations with souls of the dead who'd come up out of the earth at full moon to look at their descendants, returned to slavery. But there was an aura of uncertainty about all this, and he said he'd lived alone too long to vouch for anything.

"One man's eyes are not enough," he murmured one day, smiling. "There have to be at least two to be sure of anything, even the reality of a blade of grass."

Then he added gravely:

"Father, one pair of eyes, believe me, is always but the half of a man."

Ti Jean, disturbed by the exact likeness between their two experiences through different times and worlds, feigned not to understand.

"What do you mean, one pair of eyes is but the half of a man?"

"Don't laugh," said the other hesitantly. "But I'm not altogether sure that the present moment exists—that it isn't just another spell."

"The present moment? You mean me?" said Ti Jean, with a wan smile.

"Don't laugh, please don't laugh. At first, when things started to happen, I thought I was going mad."

"Things?"

"Well," went on Anancy with a hint of raillery, "it was when I began to die and be reborn, die and be reborn again. The first time it was at the Bellefeuille plantation, where I was well and truly hanged, like a salted eel. They left me on the rope for three days, and I didn't move. I knew I was dead and yet I could hear their words and feel the breeze on my body. When they threw me in a hole I hollowed the ground out underneath me and came out near another plantation. I didn't believe what was happening to me; it was as if it was happening in a dream. And even after the second and third time I didn't quite believe it—I thought I'd gone out of my mind. But one day I presented my body at the Sans-fâché place and the people ran away at the sight of me, shouting that they'd already hanged me, and hanged me well and truly, as recently as the year before. Then I knew I hadn't gone out of my mind, but was the victim of a spell. A spell that's still on me at this very moment," he concluded with an uncertain, equivocal smile.

During the days before the end, before his boat went to sea and was wrecked for good, Anancy's mood was strangely serene in the little cabin of eternity at the foot of Bradefort cliffs that was his last refuge on earth. Despite Ti Jean's ministrations, his left arm wouldn't come to life. It remained inert, slightly drawn back, as if trying to resume the position inflicted on it in the hanging. But his legs had recovered their agility, his tongue obeyed his will, and his eyes were beginning to see clearly, though with a slight delay that made him sometimes bump into things. He laughed, joked, and played tricks reminiscent of the little boy on the banks of the river. Lost in the clothes of the guard— black felt hat, loose shirt and trousers held up with string—he followed Ti Jean like a sort of scarecrow to the pool to watch him dive for a crayfish, a mullet, or a crab with mustaches. Or he would watch him dig up some vegetables, cut a hand of bananas, or pick guavas, cinnamon apples and tamarind berries, which the old man would peel and then carefully put in the other's mouth as though they were diamonds. No question ever crossed his lips, not even about the little black feather sticking out of Ti Jean's side. There existed between them a talking without words. There was no need for weeding and thinning out. No, everything was clear in itself. Anancy's eyes were his words— great eyes like those of a sick foal, which never left the old man, as if Ti Jean alone were the world in which the other moved, the earth on which he trod. Ti Jean, catching this glance upon him, felt a pang, and thought that with his old wanderer's face and his white hair he was now only a sort of memory of himself in Anancy's mind.

One night he heard himself being called in a dream, and opening his eyes he saw that the Young Man was sleeping peacefully. A little later the same voice was heard, but very distinctly this time, and Ti Jean opened his eyes and said: "Here I am." He got up and walked a little way around the camp. The mist was beginning to rise like steam from the seething waters of the pool. When he reached the water's edge he decided that Anancy's fate was more important than anything else in the world, and he said loudly, so that his determination should be plain to the invisible ones: "Never. No, never." At these words a wind sprang up over the pool, with many murmurs in it. Each murmur had the confidential, joking tone of the sorcerers of the plateau, and our hero repeated: "Never. No, never." Then, shaking his head, he went back into the cabin and lay down silently by his friend, resolved not to answer the call anymore. But instead of going to sleep he withdrew into himself and his head filled with wise thoughts, each one of which cost him a sigh. The gray night faded slowly without his noticing, and when the day broke he rose and said to his friend:

"Anancy, Anancy, it is time for us to part."

Without meaning to, he had called him by his name for the first time. But the Young Man paid no attention to this. Turning toward Ti Jean a face overwhelmed with astonishment, he said:

"Father, what are you saying?"

"We must part. There is a task awaiting me in which you have no place."

"Where is my place, if not with you?"

"I repeat," said Ti Jean, "there is nothing for you in what awaits me."

"There is nothing for me anywhere else."

Ti Jean gazed at his friend for a long while, then with a wide wave of his arm included all the surrounding landscape in one gesture of farewell. A few moments later they were both making their way round the pool to reach an old backwoodsmen's path leading up to La Matéliane. With a gun over each shoulder and the guard's cartridge belt round his waist, Ti Jean walked along with the measured, peaceful tread of an old mule that knows all the stones and can trust itself to the memory of its hooves. By his side, muffled down to the knees in rags, Anancy, his big feet scarcely leaving the ground, clenched his toes at every step around anything that could be gripped, as if to counterbalance the swaying of his numbed arms, which could no longer carry anything. Ti Jean strained his ears and walked meekly in the direction of the voice, followed by Anancy, humming softly and wordlessly in a sort of continuous groan. And sometimes a strange and absurd singsong would well up in him, a kind of sugar cane chant that he would sing in the traditional manner, with one finger against his eardrum, his head thrown slightly back and his eyes gazing abstractedly into the distance:

> "O my friends
> I am coming back I am coming back
> I have carried out my mission beyond the hills
> And I say to you
> Good day."

5.

The increasing cold had changed the relation between the wild lands lying fallow and those domesticated by man. Once-flourishing areas were now wilderness, and new settlements had appeared at the foot of volcanoes, near hot springs and boiling geysers, wherever underground activity offered some hope of life on the surface. A profound sadness dwelt over everything. It was as if a young woman had gone to her eternal sleep and was sending out a silent appeal from beneath her eyelids. And every time Ti Jean thought he heard that call, he increased his pace and said within himself: "Here I am. Here I am."

Following the voice of the ring all the time, the next day they reached a hill overhanging the dim traces of a road in the valley, a trail that was scarcely visible amid the vegetation. Ti Jean felt his legs give way beneath him, and he sank down in the grass. To conceal his embarrassment he put the musket across his knees and checked the flint, the powder intake, the string of the ramrod and the presence of the last silver bullet. He also checked his hands and his eye, and every beat of his heart. Anancy watched him, puzzled. On Ti Jean's instructions, he absently filled the magazine of his own gun and put a fresh bullet in the barrel. The boy neither saw nor recognized anything in the landscape; he paid attention only to the tall shape walking along in front of him, gazing at it like a faithful hound, happy and entirely trusting. Soon they came to the Bridge of Beyond and went silently along by the Rivière-aux-Feuilles until they reached the falls, where Ti Jean sniffed at the air, hesitated, sniffed again, and then made for the path leading Up Above.

Ti Jean implored his luck to hold. True, he was tense, torn between the fate of the world and that of his friend, and he toyed with the idea that the Beast might have changed islands, or leaped up to other stars, taking with it the poor sun of humans.

But halfway up the hill the voice turned off toward the mountains and the marsh, and seized with weakness again, he sat down slowly with his back against a tree and his legs bathed in sweat. Then the Eternal Young Man said to him:

"Father, can't I do anything for you?"

"There's nothing you can do," said Ti Jean.

"And must you really follow this path?"

"Must I?" said Ti Jean, laughing.

And the boy laughed with him, and both set off again, each laughing on his own account, until their bare feet finally came upon the spongy soil, threaded with streams of water, that heralded the marsh. And there, signaling to his friend to halt, our hero, more dead than alive, advanced toward the first line of reeds.

His first feeling was that he had lived through this moment before. The marsh sparkled faintly under a moon that trembled near the horizon, divesting itself of its last veils before plunging into the sea. Lying on the other side of the water, its muzzle turned toward the dying moon, the apparition was white and luminous in the shadow, and lowed painfully, lashing its sides with its tail. It seemed to be waiting for Ti Jean, and a supernatural cold spread through him, changing his sweat into runnels of frost. He turned and made a last sign to friend Anancy, a gesture begging him not to follow, to wait quietly just where he was. Then, drawing himself up to the full height of a man who knows the worlds and the worlds beyond them, the earthquakes and the landslides and the falls, he parted the line of reeds and took a few steps into the black mud that surrounded the marsh. The world-devourer shuddered, and the bright beam of its eyes lit up and slowly swept the space around it like the beam of a lighthouse. Then it got to its feet and started galloping round the marsh toward Ti Jean, who stood there, his mind blank, dreaming, trying to remember some word he knew not what, heard he knew not where nor in what time or world. He was wondering about this phenomenon, feeling neither hot nor cold in his blood, while the Beast was trotting peacefully through a landscape of mangroves and phosphorescent ferns as high as church steeples; even the biggest trunks parted before the Beast like spiderwebs. A gleam of light emanating from the monster pierced Ti Jean, flashing right into the most secret recesses of his brain. And his mind was disappearing, reeling, in that huge gaze, when a human shape emerged from a clump of trees about thirty paces to his right. A shot rang out, and the beam of light turned away as the Beast charged the marksman, now hidden behind some ferns. At the same moment a winged shape flew from the vast canopy of the monster's ear, and Ti Jean, coming to himself again, remembered old Eusebius's warning: "The strength of the Beast is not in itself, but in the bird that nests in its ear." The musket sprang to his shoulder, aiming at the bird with its wise man's brow as it rose up into the heights of the darkness. In a brief flash, Ti Jean saw the pelican start as it was hit in full flight, and at the same time, absolutely simultaneously, he saw the Beast give a great leap in the air as if the silver bullet, when it hit the bird, also hit one of the Beast's vital organs.

The bird uttered a bird's cry. The cow replied, with the sound a cow usually makes. Then, rising with difficulty, the Beast started to gallop with a kind of unreal slowness, as if dancing a pavane, one hoof to the left, one to the right, another to the left again, until it fell in a heap on the edge of the marsh, its muzzle buried in the black muddy water. Finally there was a human cry, of which it was impossible to say whether it came from a man or a woman or even from the throat of a child. Only it was a human cry; and then silence fell again over the marsh.

Anancy lay under a mahogany tree, behind a clump of ferns that had been crushed, trampled and scattered by the Beast's hooves. His eyes were open wide as if they could still see the monster approaching and were still trying to oppose the strength of a human gaze to that of the thunderbolt. That which had pursued him so long had at last overtaken him. Ti Jean sat on the grass, raised his friend and rocked him absently against his breast. He stroked the dead lad's hair for a while, then, leaning over him, saw on his face the same expression there had been on his own, the other year, the other century, in the dark, enchanted heights of Fond-Zombi: the same desperate fury, the same haughty, inexorable ardor that had been the hero's secret truth.

A few yards away the apparition lay outspread by the marsh, its muzzle buried in the mud. Ti Jean thought it was still alive, because of the phosphorescence it gave off, a thin, dim radiance. And then it struck him that this was the light of the buried worlds, and he laid Anancy gently down on the grass and asked him to excuse him for a moment. He went over to the Beast, took from his belt the machete that had belonged to the guards, and balancing on his toes, raised it with both hands, intending to strike with all his strength and weight at the middle of the Beast's body, in the way the Ba'Sonanke split open the belly of an elephant. And then a voice, a thought, restrained him, and he remembered the story of the woman with the duck's beak in the Kingdom of the Shades; the story about the cries of the living creatures imprisoned with Losiko-Siko, the hero of her village, when he tried to hack a way for himself with his knife. "Take care," they had said, "you're cutting us, you're cutting us too." Then, no longer standing on tiptoe, Ti Jean stretched out the point of his blade to just underneath the long breasts, and drew a line as delicately as he could.

It was as if he had rent some dream fabric: the pearly side had opened into a wide gap filled with black air, and there appeared before the old man's astonished eyes a golden globe which parted the lips of the wound and rose slowly above the trees with the touching fragility of a bubble, then reached the dark heights of the sky and began to shine there. The sun.

6.

Through the gaping vent under the breasts emerged a tracery of tubes that looked like glass and broke with a faint crystalline sound, giving off little whiffs of blue. It was all glass and smoke, glass turning into smoke as it encountered the light of day. The wound widened, a slit spread along the pearly skin, hollowing out deep expanses of nothingness. When it reached a breast, a milky fluid gushed out onto the ground, oily, fragrant, looking rather like a wine made from bitter oranges. As soon as this liquid touched the grasses they burst into frantic activity, twitching and swelling with sap, shooting out new leaves and branches. Then a voice spoke to Ti Jean's mind, and he opened his gourd and filled it full of the milk of darkness: the milk of the thunderbolt, as the voice of the ring had called it.

Then, saddened by the corpse, he gazed at those loins so reluctant to deliver up their secret. But lo, as his eyes began to blink, he saw that the bluish gleams were making all kinds of shapes in the air before they vanished. Mountains and valleys, rivers and human forms came from those glass entrails in exhalations, in an outpouring and press of suns and moons of all colors, which rose swiftly, flew in all directions, and disappeared suddenly in the tops of the trees. Ti Jean, leaning over that fertile womb, gazed and gazed at the wondrous spectacle of all the worlds returning to the fold, swiftly, swiftly, jostling each other as they went with a frenzy that bewildered him and brought a smiling reproach to his lips: "Gently, if you please, my friends, gently. Too much haste and the child is born without a head."

Suddenly a terrible pain seized him in the depths of his body, and he let out a cry. His body was giving off a light smoke, the smoke of well-dried wood, blue, gray, blue, like that which had come from the entrails of the Beast. He saw his arms growing gradually transparent, and then he no longer saw anything.

When Ti Jean regained consciousness he was lying face down on the grass with a strong sun shining on the back of his neck. He turned over, and his body made a sound like the click of an insect's wings. Looking down at himself, he saw that he was entirely covered with a glassy sheen, curved in places over stretches of smooth black flesh. He gazed for a moment at his chest, from which all traces of the Sonanke's spear had vanished. Then he went over to the marsh, knelt down, and saw in it the image of a huge youth with an incredible mass of hair, a face like new, and eyes that were wondering and childlike despite the two or three whiskers adorning his chin.

BOOK NINE

The end and the beginning

Lower, lower your voice
For the night is mild
And the day will soon break
Lower, lower your voice . . . *

* Jacques Roumain, *Gouverneurs de la rosée.*

For three months Ti Jean remained in the shade of that straight unbending mahogany tree near which he had buried his friend. By day the world was nothing but a flood of colors, and he thought how Anancy could see none of it, he who had rekindled the sun. And then the air grew steeped in green, and turned to night; the mountain fell in purple masses toward the sea; and he arose and went hunting. And they were strange expeditions in which he was at once the dog and the agouti, because of a gift which had come to him since the death of the Beast, a way of drawing his prey to his feet from a distance, and then gently sending them to sleep by an effort of the mind. Then he would light a fire by the mahogany tree, bend his lips to the food, and eat.

One afternoon as he was dreaming under the tree, shots rang through the mountains and for the first time he heard voices floating up from the valley. Men were coming and going somewhere under the clouds, between heaven and earth, and it was on this earth that he had to walk, yes, even if it burned his feet like a red-hot iron. Thus, through one dream after another, the knots came undone inside him, and there arose from within a murmur, a word of acquiescence. And suddenly making up his mind, with his eyes shut, our hero projected his vision to the foot of the slopes, not far from Ma Vitaline's tavern.

His antennae went to and fro in a survey of everything, calculating the extent of the disaster as after a cyclone. He counted the huts, which had been put up again and were still tottery, and then the people inside the huts. And two or three times he thought he recognized people who had been swallowed by the Beast on that olden day when it had made its entry into the village, galloping and bellowing in a frenzy, as if it was already invading men's hearts. He stopped and threw off the delusion which used to come to him in his youth, though he had never lost his bearings under his white hair. Suddenly he was struck by a figure at the back of a hut, and looking at it carefully and bending his mind over the face of the sleeping child, he definitely recognized the little girl with the goat who had sung a little sarcastic song before she disappeared in the breath of the Beast, drawn in alive and unscathed.

> "My mother has gone away
> With the jar of sugar . . ."

At that moment everything blurred and he rubbed his eyes for a long time like someone cleaning his glasses, until he could see clearly and accurately again. Then, passing the empty space where the Kayas used to live, he came to the end of the village, where Ma Eloise's hut awaited him, set up again on its four stones. The walls were held together with long poles, and chevalier-du-midi vines swarmed over the stones, changing them into dazzling multicolored flowerbeds. Inside, a girl was sitting on a little empty packing case, looking out expectantly onto the street. Her neck was smooth, her hair drawn back over her temples, she was simply dressed in a frock made of "France" flour sacks. But the girl's serenity, her air of majesty and poise, even the little dash of gaiety lent by her dress being freshly washed and ironed and starched—all these could only belong to another, although that other was also Egea. Suddenly her eyes lost all their brightness, and putting her hand in front of her mouth as if to hide her teeth, she sang softly, in a sudden fit of melancholy:

> "They have called me luckless
> They say I am not rose-colored
> But if not rose I am green
> And my luck will come, for I have my hope."

Then, finding her again as she was, a Negress without disguise or affectation, neither one extreme nor the other, who concealed neither ugliness nor glory with the palm of her hand, Ti Jean swiftly opened his eyes under the leaves of the mahogany tree where his body rested like a moored ship. And snatching up bag and musket, not forgetting the gourd which hung from one of the lower branches, he bowed to the grave, bowed again, then rounded the marsh and went down again into the valley.

When he had crossed the Bridge of Beyond, the wind drove a flock of clouds before it and there was complete darkness, just pricked with thin, dim gleams, some falling from the sky and others flickering on either side of the road in the huts which were inhabited. Ti Jean, walking in the middle of the road in a zone of shadow which the faint oblique rays from the huts could not reach, advanced with the slow and measured pace of an Ancient, as if, he thought with surprise, he still had an old man's heart inside the smooth and swelling chest of a young one. Inhabited huts were few, and rebuilt with odds and ends, while all that was left of the others were a few rotten planks sticking out of a mass of greenery. All the huts where old people had lived were in ruins, and in the others, those which had come to life again, the doors, closed against the spirits of darkness, sheltered no white hairs. No dog strayed across his path; there were no groups of people. Only silence, and the faint lights which didn't reach the middle of the road along which Ti Jean shambled slowly, his young shoulders weighed down with ghosts. Sometimes he would be roused by an impulse of immense veneration and would quicken his pace; only to slow down again as much as he could, stiffened by determination to preserve the gait his spirit had learned. During all these years, which for him had seemed to last a lifetime, when he dreamed about Fond-Zombi he had always seen his return as an end, the conclusion of the story Wademba had foretold on the night of his death; a story called sadness, darkness and blood, the old man had said in a strange, perhaps sorrowful voice, as the child looked at him out of eyes burning with impatience. But now he saw, did our hero, that this end would be only a beginning: the beginning of something that awaited him there among the groups of tumbledown huts, those makeshift shelters beneath which people quietly told each other their stories, and dreamed, and already eagerly invented life anew by the light of torches stuck in the earth.

SIMONE SCHWARZ-BART

WRITES ABOUT HERSELF

Born in September, 1938, in Guadeloupe. . . . Childhood in a remote hamlet of the island, where her mother teaches school. . . . The father is at war in the Free French Forces and comes back after five years of absence during which there is not a word of news about him. Mother and daughter pass their time in waiting, living the miserable life of peasants, subject to the police vexations of the colonial administration, which is Petainist. For Simone Schwarz-Bart, the essence of Guadeloupe will always be the most oppressed and proudest Negroes of the island, "unbroken and unbreakable," as she says. She early dreams of speaking about them someday, so that justice may be done for them.

At twenty, having come to France to continue her studies, she meets a poor young man who speaks to her in the language of her country, the Creole of the Antilles. He is a Jew, thus not really white in the eyes of the peasant girl from Guadeloupe, who has heard of the Holocaust. He speaks vaguely of a manuscript that he has just delivered to a publisher. Several months later, The Last of the Just *appears.*

After their marriage, the couple divide their life among Africa, Guadeloupe, Europe, and Israel, where they intend to settle. Two children: Bernard, born in 1961 at Dakar, and Jacques, born in 1962 at Point-à-Pitre, Guadeloupe. . . .

Her first literary attempt in 1967, in collaboration with her husband. . . . Then a novel, written in memory of an old peasant woman of her village who was her friend: Telumee-Miracle, the heroine of The Bridge of Beyond. *Her second novel, also devoted to her people, the peasants of Guadeloupe, is* Between Two Worlds.